Kindling Hope:
Stories Awakening the Heart

Donald T. Iannone, PhD

DEDICATION

To all storytellers whose words awaken our hearts with gifts of hope, goodness, inspiration, and wisdom, and to the spirits that speak through the storytellers' words.

TABLE OF CONTENTS

ACKNOWLEDGMENTS

Kindling Hope: Stories Awakening the Heart exists because of the countless sparks of hope I have encountered throughout my life. In the face of life's uncertainties and the relentless challenges of today's chaotic world, hope is the light that guides us, the anchor that steadies us, and the fire that sustains us. It is hope that keeps us moving forward, even when the path is unclear, and it is hope that reminds us of our shared humanity, no matter how divided the world may seem.

To those who give hope to others in times of crisis and despair—whether through words, actions, or simply their presence—you are the true keepers of the flame. Your courage and compassion inspire others to believe in the possibility of better days, even when all seems lost. This book is a tribute to you and the powerful ways your hope has made a difference.

I am deeply grateful to my family, whose love has been my foundation, and to my friends, who have stood by me through life's joys and sorrows. To my teachers and mentors, who taught me to see the world not just as it is, but as it could be. Thank you for your wisdom and guidance. To my students, who continually remind me of the boundless potential of the human spirit. You have given me as much as I could ever give you. To my readers, who share in this journey, your willingness to engage with these stories gives them life and meaning beyond the page. Finally, to the spirits who speak to me often in my dreams. And trust me, they are real!

Finally, to all those who have given me hope through their life stories—whether shared in moments of vulnerability, resilience, or quiet strength—you have shaped this work in ways words cannot fully express. Your hope is what makes us truly human.

This book is dedicated to the fire within each of us—a fire that may flicker but never truly dies. May these stories kindle that flame and remind us of all of the enduring power of hope.

INTRODUCTION

In a world that often feels fractured, where the noise of division drowns out the soft voices of unity, there is one enduring light that has the power to guide us through the chaos: hope. *Kindling Hope: Stories Awakening the Heart* is a collection of short stories born from that light—a tribute to the moments, people, and acts that remind us of our capacity to endure, connect, and find hope.

Hope is not merely a feeling; it is a force—a quiet yet powerful energy that can transform despair into resilience and isolation into connection. In today's chaotic world, where the weight of uncertainty presses heavily upon us, hope becomes not just a luxury but a necessity. This book invites you on a journey of hope, one story at a time, drawing on the quiet strength of ordinary people and the extraordinary acts that arise when kindness and courage meet.

The stories within these pages reach across American history and geography, reflecting the diverse experiences that compose the rich tapestry of our shared humanity. Yet they are all bound by a single, unshakable truth: even in our darkest moments, hope can be found in the simplest of acts—an outstretched hand, a kind word, or a heart willing to give. These narratives are not just tales of the past; they are mirrors reflecting the timeless values that continue to shape our lives today.

In "The Lantern Parade," set during the Great Depression, a group of children from different neighborhoods come together to create light in a time of darkness. Their collaboration transcends social and cultural barriers, sparking a sense of unity that lifts their entire community. The lanterns they carry are more than sources of illumination; they are symbols of hope, crafted by innocent hands yet powerful enough to inspire even the most disheartened souls.

Similarly, "The Thanksgiving Visitor" tells the story of a lonely widower who finds solace and joy in a neighboring family's feast. Invited by a group of children he barely knows; he experiences the warmth of inclusion and the healing power of shared holiday traditions. Around a table filled with carefully prepared dishes, barriers dissolve, and the simple connections between people come to light. The act of coming together highlights the beauty of unity and the profound impact that gratitude and kindness can have on a person's life.

Acts of kindness often serve as the seeds of hope, transforming not just individuals but entire communities. In "The Snowflake Inn," an innkeeper shelters stranded travelers during a Christmas Eve snowstorm. What begins as a reluctant act of hospitality becomes a transformative experience for all involved. Strangers become friends, and the warmth of human connection melts away the coldness of isolation. The inn, once merely a place of business, becomes a sanctuary where stories are shared, and hope is rekindled.

In "The Forgotten Toy Drive," a young boy's determination to bring joy to others during the Korean War demonstrates that generosity can flourish even in times of great adversity. Faced with the harsh realities of conflict, the boy initiates a toy drive to collect gifts for children affected by the war. His unwavering spirit ignites a movement within his community, showing that one person's hope can inspire collective action. The story underscores the idea that even the smallest gestures can have far-reaching impacts, touching lives in ways we may never fully comprehend.

"Redemption" reminds us that while we cannot undo the past, we can learn from it and redeem ourselves by giving selflessly to others. Redemption holds the power to transform even the deepest wounds into opportunities for growth and renewal, reminding us that change is always possible. It offers a path to reclaim our humanity, rebuild trust, and embrace the hope of a brighter, forgiven future. In the story, Peter Di Lonzo swindles his insurance customers and uses their accounts to launder organized crime money. As an act of redemption, he anonymously gives back to them what he has stolen and more, proving that even the most flawed actions can lead to meaningful change.

Other stories explore the quiet courage that accompanies acts of hope. In "The Pumpkin Wagon," a young Native American boy joins a farming family to deliver Halloween cheer during the Dust Bowl. Despite the pervasive hardship and scarcity, they manage to bring moments of joy to their neighbors. The boy's participation bridges cultural divides, teaching the importance of gratitude in the most challenging times.

In "The Last Sleigh Ride," a retired mailman embarks on a final journey to deliver Christmas letters. His trek through the snowy countryside is not just about fulfilling a duty but about reconnecting with the community he has served for decades. Each letter he delivers carries messages of love, hope, and reconciliation. The journey rekindles his sense of purpose and leaves a lasting imprint on those who receive his unexpected visit.

At their core, these stories are a celebration of resilience, connection, and the transformative power of hope. They ask us to look beyond ourselves, to recognize the humanity in others, and to embrace the courage it takes to care. Through grand gestures and small acts alike, they illuminate the ways hope can heal, inspire, and guide us through the most challenging times.

This book also honors the mysterious ways hope finds us—often through dreams and whispers of inspiration. In "Stories from Dreams," the unseen threads of the subconscious weave together to ignite acts of kindness and compassion. The protagonist receives vivid dreams that compel him to reach out to others, demonstrating that even in moments of solitude, hope can be a steadfast companion. These stories remind us that paying attention to the stirrings of our own hearts can lead us to impact others in profound ways.

As you turn these pages, you will meet people from diverse walks of life and cultural backgrounds, united by their capacity to care. You'll encounter characters like Rosa Schmidt, a German immigrant mother whose journey reflects the struggles and triumphs of many seeking a better life. Her story highlights the universal quest for belonging and the hope that fuels it. You'll walk alongside a soldier in "Letters from the Homefront," who finds solace and purpose through correspondence with a stranger during wartime. Their exchange becomes a lifeline, proving that words can bridge even the widest of chasms.

These stories reflect how gratitude can transform pain into healing, how courage can conquer fear, and how kindness can light even the darkest of paths. They serve as a testament to the enduring spirit of humanity—a spirit that persists even when tested by the harshest of circumstances.

Hope is what makes us human. It is the light we pass to one another, a flame that refuses to be extinguished even in the fiercest storms. In times of crisis and despair, it is hope that anchors us. *Kindling Hope: Stories Awakening the Heart* is an invitation to tend to that flame—to nurture it within yourself and to ignite it in others. It's a call to action, urging each of us to become beacons of hope in our own spheres of influence.

May these stories remind you of the hope you have received, the kindness you have given, and the immense power we hold to bring light to the world. May they inspire you to carry hope forward, creating ripples of goodness in a world that needs it now more than ever.

As you embark on this journey, consider the ways in which you can be a catalyst for hope. Reflect on the moments when others have lifted you up and how those experiences have shaped who you are. Remember that every act of kindness, no matter how small, has the potential to ignite a spark in someone else's life. Together, we can weave a tapestry of hope that spans communities, cultures, and generations.

In closing, I invite you to not only read these stories but to live them. Let them awaken your heart and inspire you to be a bearer of hope in your own right. The challenges we face are great, but so is our collective capacity to overcome them. By kindling hope within ourselves and others, we can illuminate even the darkest corners of our world.

Welcome to a journey of hope. May it leave an indelible mark on your heart, as it has on mine.

A CHRISTMAS PROMISE

The Homefront During World War II

The early morning light stretched across the rooftops of Hazelwood, a small Upstate New York town nestled between rolling hills and fields that had turned to mud in the winter rain. Thaddeus Meriwether walked the familiar path to Hazelwood Elementary, his breath misting in the chill December air. He paused for a moment outside the school gate, taking in the quiet. It was hard to believe another Christmas was almost here. Harder still to believe it would be his second Christmas without Margaret.

Margaret had been the light of Thaddeus's life, her laughter filling their small home even on the darkest days. But the winter of 1943 had brought a sudden illness—pneumonia—that gripped her lungs with a fierce and unrelenting hold. Despite the doctor's best efforts, she slipped away in a matter of days, leaving Thaddeus with an emptiness he hadn't known was possible. He had buried her on a cold February morning, the ground frozen hard as iron, signaling his insurmountable difficulty in letting her go.

Thaddeus had thrown himself into his work over the past year. It was the only way he knew how to cope with the loss, to drown out the silence that echoed through the empty rooms of their small home. He straightened his shoulders, shaking off the memories as he approached the front door of the school. Today wasn't about him. It was about the children—his children, he liked to think of them. They needed him now more than ever.

Inside the schoolhouse, the familiar smell of chalk and old wood greeted him. Thaddeus set his satchel down on the worn desk at the front of the room. He glanced out at the empty desks, each one representing a story, a family, and lately, a great deal of hardship. Hazelwood was a melting pot of European immigrant families who had settled there over generations: Polish, German, Italian, and Hungarian families who had come seeking work and a fresh start.

The metalworking factory was the town's heartbeat, its lifeline, churning out supplies for the soldiers overseas. But the war had taken its toll here too. Many of the men—fathers, older brothers—had been drafted or volunteered, leaving the women and children to hold the town together. The strain showed in the small things: the drawn faces of mothers, the worn shoes of the children, the quiet, hollow look in their eyes as Christmas approached.

As the students began filing in, Thaddeus greeted each of them with a nod or a kind word. There was Emilio Rossi, the youngest son of the Italian-American Rossi family, whose father had gone to fight in the Pacific. Next was Rachel Kowalski, a bright girl with pigtails who clutched her tattered coat tight around her shoulders. Her brother was overseas too, serving as a field medic in Europe. Thaddeus could see the worry etched on her face, the same look her mother wore when she came to the schoolhouse.

"Good morning, Mr. Meriwether," Rachel said with a small, brave smile.

"Good morning, Rachel," Thaddeus replied, giving her shoulder a gentle squeeze. "How's your mother holding up?"

"She's all right," Rachel said, her voice softer now. "We got a letter from my brother Tom yesterday. He's safe."

Thaddeus felt a wave of relief for her, but it was tinged with the familiar sting of loss. He remembered the letters he'd once received from Margaret when she was away caring for her sick mother, and the crushing silence that followed when the letters stopped coming. He pushed the thought away.

"That's wonderful news," he said, smiling warmly at Rachel before she scurried off to her desk.

As the rest of the children settled in, Thaddeus noticed a tension in the room, a restlessness that hadn't been there before. It wasn't just the usual excitement that came before the holidays. It was something heavier, a quiet fear that clung to the air like the scent of burning wood from the factory chimneys.

Thaddeus cleared his throat and began the morning lesson, but his mind was elsewhere. He could see it in their faces—the hollowed cheeks, the nervous glances. The war had stolen more than just their fathers. It had taken their sense of security, their belief that the world was a safe place. And now, with Christmas around the corner, the absence of joy was palpable.

He set down his chalk and turned to face the class.

"Let's take a little break," he said, surprising himself as much as the children. "I want to tell you all a story."

The children leaned forward, curious. It wasn't often that Mr. Meriwether paused his lessons for a story. He pulled up a chair and sat down, looking at the faces before him—so young, yet marked by worry beyond their years.

"Many years ago," Thaddeus began, "when I was not much older than you are now, there was a Christmas that almost didn't happen. It was a difficult time for everyone. People were tired, cold, and uncertain about the future. But one small act of kindness changed everything."

The room fell silent. Even the youngest children, who usually squirmed in their seats, were captivated. Thaddeus wasn't sure where the story was going, but he could see the glimmer of hope in their eyes. He hadn't seen that in a long time.

"And that's when I got an idea," he continued, smiling a little as he saw Emilio and Rachel exchange glances. "This year, we're going to make sure everyone feels the magic of Christmas. We're going to do something special—together."

He stood up and looked around the room, taking in each child's expression, from the skeptical raise of little Anton Kaczmarek's eyebrow to the hopeful tilt of Diedre Milbaugh's head.

"We're going to have a secret Santa gift exchange," Thaddeus announced, his voice filled with conviction. "But it won't be about spending money. It'll be about giving something from the heart. Something handmade, or a small token that means something to you."

A murmur of excitement rippled through the room, mixed with a bit of uncertainty. Thaddeus could see the children's minds working, already thinking about what they could give despite having so little.

"But what if we don't have anything to give, Mr. Meriwether?" asked Tony Müller, his voice small but filled with genuine worry.

Thaddeus walked over and knelt beside Tony's desk, meeting the boy's eyes.

"Tony," he said softly, "everyone has something to give. A drawing, a poem, a story, even a smile. It's not about the gift itself—it's about the love behind it."

Tony nodded, looking down at his desk, and Thaddeus patted his shoulder before standing up.

"All right, class," he said, clapping his hands together, a new energy filling the room. "Let's get started. We have some work to do, and only a few weeks left before Christmas."

For the first time in a long while, Thaddeus felt a flicker of excitement himself. Perhaps, just perhaps, this Christmas would be different. It might not be filled with the familiar joy of the past, but it could be something new—something born out of shared hardship and the small, quiet acts of love that bind a community together.

And that, he thought, might be the greatest gift of all.

The idea of a secret Santa gift exchange lingered in Thaddeus Meriwether's mind long after the school day ended. He could still see the children's weary faces, marked by the absence of holiday cheer. He knew they needed something to lift their spirits—a reminder that Christmas was about more than just gifts. It was about connection, kindness, and the joy of giving.

He spent the evening crafting his plan, sitting by the fireplace with a notepad and pencil. He wanted this to be special, but he also knew it needed to be simple. Most families in Hazelwood were struggling to make ends meet. It had to be something that didn't require money—something handmade or meaningful from their own homes.

The next morning, he arrived at school early, determined to set things in motion. He had already spoken to a few of the parents, testing the waters to gauge their support. The reaction had been mixed. Some were enthusiastic, eager for a bit of holiday cheer in a difficult year. Others were more hesitant, overwhelmed by the daily grind of rationing and worrying about loved ones overseas.

As the children filed into the classroom, Thaddeus noticed a new sense of anticipation. They had sensed that something was different. He hadn't told them his full plan yet, but he knew he needed help to make it work.

Enlisting Mrs. Kowalski's Help

That afternoon, Thaddeus paid a visit to Mrs. Kowalski's sewing shop. The Polish immigrant had lived in Hazelwood for nearly two decades, becoming a beloved figure in the community. Her fingers flew deftly over her sewing machine as he explained his idea.

"A secret Santa gift exchange," she repeated thoughtfully, pausing her work. "And you want the children to make their own gifts?"

"Yes," Thaddeus said. "I want them to focus on creating something meaningful rather than buying presents. I was hoping you might help some of the girls with sewing small items—handkerchiefs, sachets, things like that."

Mrs. Kowalski's eyes softened, and a smile spread across her face. "It's a wonderful idea, Mr. Meriwether. The children need something to look forward to. I'll teach them how to make little pouches and lavender sachets. I have plenty of fabric scraps I've saved over the years. It will keep their hands busy and their minds off their worries."

As Thaddeus left the shop, he felt a surge of optimism. This was already becoming more than just a classroom project. It was a community effort.

The Carpenter's Workshop

Next, Thaddeus made his way to Wilhelm Schneider's woodworking shop. Wilhelm had lived in Hazelwood since before the war, a German-American who had faced prejudice as tensions rose. Despite this, he remained a respected craftsman, known for his skill and quiet strength. Thaddeus found him in the back of the shop, carving a small wooden bird.

"Wilhelm," Thaddeus began, "I'm organizing a secret Santa exchange for the children. I was wondering if you might be willing to help. The boys might like to carve small toys or ornaments. It doesn't have to be fancy—just something made with care."

Wilhelm looked up, his hands stilling on the carving knife. "Carving toys?" he asked, a faint smile forming on his lips. "I haven't done that in years. My son loved making little boats when he was a boy."

Thaddeus nodded, understanding the unspoken grief behind Wilhelm's words. "It would mean a lot to the children," he said gently. "And to the community."

Wilhelm gave a slow, thoughtful nod. "I'll bring some wood scraps by the school. It will be good for them. And for me, I think."

The Children's Excitement Grows

By the end of the week, the project was well underway. Mrs. Kowalski had brought a basket of fabric pieces to the classroom, and the girls were gathered around her, learning how to sew small sachets filled with dried herbs. Wilhelm arrived with a box of wood scraps, and the boys eagerly took to carving under his guidance, their faces lighting up as the rough pieces of wood transformed into little animals, ornaments, and spinning tops.

Deidre Milbaugh, who had been quiet all week, shared that she was writing a poem for her gift, inspired by the lullabies her German grandmother used to sing. Emilio Rossi decided to write out his grandmother's biscotti recipe, a family treasure passed down through generations. Even Anton Kaczmarek, who initially thought he had nothing to give, spent hours polishing a river stone until it shone like glass, imagining it as a lucky charm for its recipient.

The children worked with a newfound energy, chattering with each other about their secret projects. There was an unspoken understanding that this wasn't just about the gifts—it was about the joy of creating something for someone else, the anticipation of giving rather than receiving.

Overcoming Doubts and Skepticism

Despite the growing excitement, Thaddeus faced resistance from a few parents. Mr. Gillespie, whose eldest son was fighting in the Battle of the Bulge, voiced his frustration during a community meeting.

"We should be focusing on the essentials," he said, his voice edged with tension. "The war has taken so much already. There's no time for frivolities like this."

Thaddeus took a deep breath, feeling the weight of the room's collective worry. He understood their fears—their need to conserve every bit of energy and resource for the war effort. But he also knew that the children needed this small moment of joy.

"Our children are living through a war," he said, his voice calm but resolute. "They've seen their fathers and brothers leave, and they live with uncertainty every day. This isn't about frivolities—it's about hope. It's about giving them a chance to feel the spirit of Christmas, even if just for a moment."

Mr. Gillespie's expression softened, and slowly, he nodded. Around the room, other parents murmured in agreement. They had been reminded, if only briefly, of their own childhood Christmases—the magic, the wonder, the feeling of safety.

A New Kind of Christmas

Back at the school, the secret Santa preparations continued. The children's excitement filled the room, and for the first time in months, it felt like the holidays. Thaddeus watched them with a quiet smile, feeling a flicker of warmth in his chest. The laughter, the joy—they were building more than just gifts. They were rebuilding their sense of connection, of community, of hope.

And as the snow began to fall softly outside the classroom window, Thaddeus knew that they had found something far more valuable than any gift. They had found a way to give each other a piece of light in a dark time.

Christmas Eve arrived in Hazelwood with a light dusting of snow that clung to the bare branches of the trees lining the schoolyard. Inside the small, one-room schoolhouse, the children had gathered, their faces bright with anticipation despite the chill in the air. The room was transformed—strings of paper garlands draped across the ceiling; pine branches adorned with handmade ornaments resting on the windowsills. Each decoration told a story, reflecting the rich tapestry of the town's families: delicate paper snowflakes from the Rossi children, brightly colored Polish stars from the Kowalskis, and small carved wooden birds shaped by Wilhelm Schneider's hands.

Thaddeus Meriwether stood at the front of the room, taking it all in. He could see the pride in the children's faces, the way they marveled at the festive scene they had created together. It was more than he had hoped for—a moment of true, shared joy, a brief reprieve from the weight of the war.

"All right, class," Thaddeus said, his voice steady but warm. "It's time for our gift exchange. Remember, this isn't about what we receive. It's about what we've created for each other, from the heart."

The children nodded, eager and a little shy, glancing at the small bundles and packages they held in their hands. One by one, they stepped forward to share their gifts. There was a hushed reverence in the room as each child presented their offering, accompanied by a few quiet words.

Emilio Rossi went first, holding a small package wrapped in brown paper. He handed it to Anton Kaczmarek, whose eyes widened with surprise.

"It's my grandmother's biscotti recipe," Emilio explained. "I thought your family might like to try it. It's her way of saying thank you for the bread your mother shared with us last winter."

Anton's face broke into a grin, and he gave Emilio a quick, awkward hug, their shared laughter filling the room.

Next was Diedre Milbaugh, who presented a neatly folded piece of paper to Rachel Kowalski. "It's a poem," Diedre said, her cheeks flushed with nerves. "I wrote it for you, Rachel. It's about the lullabies my Oma used to sing when I was little. I hope it brings you some comfort."

Rachel's eyes shone as she read the first few lines, her voice catching on the words. She hugged Diedre tightly, whispering her thanks.

Around the room, the gifts continued—small, simple tokens, each one carrying a deeper meaning than anything money could buy. Tony Müller gave a carefully polished river stone to Diedre, telling her it was a lucky charm. Rachel gifted Anton a sachet filled with lavender, stitched by her own hands, and whispered that the scent was meant to bring peace and good dreams.

Thaddeus watched it all unfold, feeling an unfamiliar warmth settle in his chest. The children's laughter, the shared stories of their families and loved ones overseas—it was as if, for this brief moment, the war didn't exist. They had found something greater than the fear and uncertainty that had clouded their days. They had found a way to hold on to hope.

A Gift for Thaddeus

Just as the last gift was exchanged, Emilio stepped forward again, this time holding a large, wrapped bundle. He hesitated, glancing back at the other children, who nodded and urged him on.

"Mr. Meriwether," Emilio said, his voice small but clear. "We have a gift for you too."

Thaddeus's brow furrowed in surprise. He hadn't expected anything. "For me?" he asked, a soft smile tugging at his lips. "You didn't have to do that."

"We wanted to," Diedre said, stepping up beside Emilio. "You've done so much for us, and we wanted to show you how much it means."

The children gathered around as Thaddeus carefully unwrapped the bundle. Inside was a scrapbook, its cover handmade from scraps of fabric and bits of ribbon. He opened it slowly, his breath catching as he saw the first page: a drawing of him standing at the front of the classroom, surrounded by smiling faces.

"It's from all of us," Tony Müller explained. "We each made a page. There are drawings, notes, and stories… things we wanted to share with you."

Thaddeus turned the pages, his eyes filling with tears as he took in each child's contribution. There were sketches of their favorite memories from the year, little notes thanking him for his kindness, and stories about their families. He paused on a drawing of himself and Margaret, sketched by Diedre Milbaugh, her pencil lines delicate and full of emotion. It was the two of them standing under the Christmas tree, the way they had been before she fell ill.

For a moment, Thaddeus couldn't speak. He ran his fingers over the page, feeling the familiar ache of grief, but also something new—something like healing.

"Thank you," he managed, his voice thick with emotion. "This… this is the most beautiful gift I've ever received."

The children crowded around him, hugging him tightly, their small arms offering a warmth that seemed to fill every crack in his broken heart.

The Final Scene

As the children began to leave, their laughter trailing into the cold evening air, heavier snow began to fall. Thaddeus stood by the doorway, watching them go, feeling a peace he hadn't known in years. The snow fell softly, covering the ground in a white blanket, muffling the world in a quiet hush.

He looked down at the scrapbook in his hands, feeling the weight of it, the love poured into each page. For the first time since Margaret's passing, he felt her presence, as though she were standing beside him, her hand resting on his shoulder. It was as if she were telling him it was all right to let go of the sorrow, to hold on to this moment of grace.

Just as he was about to close the door, a small figure ran back toward him. It was Rachel Kowalski, her breath puffing in the cold air, her cheeks rosy.

"Merry Christmas, Mr. Meriwether," she said, throwing her arms around his waist. "We couldn't have done it without you."

Thaddeus hugged her back, his eyes closing against the tears that threatened to spill over. "Merry Christmas, Rachel," he whispered. "Thank you."

He watched her run back to her family, then stepped outside, standing alone in the gentle snowfall. He looked up at the night sky, the stars barely visible behind the drifting clouds, and for the first time in a long time, he felt a sense of hope—real, tangible hope.

The world was still broken, the war still raged on, but here, in this small town, they had found a way to hold on to what mattered. They had given each other the gift of light in the darkness.

Thaddeus took a deep breath, letting the cold air fill his lungs. He smiled, feeling a renewed sense of purpose and the quiet, steady warmth of the community he loved.

And as he turned to head back inside, he knew one thing for certain: This Christmas had been a promise kept—not just to the children, but to himself.

REFLECTIONS BY THE FIRE

Embers of Memory

Orson Baines sat alone in his study, a room thick with shadows and the comforting scent of old books. The fire was the room's only light, its glow casting a dance of orange and gold across the faded wallpaper. He leaned back in his worn leather chair, feeling its familiar creak, and let the sound of the crackling wood fill the silence. It was a rare indulgence tonight—both the solitude and the whiskey he cradled in his hand. He took a slow sip, savoring the warmth that settled in his chest.

The flames held his gaze, as if they were the final chapter of a book he had read a thousand times. Each flicker, each spark, pulled memories from the depths of his mind, memories that had both warmed and burned him, leaving scars like the blackened edges of a smoldering log. He let himself drift back, allowing the years to blur together, letting the fire carry him away.

He was a young man again, seated at a café table in the city, scribbling furiously into a notebook. The words came easily then—sharp, inspired, unburdened by the weight of life's regrets. Across the table from him sat Eliza, her laughter filling the air like a melody he hadn't heard in years. She was his muse, his first love, and for a brief, brilliant moment, the world had revolved only around the two of them. He could still see the way the sunlight danced in her eyes, how her smile had seemed to promise endless possibilities.

But he hadn't pursued it. He had chosen his words, his writing, over her. He had told himself it was the right decision, the sensible one. He'd been too young, too ambitious, and too certain that there would always be more time. Now, sitting by the fire, he could see the folly in that. The moments of passion they shared had been fleeting, but their memory lingered like the dying embers before him—beautiful and agonizingly out of reach.

The room seemed to grow colder as he thought of Eliza. He took another sip of whiskey, feeling the burn this time. He'd tried to capture her in his writing over the years, to immortalize the love he had let slip away, but the words had never felt right. They had always fallen short, a pale imitation of the truth. He could admit that now, here in the silence, with only the fire as his witness.

He glanced over at his desk, where his unfinished memoir lay in a neat stack of papers. It was a lifetime's worth of stories, filled with triumphs and broken moments, carefully crafted yet incomplete. He had always been a storyteller, but tonight, as he looked back on his life, he realized he had often been telling the wrong story—the one where he was always the hero, always in control.

The fire crackled, sending a shower of sparks into the chimney. Orson closed his eyes and let the sound carry him deeper into his memories. He could see the faces of friends long gone, the places he'd once called home, the children who had grown up and moved away. They were all there, in the smoke and the flames, dancing just out of reach.

He opened his eyes again and stared into the fire. It was dying down now, the flames shrinking, the light dimming. The passage of time felt heavy in the room, as if the very air was saturated with the weight of missed opportunities and paths not taken.

Orson leaned forward, feeling the ache in his bones, the reminder of his own frailty. He raised his glass in a silent toast—to Eliza, to the dreams of his youth, to all the things he would never say aloud. He took the final sip of his whiskey and set the glass down beside him.

The fire was no longer a blaze, but a soft, glowing ember, its warmth fading. He felt a sudden urge to add another log, to rekindle the flames, but he resisted. There was a kind of peace in letting it die down, in sitting with the fading heat and the memories that lingered like smoke in the air.

The room grew dimmer, the shadows longer. He leaned back in his chair and let out a slow, weary sigh. It was enough, he decided. Tonight, it was enough.

The Smoldering Struggles

The fire had dimmed to a soft, sullen glow, casting long shadows that crawled up the walls like echoes of a forgotten past. Orson Baines leaned forward in his chair; the empty whiskey glass heavy in his hand. He felt the chill of the room seep into his bones, mingling with the familiar ache of old regrets. Tonight, he wasn't just an old man reminiscing by the fire; he was a father haunted by the ghosts of choices he could never take back.

He glanced down at his hands, the skin thin and veined like crumpled paper. These were the hands that had once held his children, cradled them close, and promised to keep them safe. How many times had he let them slip away to chase after his own dreams? The memories of those small, trusting faces rose unbidden, and he felt a sharp pang of loss—deeper and more raw than he had ever allowed himself to acknowledge.

Orson stared into the fire, watching the embers pulse with a faint, dying light. He saw himself in that glow, burning brightly once, now fading away. The silence in the room seemed to press in around him, thick and heavy, as he let his mind drift back to those early days when everything had seemed possible. He had been a young writer then, full of ambition and eager to carve out a name for himself. He could still recall the thrill of his first published story, the way it had felt like he had finally found his place in the world.

But that thrill had come at a price. He had thrown himself into his work with a single-minded passion, writing late into the night while his wife slept alone, waiting for him to come to bed. He remembered the mornings when she would find him slumped over his desk, pen still in hand, and the look of resigned sadness in her eyes. He had brushed it off at the time, told himself she would understand. It was for their future, he had insisted, for the life he was building for them all.

Yet now, sitting here in the dim light of the dying fire, he could see the truth he had ignored for so long. It wasn't for their future he had been writing—it was for himself. It had always been for himself.

He thought of his son, Robert, and the rift that had grown between them like a deep, unbridgeable canyon. When Robert was a boy, he had idolized Orson, following him around, mimicking his every move. Orson could still picture the way Robert's eyes would light up whenever he read his father's stories. It had been the pure, uncomplicated love of a child who believed his father could do no wrong.

But that love had withered as Robert grew older and began to see his father for what he truly was—a man consumed by his own work, always distant, always distracted. Orson could still hear the sharp edge of his son's voice, filled with a bitterness that cut deeper than any critic's review.

"You care more about your damn stories than you do about us," Robert had shouted one night, slamming the door so hard the whole house seemed to shake.

Orson had yelled back, his pride wounded, his defenses rising. He had thrown out accusations, tried to justify his choices, but even then, he knew he was losing something far more precious than an argument. The look in Robert's eyes had been one of betrayal, and Orson knew it was a look that had lingered long after the shouting stopped.

He ran a hand over his face, feeling the rough stubble of his unshaved beard. How many times had he replayed that scene in his mind, wishing he could go back and say something different? He had spent his life weaving stories, crafting perfect dialogues, yet when it mattered most, he had been unable to find the right words.

A shiver ran through him as he leaned back, the coldness of the room settling over him like a shroud. He picked up the stack of papers from his desk, his unfinished memoir, and flipped through the pages. Each line felt like a piece of himself, raw and exposed. He paused at a single, yellowed sheet tucked between the chapters—a letter he had written but never sent. The creases were deep, the ink smudged in places where his tears had stained the paper.

With a deep breath, he unfolded the letter, his hands trembling slightly. He knew every word by heart, yet he had never dared to read it aloud. Tonight, it felt different. The silence seemed to demand it, as if the room itself were waiting for him to finally confront the truth.

"*My dear Robert,*" he began, his voice barely above a whisper, "*I know I have hurt you in ways I can never undo. I chose my stories, my characters, over you, and I see now what a terrible mistake that was. I don't expect your forgiveness. I only hope you understand that writing was the only way I knew how to make sense of the world. It wasn't because I loved my stories more than you; it was because I was afraid. Afraid of being a father, afraid of being vulnerable. You are everything I wish I could have been. Please know that I love you, even if I never found the right words to say it.*"

His voice broke on the last line, and he let the letter fall to his lap. He felt the tears well up, hot and unbidden, spilling down his cheeks. He didn't wipe them away this time. He let them fall, let himself feel the weight of every unsaid word, every missed moment.

The room felt different now—emptier, but also lighter, as if he had finally set down a burden he'd been carrying for far too long. He looked at the fire, nearly out now, just a few smoldering coals left in the grate. It seemed a fitting metaphor for his own life—still warm, but the flames almost spent.

He leaned forward, placing another log on the fire. He watched as the flames licked up around the wood, slowly coming back to life. It wasn't much, but it was something.

He wiped his eyes and took a deep breath, feeling a strange, quiet solace settle over him. He couldn't change the past, but he could change the way he told the story. He could write a better ending, one where he didn't pretend to be the hero but simply a man, flawed and full of regrets, trying his best.

Orson leaned back, the warmth of the fire seeping back into the room. It was a small comfort, but it was enough.

For tonight, it was enough.

The Final Flame

The fire was down to its last embers, a soft, red glow that barely lit the room. The shadows crept closer, long fingers of darkness that stretched across the floor, brushing against the worn leather of Orson's chair. He could feel the chill seeping in now, wrapping around his ankles like the breath of winter. He knew it might be the last winter he spent here, beside this hearth that had witnessed so many nights like this—nights filled with silence, regret, and the company of his own thoughts.

He leaned back, letting the quiet settle over him. The whiskey glass sat empty on the table, but he didn't reach for more. He wanted to feel everything tonight, unfiltered and raw. It was a night for endings, for letting go of the things he had held onto for far too long.

He turned his gaze to the stack of papers on his desk, his final memoir—unfinished, yet complete in its own way. It was a collection of stories, fragments of a life that he had pieced together in these last years. The room felt heavy with the weight of those words, the culmination of a lifetime of writing. He knew, as he picked up the manuscript, that these were the last words he would ever write. The realization brought a sense of calm, as if a door was gently closing on a chapter that had run its course.

Orson ran a hand over the cover page, feeling the indentations of his pen. He thought of the countless hours he had spent here, bent over his desk, shaping sentences like a sculptor carving marble. He had always believed that his words could outlast him, that they could speak for him when he was gone. But tonight, he wasn't so sure. Tonight, the words felt fragile, like the embers in the grate—beautiful but fleeting.

He cleared his throat, speaking softly into the silence, as if addressing an unseen audience. "If you're reading this," he began, "then you've found the last thing I must give. It's not a perfect story. It's not even a complete one. But it's mine. It's the truth as I've known it."

He paused, the room feeling strangely alive, as if it were listening. He felt a pull deep within him, a need to speak plainly, without the guise of fiction or the comfort of metaphor. He set the manuscript down and leaned forward, his voice steadier now.

"I spent my life trying to understand love, to write about it in a way that made sense. But I realize now that I got it wrong. I thought love was something you could capture in words, something you could hold onto if you just tried hard enough. But love isn't a story you can write. It's a feeling you live with, a choice you make every day. And sometimes… sometimes you make the wrong choices."

His voice broke, the words hanging in the air like a confession. He thought of Eliza, her face as vivid in his mind as it had been all those years ago. He had loved her with a kind of reckless abandon, the kind of love that could set the world on fire. But he had let her go, believing that his writing was his true calling. It was a choice he had made, and one he had lived with every day since.

He closed his eyes and whispered, "Goodbye, Eliza." It wasn't the first time he had said it, but it felt different now. It felt final, like the closing of a book. He could almost see her smile, that soft, knowing look that had always made him feel seen, truly seen.

Orson took a deep breath, feeling a lightness in his chest that he hadn't felt in years. It was as if he had released something, a burden he hadn't even realized he was carrying. He looked back at the manuscript, thinking of his children—of Robert, who might never read these words, and of his daughter, who had always understood him in ways that surprised him.

"I hope you find this someday," he said quietly, as if speaking directly to them. "I hope you read these words and see the man I was trying to be, not the one you remember. I wasn't always good at showing it, but I loved you. I loved you more than I loved my stories, more than I loved anything."

He fell silent, the room growing colder as the last of the embers faded. He felt a deep, aching sense of loss, but also a strange, unexpected peace. He had spent so many years wrestling with his regrets, trying to rewrite the past in his mind. But tonight, he was done fighting. He was ready to accept the story for what it was.

He leaned forward, picking up a small candle from the table. It was the same candle he had lit so many nights when the power went out, when the fire wasn't enough to keep the darkness at bay. He brought it close to his lips and blew softly. The flame flickered, danced for a moment, then went out, leaving the room in complete darkness.

For a moment, he just sat there, listening to the silence. It was a deep, restful silence, the kind that comes after a long storm. He felt a smile tug at the corners of his mouth, a small, private smile. It wasn't the ending he had planned, but it was enough. He had told his story, as best as he could. And now, he could finally rest.

THE SNOWFLAKE INN

Winter's Chill

Snow fell in soft ripples over the frozen landscape of northern Wisconsin, blanketing the world in a quiet that was both serene and unsettling. The village of Winter Hollow lay nestled between thick pine forests and the jagged shores of Lake Winnemara, a place where stories of long winters and longer memories lived in every cabin and shadowed corner. At its heart stood the Snowflake Inn, an old Victorian manor that had once been the pride of the town but now stood like a solemn relic of another time.

Fiora Lovett, the innkeeper, stared out from the large bay window, her reflection blending with the falling snow. Her auburn hair, streaked with the silver of passing years, framed a face that was still beautiful but softened by time and loss. Tonight, something felt different. The air was heavy with more than just the promise of a snowstorm. It was as if the entire village was holding its breath, waiting for something unseen.

"Winter Hollow has its ghosts," her father used to say, his gravelly voice sent shivers down her spine. Fiora never truly believed him — until tonight.

The Snowflake Inn had belonged to her family for generations. Her mother, a lively woman with a heart full of Christmas cheer, had turned it into a haven for weary travelers. Her father, ever the stoic, had filled its halls with stories of the old days — tales of lumberjacks who braved the northern woods and fishermen who disappeared into the icy depths of the lake. But there was one story he never told in full, a story that lingered in the silence of Christmas Eve.

Fiora could almost hear his voice now, warning her not to dwell on the past. Yet, as she gazed at the empty lobby, lit only by the soft glow of candles and the flickering flames in the hearth, the memories felt closer than ever. Fifty years ago, on a night just like this, a man had vanished from one of the inn's upstairs rooms. No one had seen him leave; his bed was untouched, his coat still hung by the door. It was as if he had walked into the snow and simply disappeared.

The villagers called it The Christmas Vanishing, and every year, the tale was whispered over mulled wine and crackling fires. Some said the man's spirit still roamed the halls of the inn, searching for something he lost long ago. Fiora didn't believe in ghosts, but tonight, as the snow piled up against the windows and the wind howled through the eaves, she couldn't shake the feeling that she wasn't alone.

A gust of wind rattled the front door, and the old brass bell above it jingled. Fiora jumped, her heart pounding in her chest. It had been years since that sound startled her. She smoothed down her apron and hurried to greet the first guests of the night.

A young family stumbled in, covered in snow and shivering from the cold. The father, a tall man with dark, tired eyes, clutched a small child wrapped in a thick blanket. The mother, pale and trembling, held a bag tightly against her chest, her knuckles white.

"Please," the man said, his voice edged with desperation. "The roads are blocked. We need shelter."

Fiora forced a smile, her unease pushed aside by the instinct to help. "Of course. You're safe here," she said, guiding them inside. The fire's warmth enveloped them, and the child stirred, letting out a soft whimper.

"Thank you," the mother whispered, her eyes darting around the lobby. She seemed almost afraid, as if she expected someone — or something — to follow them inside.

"What's your name, dear?" Fiora asked gently.

"I'm Sofia," the woman replied, her voice barely above a whisper. "This is my husband, Alexei, and our daughter, Anya. We've been traveling for days."

"Well, Sofia, you've found the right place," Fiora said, her smile turning genuine for a moment. "The Snowflake Inn may be old, but it has a way of making people feel at home."

Before she could say more, the door creaked open again, carried by a sharp gust of icy wind. A man stepped inside, shaking snow from his broad shoulders. He was tall and gruff-looking, with a face that seemed carved from the rugged granite of the northern cliffs. He looked around with a frown, as if disappointed by what he saw.

"Is this place still open?" he demanded, his voice rough like gravel crunching under boots.

"Yes, we're open," Fiora replied, meeting his gaze. There was something unsettling about his eyes — a sharpness that felt out of place in the warmth of the inn. "And you are?"

"Whitaker," he said curtly. "Thomas Whitaker. Got stuck on the road when the storm hit. Need a room, and I'm not picky."

"There's hot coffee by the fire," Fiora said, gesturing toward the hearth. "Warm yourself up while I get your room ready."

Whitaker nodded stiffly, tossing his wet coat over a chair. Fiora watched him for a moment, sensing a heaviness in his presence. He was like so many travelers she'd seen — hardened by the road, carrying secrets like stones in his pockets.

The bell chimed once more, and a couple entered, their faces flushed with cold. They seemed well-dressed but frazzled, as though they'd been arguing moments before. The woman's eyes were red-rimmed from crying, and the man's expression was a mask of forced calm.

"We need a room," the woman said, her voice brittle. "Just for tonight."

Fiora's smile faltered, replaced by a look of deep understanding. "You've come to the right place," she said softly. "Here, everyone finds shelter."

As she led them toward the fire, a shadow moved at the top of the staircase. It was there only for a split second, but Fiora's heart skipped a beat. She blinked, and it was gone, leaving her with the eerie sensation that someone — or something — had been watching.

The storm raged outside, but inside the Snowflake Inn, a deeper storm was brewing. Fiora glanced at the old portrait of her parents above the mantle. In the flickering candlelight, it almost seemed like their painted eyes were following her, gleaming with a life that shouldn't have been there.

For the first time in years, Fiora wondered if the stories were true. If tonight, on this snowbound Christmas Eve, the past had finally returned.

The Gathering Storm

The wind roared against the windows like a living thing, rattling the glass as if it sought to break into the warm sanctuary of the Snowflake Inn. The storm outside had escalated into a blizzard, wrapping Winter Hollow in a blanket of white that smothered the town's flickering lights. Inside, the inn felt like an island adrift in a sea of snow, cut off from the world.

Fiora Lovett stoked the fire, her hands moving with practiced ease, though her eyes darted to the darkened corners of the room. The guests had gathered by the hearth, and the heat from the flames cast a golden glow over their faces. Yet the warmth did little to thaw the chill of unease that hung between them.

Thomas Whitaker, the traveling salesman, leaned back in his chair, his eyes narrowed as he scanned the room. He had shed his coat, but the hardness in his expression hadn't softened. He took a long sip of his coffee, the steam rising like smoke from a smoldering fire.

"So, where exactly did you folks come from?" he asked, his voice dripping with suspicion. He directed his gaze at Alexei and Sofia, the young immigrant couple who huddled close together with their daughter, Anya, asleep on her mother's lap.

"We're from Ukraine," Alexei replied, his accent thick, his words clipped. He did not elaborate, but the weight of their journey hung heavily in the room. It was written in the exhaustion on their faces, the way Sofia held Anya close as if she might vanish into the night.

Whitaker smirked, swirling his coffee. "Long way from home, aren't you? What brings you to a place like this?"

"We came for a better life," Sofia said softly, her eyes downcast. "The war... it's too dangerous. We wanted a fresh start for Anya."

Fiora felt a pang of empathy. She knew the look in Sofia's eyes — the look of someone who had been running for so long, they'd forgotten how to stop. "You're safe here," she said gently. "The storm will pass by morning, and we'll help you find your way."

"Safe?" Whitaker snorted, leaning forward. "You think this place is safe? You don't know the stories they tell in this town, do you? About the people who've disappeared — just like that." He snapped his fingers, the sound echoing in the quiet room.

The couple exchanged a glance, unease flashing between them. Even the well-dressed couple, sitting stiffly at the edge of the room, seemed to tense. The woman's red-rimmed eyes darted to the staircase, as if she expected something to appear there.

"Enough, Thomas," Fiora said, her tone sharp but controlled. "There's no need to frighten anyone. It's just a storm, nothing more."

Whitaker chuckled, settling back into his chair. "If you say so, innkeeper. But I've heard the stories. A man goes missing on Christmas Eve, and no one ever finds him. Maybe he's still here — in the walls, in the shadows."

"Stop it!" the woman snapped, her voice trembling. Her husband reached for her hand, but she pulled away, tears welling in her eyes. "I can't take any more of this."

Fiora stepped closer, her expression softening. "It's alright," she said gently. "The storm can make us all feel a bit on edge. Why don't we share a little bit about ourselves? It might help pass the time."

For a moment, the room fell silent, save for the crackling of the fire. Then, to Fiora's surprise, Alexei spoke.

"We came to America because we had no choice," he said quietly. "We left everything behind — our home, our family. All we have now is each other. And we are grateful for that, but..." His voice faltered, and Sofia squeezed his hand, a tear slipping down her cheek.

"But it is hard," she finished for him. "Harder than we expected. We are trying to be brave for Anya, but some nights, it feels like the world is against us."

Fiora's heart clenched. She knew that feeling well. "You are brave," she said simply. "And you are not alone tonight."

Whitaker cleared his throat, looking uncomfortable. He rubbed the back of his neck, as if trying to dispel his own discomfort. "Yeah, well, the road can be a lonely place, too," he muttered. "I've been selling for thirty years. Seen every kind of town, every kind of person. But there's nothing lonelier than a cheap motel room on Christmas Eve."

He glanced at the couple sitting apart, as if daring them to share. The woman's face softened, and she reached for her husband's hand once more. This time, he didn't pull away.

"We're... we're going through a rough patch," she admitted, her voice barely above a whisper. "We've lost sight of each other. Of what matters." She squeezed his hand, tears glistening in her eyes. "But maybe tonight, we can find it again."

Fiora watched them, her heart swelling with a strange kind of joy. This was the magic of the inn, the magic her mother had always believed in. The storm outside howled, but here, in the glow of the fire, something was beginning to heal.

Just as she thought the moment couldn't be more perfect, the lights flickered. Once, twice, then plunged the room into darkness.

A collective gasp filled the air. Anya stirred in her mother's arms, whimpering softly. Fiora moved quickly, lighting candles and placing them on the mantle. The flames flickered to life, casting a warm, golden light that softened the shadows.

"Don't worry," she said, her voice calm. "We've been through worse storms. The power will come back soon."

But even as she spoke, a chill crept up her spine. She couldn't shake the feeling that something was different tonight, that the darkness held more than just the absence of light.

The guests huddled closer together, the flickering candles casting their faces in an otherworldly glow. Whitaker's eyes darted to the staircase, and for the first time, Fiora saw fear in them.

"Maybe the stories are true," he muttered. "Maybe we aren't as alone as we think."

Fiora forced a smile, but the shadows in the corners seemed to dance with a life of their own. The snow battered the windows like a thousand icy fingers, and somewhere in the distance, a low, mournful wail echoed through the night.

"Let's sing," she said suddenly, her voice bright and cheerful. "A carol, to lighten the mood."

The guests hesitated, but then Alexei began to hum, a soft, sweet melody that filled the room. One by one, they joined in, their voices blending in a harmony that felt like a balm against the storm.

As they sang, Fiora glanced at the portrait of her parents above the mantle. In the candlelight, their painted faces seemed to smile, as if they, too, were part of the gathering. And for a fleeting moment, the inn felt like it had when she was a child — full of laughter, full of life.

But even as the song lifted her spirits, Fiora couldn't shake the sense that something was watching from the shadows. Something that had been waiting for this very night.

The power will come back, she told herself. The storm will pass. And yet, she knew that before the night was over, the secrets of the Snowflake Inn would demand to be heard.

The Light of Dawn

The blizzard's fury slowly waned, and the relentless howl of the wind gave way to a deep, muffled silence. It was as if the storm, having spent its wrath, had finally surrendered to the stillness of the northern Wisconsin night. Inside the Snowflake Inn, the guests huddled close, their faces illuminated by the flickering candles. The room was filled with an almost palpable sense of shared vulnerability — and a growing warmth.

Fiora Lovett stood at the edge of the circle, her eyes sweeping over the group. The young immigrant family, the couple who had walked in with their broken hearts, and Thomas Whitaker, who seemed more lost than any of them. For a moment, it felt as if time had slowed, holding them all in a quiet, fragile suspension.

"Is it over?" Sofia's voice was barely a whisper, her arms wrapped protectively around her sleeping daughter, Anya. The little girl's soft breathing was the only sound in the room.

Fiora nodded. "Yes," she said gently. "The worst has passed. By morning, the snow will start to melt away."

But it wasn't just the storm outside that was easing. Fiora could feel the tension among the guests softening too, like ice breaking apart on the first warm day of spring. They had come together, strangers bound by a shared need for shelter, and in the dark hours of the night, something had changed.

Sofia turned to her husband, Alexei, her eyes shining with unshed tears. "We made it," she whispered, reaching for his hand. He took it, squeezing it tightly, and for the first time since they arrived, a genuine smile crossed his face.

"We did," he said, his voice choked with emotion. "We have each other, and that's enough."

The couple at the edge of the room, who had barely spoken to each other since they arrived, exchanged a look that held years of unsaid words. The woman, still teary-eyed, took a deep breath. "I'm sorry," she said quietly, her voice raw. "I've been so angry, so hurt. But I never stopped loving you."

Her husband looked down at their joined hands, as if seeing them for the first time. "I've been a fool," he admitted, his voice thick with regret. "I let my pride come between us. But I'm here now, and I don't want to lose you."

She leaned into him, resting her head on his shoulder. "We're still here," she murmured. "That's what matters."

Whitaker, who had been sitting with his arms crossed, looked away, blinking rapidly. The hardness in his face seemed to dissolve, and he let out a long, weary sigh. "Maybe I've been wrong about a lot of things," he said, almost to himself. "I've spent my life on the road, selling things people don't need, thinking it made me important. But sitting here tonight... I see what I've been missing."

Fiora stepped closer, placing a gentle hand on his shoulder. "It's never too late to change your path," she said softly. "You've still got time to find what you're looking for."

Whitaker met her eyes, and for the first time, he looked vulnerable. He nodded, a small, grateful smile tugging at his lips. "Maybe I'll try," he said. "Maybe it's time to stop running."

The fire crackled, sending up a shower of sparks, and the room fell into a peaceful silence. Outside, the first light of dawn crept over the horizon, casting a pink glow across the snow-covered landscape. The storm had left a pristine world in its wake, untouched and full of promise.

Fiora turned toward the window, her heart swelling with a quiet joy. The inn, her parents' legacy, had become what it was always meant to be — a place where strangers found comfort, where broken hearts could heal. She felt a presence beside her and looked up to see the well-dressed woman who had arrived with the arguing couple.

"I never introduced myself," the woman said with a kind smile. "My name is Meredith Blake. I'm a consultant for small businesses, and I couldn't help but notice the charm of this place. It's rare, you know, to find an inn like this — so full of history and heart."

Fiora laughed softly, a lightness she hadn't felt in years bubbling up inside her. "It's seen better days," she admitted. "But it's always been special to me."

Meredith nodded thoughtfully. "I think it could be special to a lot of people," she said. "With a bit of investment, this inn could become a hub for the community — a place for gatherings, events, even retreats. I'd love to help you make that happen."

Fiora's breath caught. She had spent so many nights worrying about the inn's future, fearing she would lose it forever. Now, this unexpected offer felt like a lifeline thrown just when she needed it most. "Are you serious?" she asked, her voice tinged with hope.

"As serious as the snow outside," Meredith said with a grin. "Think about it, Fiora. You have something here that people crave — a sense of home, of belonging. Let's bring it to life together."

Fiora felt a tear slip down her cheek, but this time it wasn't from sadness. It was from the overwhelming relief of realizing that she didn't have to fight this battle alone. "I'd like that," she said, her voice breaking. "I'd like that very much."

The guests, sensing a shift in the room, turned to look at Fiora. There was a collective sigh of contentment, as if everyone had been holding their breath and could finally let go. The firelight danced in their eyes, and someone — perhaps Alexei — began to hum a carol. One by one, the others joined in, their voices rising together in a soft, harmonious song.

Fiora stood by the window, watching the snowflakes drift lazily to the ground. The storm had passed, but its magic lingered in the air. She thought of her parents, of the love they had poured into this place, and she knew they were smiling down on her.

The Snowflake Inn was alive again, filled with laughter, music, and the warmth of human connection. It had become more than just a building; it was a refuge, a place where miracles could happen — especially on Christmas Eve.

As the morning light streamed through the windows, Fiora felt a deep, abiding peace settle over her. She wasn't just an innkeeper. She was the keeper of a thousand untold stories of hopes and dreams wrapped in the wisping snow. And she knew, with every beat of her heart, that this was just the beginning.

The snow fell gently outside, like a benediction. And inside, the spirit of the Snowflake Inn shone bright and true, lighting the way for all who sought shelter from the storm.

LETTERS FROM THE HOMEFRONT

A Letter Unwritten

The leaves of Willow Creek had turned to shades of amber and crimson, swirling around like tiny dancers in the crisp October breeze. Janelle Madison kicked a pile of them as she walked home from school, watching them scatter like memories she couldn't quite grasp. The creek babbled nearby, its familiar sound comforting yet distant, as though it belonged to another time, a time before the letter arrived.

It was a Tuesday morning when Janelle's world changed. She remembered the way her mother's hands shook, the letter crumpled in her grip. The words *We regret to inform you* had sliced through their living room like a cold wind. David, her older brother — gone. Just like that. The laughter they shared by the creek, the games, the secrets, all of it swallowed by a place she couldn't even picture: Vietnam.

Janelle shook off the memory as she reached the steps of Willow Creek Elementary School, the red bricks warm in the afternoon sun. She was greeted by the familiar chaos of kids spilling out of the building, their shouts and laughter mingling with the sound of the creek. It felt strange to her, how life seemed to go on so easily for everyone else.

"Hey, Janelle! Wait up!" called out her best friend, Becky Carlson, her blond pigtails bobbing as she ran to catch up.

"Hey," Janelle said, forcing a smile. She hadn't told Becky about David yet. How could she? It made everything too real.

"Did you hear about the project Mrs. Porter's got for us?" Becky asked, her eyes wide with excitement.

Janelle frowned. "No, what project?"

Becky tugged on her sleeve. "Come on! You'll see."

Inside the classroom, Mrs. Porter stood at the front, her kind eyes crinkling behind her glasses as she clapped her hands for attention. "Alright, everyone, settle down. I've got something special for you today."

The chatter died down, and Janelle slid into her seat, her fingers tracing the wood grain of the desk. She had loved Mrs. Porter's projects in the past, but today her heart wasn't in it. Nothing seemed important anymore, not since David…

"We're going to write letters," Mrs. Porter announced, her voice bright and full of encouragement. "Not just any letters. These are going to soldiers stationed overseas. I know some of you may have family members serving, and I think it's important they know we're thinking of them."

Janelle's heart clenched. She stared down at her desk, her vision blurring. This project wasn't special. It was cruel.

Mrs. Porter must have noticed her expression because she softened her tone. "I know it might be hard for some of you," she said gently, her eyes meeting Janelle's. "But sometimes, sharing our thoughts can help us heal. And you never know who your words might reach."

Janelle nodded; her throat tight. She wanted to run, to hide in the safety of the creek's whispering reeds, but instead, she picked up her pencil. The words came slowly, each stroke of the pencil feeling like she was digging into her own heart.

"Dear Soldier,"

She paused. What could she possibly say? Her mind flashed back to the summer festival in Willow Creek, the smell of kettle corn in the air, David lifting her onto his shoulders so she could see the fireworks. It felt like a dream now, one she couldn't get back to.

Janelle bit her lip and began to write again, her hand trembling.

"My name is Janelle Madison. I'm from a small town called Willow Creek. It's a quiet place, with a creek that runs right through the middle of it. My brother used to say it was the most peaceful sound in the world…"

She stopped, pressing her fingers to her eyes to keep the tears from falling. She couldn't write about David. It hurt too much. Instead, she wrote about the town, the festivals, the way the leaves turned gold and red in the fall.

"I hope you're doing okay," she wrote. *"I can't imagine what it's like over there, but I wanted you to know that someone is thinking of you. I pressed a flower from the creek inside this letter. It's my favorite place to go when I need to think. Maybe it can bring you a bit of peace, too."*

Janelle stared at the page, her emotions swirling like the leaves outside. Was this letter silly? Pointless? She almost crumpled it up, but something stopped her. It was as if she could feel David's hand on her shoulder, giving her the smallest, gentlest push.

She carefully pressed a small purple flower from the creek between the pages, the petals delicate and perfect. It was the kind David used to pick for her, making her laugh when he put them behind her ear like a crown.

"Alright, class, finish up your letters and bring them to the front," Mrs. Porter said. "We'll send them off this week."

Janelle folded her letter slowly, her hands shaking as she sealed the envelope. It felt like she was sending a piece of herself far away, into a world she couldn't see. As she walked up to the desk, Mrs. Porter gave her a small, encouraging smile.

"I'm proud of you, Janelle," she whispered. "I know this wasn't easy."

Janelle nodded, unable to speak. She slipped the letter into the pile with the others, then turned and walked out of the classroom, the cool autumn air hitting her cheeks as she stepped outside.

The sun was setting, casting a golden light over the creek. She wandered down to the water's edge, watching the leaves float by like tiny ships. The creek had always been her safe place, a place where everything made sense. But now, it felt different — like it was keeping a secret, whispering something she couldn't quite hear.

Janelle knelt by the water and cupped her hands, letting the cold water run through her fingers. "David," she whispered, her voice breaking. "I hope you can hear me."

The wind picked up, rustling the trees, and for a moment, she thought she heard his laughter, faint and far away.

"Maybe this is just a letter," she said aloud, standing up and wiping her tears. "But maybe it's more than that."

With a deep breath, she turned and headed for home, the autumn leaves swirling around her like a promise.

The mailbox stood tall at the end of her driveway, a silent sentinel. Janelle hesitated for a moment, then slipped the letter inside. As she closed the lid, she felt a shiver run down her spine, like a breath of cold air. She turned quickly, but there was no one there — only the fading light and the sound of the creek.

"It's just the wind," she whispered, but a part of her wasn't so sure.

She stood there for a long moment, staring at the mailbox, feeling as if she had sent something far more significant than a letter. It felt like she had sent out a prayer.

And somewhere, far across the ocean, someone was waiting to receive it.

The Heart of the Battlefield

The air in Vietnam was thick, a damp, cloying heat that pressed down on Private Marcus King like a wet blanket. He wiped the sweat from his brow, feeling the sting of salt in a cut just below his hairline. The jungle around him was alive, buzzing with unseen life — cicadas, frogs, the distant squawk of a bird. But for Marcus, it was the sounds he couldn't hear that haunted him: the muffled cries in the night, the whispers of men who never came back from their patrols.

Marcus trudged along the narrow, muddy path, his rifle slung over his shoulder, his eyes scanning the dense canopy above. It had been months since he left Harlem, but the memory of home still clung to him like a second skin. He could almost hear the rhythm of the jazz clubs, the laughter of his sister as they danced in the kitchen. Now, the only rhythm was the thrum of helicopters overhead and the distant thud of artillery fire.

The platoon had been on edge for days, moving through hostile territory with the constant fear of ambush. But the danger outside the camp wasn't what weighed heaviest on Marcus's mind. It was the isolation — the way some of the white soldiers glanced at him when they thought he wasn't looking, the unspoken barrier that had followed him even into this godforsaken jungle.

"Mail call!" a voice shouted, breaking the humid silence. Sergeant Thompson, a burly man with a permanent scowl, held up a canvas bag filled with letters, waving it like a prize. The soldiers gathered around half-heartedly, most of them too exhausted or jaded to care.

Marcus lingered at the edge of the group, his eyes on the ground. He hadn't received a letter in weeks, and the hope of hearing from home had dimmed. He was about to turn away when something caught his eye — a small, cream-colored envelope peeking out from the pile, a pressed purple flower sealed inside the flap.

"King," Thompson called, shoving the envelope into his chest. "Looks like someone's thinking of you."

Marcus took the letter gingerly, staring at the neat handwriting on the front: From Willow Creek, Ohio. He didn't know anyone from Ohio, but something about the letter made him pause. It was small and delicate, so out of place in this land of mud and gunfire.

He retreated to a quiet spot under the shade of a banyan tree, the sounds of the jungle fading into the background. He slipped a finger under the flap and opened it, careful not to tear the flower. As he unfolded the letter, the scent of the pressed petals filled his nose — a soft, sweet reminder of a place far removed from the brutality of war.

"Dear Soldier," it began.

Marcus's breath caught in his throat as he read the words. It was a child's handwriting, but the message was anything but childish. She wrote about the creek that ran through her small town, the way it sounded like music when it rushed over the rocks. She mentioned her brother, David, who used to take her there to skip stones. The letter was filled with small, vivid details — the smell of her mother's pie baking in the kitchen, the sound of the wind in the tall oak trees.

As he read, something inside Marcus shifted, like a heavy door swinging open after years of rust and neglect. He could almost see the little girl's face, her wide eyes staring up at him from across a distance he couldn't fathom. She had lost her brother to this war, just as he had lost so many friends. Her pain, raw and unfiltered, bled through the page.

He turned the letter over and found a small sketch on the back — a simple drawing of a creek with two stick figures standing by the water's edge. One of them had a flower tucked behind its ear.

"Damn," Marcus whispered, wiping at his eyes with the back of his hand. He hadn't cried in months, but this letter had reached a part of him he thought was buried deep beneath the surface. It was as if this girl, this stranger, had somehow touched his soul across the ocean.

That night, as the platoon gathered around the campfire, Marcus sat a little apart from the others, staring at the letter in his hands. He could feel the eyes of the other soldiers on him, their whispers barely masked by the crackle of the fire.

"What you got there, King?" Corporal Hendricks asked, a smirk on his face. "Love letter from some girl back home?"

Marcus looked up, meeting his gaze with a steady calm. "Something like that," he said quietly.

He turned back to the letter, ignoring the laughter that followed. It wasn't a love letter — it was something more. It was a connection, a lifeline to a world that still had hope and innocence, a world he had almost forgotten existed.

He pulled a scrap of paper from his pocket and began to write back, the words flowing out of him like water.

"Dear Janelle,"

He hesitated, the tip of his pencil hovering over the page. What could he say to her? How could he put the reality of his world into words without scaring her? He decided to keep it simple, focusing on the small moments of beauty he could find.

Thank you for your letter. You don't know me, but your words meant more than I can say. It's not easy over here, but I've seen things that would amaze you. The jungle is alive at night, the air filled with sounds you can't imagine. Sometimes, when it rains, it feels like the whole world is singing. I drew a picture of what I think your creek looks like. I hope it's close.

He sketched a small scene at the bottom of the page — a winding creek with tall trees and two figures standing side by side, just like in her drawing.

Keep writing, if you can. It helps. More than you know. — Marcus

He folded the letter carefully, placing it in a new envelope. He knew there was a chance she might never receive it, that it could get lost in the chaos of war. But he had to try. He had to believe that his words might find their way back to her, just as hers had found their way to him.

The next morning, as the sun rose over the jungle canopy, Marcus slipped the letter into the mail bag, a small smile on his lips. For the first time in months, he felt something other than fear or anger. He felt hope.

Thousands of miles away, Janelle stood by the mailbox in Willow Creek, her fingers tracing the rough edge of the lid. She couldn't explain it, but she felt a tug in her chest, a pull toward something far beyond the horizon. She had no idea that her words had already crossed oceans and jungles, that they had reached a man who needed them more than she could ever know.

She turned and walked back home, the leaves crunching under her shoes. Behind her, the creek bubbled softly, as if it knew a secret she hadn't yet discovered.

Letters of Hope

The letters became a rhythm Janelle Madison could count on, like the gentle flow of Willow Creek itself. Each week, she would race to the mailbox, the metal cool beneath her fingers as she opened the lid with a mix of hope and trepidation. And every time she saw Marcus's handwriting on the envelope, her heart would leap.

Inside, his words painted vivid pictures of a world she couldn't imagine. He wrote about the monsoon rains, the thick fog that rolled in from the jungle like a living thing, and the camaraderie he found among the men who became his brothers. But there were darker notes, too, hints of battles fought in the dead of night, the fear that clung to them all like a shadow.

In return, Janelle shared stories of summer fairs in Willow Creek, the laughter of children running barefoot through the grass, the scent of sweet corn roasting on the grill. She described the way the sun danced on the surface of the creek, turning it into a river of light. With every letter, she felt a little more of her own sorrow slip away, replaced by something she hadn't felt in a long time — a sense of purpose.

It was as if the letters had become a bridge, stretching from her quiet Ohio town to the heart of a distant battlefield. Janelle could almost hear Marcus's voice in her head, see his smile as he read her stories. She didn't know why, but she felt certain that her words mattered, that they were a lifeline for him as much as his were for her.

But then, one day, the rhythm broke.

The mailbox was empty.

Janelle frowned, peering inside as if she had somehow missed it. But there was no letter. Just the hollow echo of her own heartbeat. She told herself it was nothing, that the mail was simply delayed. But as the days turned into weeks, the silence grew louder. The vibrant colors of summer faded, and the joy she had found in their correspondence slipped away, replaced by a gnawing fear she couldn't shake.

"What's wrong, honey?" her mother asked one morning, noticing the way Janelle sat listlessly at the kitchen table, her toast untouched.

"It's nothing," Janelle lied, forcing a smile. "I'm just tired."

But it wasn't nothing. She knew something had happened. She felt it in her bones, the same way she had felt the moment David was gone. It was as if the creek itself had gone quiet, its babbling replaced by a mournful hush.

In the jungles of Vietnam, Marcus lay in the mud, his body battered and broken. The ambush had come out of nowhere, a flash of fire and metal in the darkness. He remembered diving for cover, the sharp pain in his side as shrapnel tore through him. Now, he could feel the blood soaking through his uniform, the ground beneath him cold and unforgiving.

He closed his eyes, thinking of the letters tucked in his pocket. Janelle's last words to him had been about the creek, how she wished she could show it to him in person someday. He clung to that thought, imagining the cool water washing over his wounds, the sound of her laughter like a balm against the pain.

"Hang on, King," someone shouted, the voice distant and hazy. "We're gonna get you out of here."

But Marcus didn't know if he had it in him to hold on. The pain was too much, the darkness too deep. He felt himself slipping, his grip on the world loosening like a leaf falling from a tree.

Back in Willow Creek, Janelle stood by the creek's edge, her eyes closed, listening to the sound of the water. She whispered a prayer, her voice carried away by the wind. "Please," she begged, not knowing who she was speaking to. "Please let him be okay."

The summer faded into autumn, and still, there was no word from Marcus. Janelle had stopped running to the mailbox, her hope turning brittle and fragile. She began to dream about him, strange, fragmented visions of a figure walking through the jungle, alone and lost. She would wake up with tears on her cheeks, clutching her pillow as if it were his letters.

Then, one crisp October morning, the mailbox creaked open, and there it was — a battered envelope, stained and torn, but unmistakably his. Her hands shook as she pulled it out, her breath coming in short gasps.

Inside was a single sheet of paper, the handwriting slanted and shaky.

Dear Janelle,

I don't know if you'll get this letter. I've been hurt, bad. I can't say where I am or what happened, but I want you to know your words kept me alive when nothing else could. I thought about the creek, the way you described it, and it gave me something to hold onto. I'm coming home, if I can. And if I make it, I'd like to see that creek for myself. —
Marcus

Tears streamed down Janelle's face as she read the letter, her hands clutching it tightly as if it might disappear. He was alive. He was coming home. She laughed through her sobs, the sound echoing across the water.

Two weeks later, Willow Creek held a small ceremony for the returning soldiers. The whole town turned out, waving flags and cheering as the bus pulled up to the square. Janelle stood apart from the crowd, her heart pounding in her chest. She scanned the faces, searching for the one she knew only from her dreams.

And then she saw him.

He was thinner, his face lined with pain, but he was standing tall, leaning on a cane. His eyes searched the crowd, and when they found hers, a slow, wide smile spread across his face.

Janelle ran to him, her feet barely touching the ground. She threw her arms around him, feeling the solid warmth of him, the reality that he was here, alive.

"You made it," she whispered, her voice choked with tears.

"I told you I would," Marcus replied, his voice low and rough. He pulled back, looking into her eyes. "Show me the creek," he said softly. "The one you wrote about."

They walked together, hand in hand, to the edge of the water. The sun was setting, casting a golden light over the surface. Janelle knelt, trailing her fingers through the cool water.

"This is it," she said, her voice filled with wonder. "This is our creek."

Marcus sank down beside her, dipping his hand into the water. He closed his eyes, a smile spreading across his face. "It's just like I imagined," he said.

They sat together in silence, the creek babbling softly between them, the leaves rustling overhead like a gentle applause. It was a silence filled with understanding, with shared pain and healing. And for the first time, Janelle felt a sense of peace settle over her, like the closing of a long, painful chapter.

The war was over for both of them, and a new story was just beginning.

THE FORGOTTEN TOY DRIVE

Chicago, December 1952

The wind swept cold off Lake Michigan, carrying the sting of winter through the narrow streets of Albany Park, a neighborhood in Chicago filled with brick buildings, modest storefronts, and the bustle of immigrant families trying to carve out a new life. The holiday season had arrived, but the usual cheer was missing this year. Lights hung across the windows of the corner grocery store, but many of the bulbs were burnt out, casting dull shadows against the brick. Wreaths decorated a few doors, but they looked dry and thin, the green needles brittle from the harsh, early frost.

The Korean War had left its mark here too, far from the battlefields overseas. In Albany Park, where families from Europe, Asia, and Latin America shared crowded tenements, the impact was felt in the worried glances exchanged at the local diner, in the silent prayers at St. Edward's Church, and in the worn faces of mothers clutching letters from sons who had gone off to fight. The neighborhood had become quieter, the noise of everyday life softened by the weight of uncertainty and loss.

The cold bit through wool coats, weaving its way down the wide avenues and into the small alleyways where children usually played. Life continued, as it always did in Chicago, but there was a tension in the air, a sense of holding back. The bakery on Lawrence Avenue still filled the air with the sweet smell of freshly baked bread, but fewer people lingered by the windows. The children who used to race down the sidewalks now walked more slowly, their voices subdued, muffled by the worries they'd overheard from the adults. Christmas was coming, but this year it felt thin and distant, like a song played too softly to be heard clearly.

Yoon-Ji Kim stood alone at the edge of the playground behind Haugan Elementary School, watching the other kids on the swings and monkey bars. Her coat was far too big for her small frame, a secondhand purchase her mother had altered to fit as best she could. The wind blew strands of her black hair across her face, but she didn't push them away. Instead, she stared down at her scuffed shoes, drawing small patterns in the slushy snow beneath her feet.

She had only been in Albany Park for a few months, but every day felt like a struggle. The school, filled with the noise of kids chattering in fast, clipped English, overwhelmed her. Words tumbled past her like rushing water, their meanings slipping away before she could grasp them. The teachers tried to help, but their patience was limited; they had too many students and not enough time. Her classmates mostly ignored her, not out of unkindness, but because she was different—quiet, a shadow at the edge of their busy games.

Her only comfort was the small doll she kept hidden in her coat pocket. It was worn, its fabric faded from years of being held close. The doll wore a tiny hanbok, the traditional Korean dress, with a pink skirt and a yellow top. Its black yarn hair was tied with a red ribbon, just like the ones Yoon-Ji remembered her grandmother wearing back in Seoul. She clutched the doll in her pocket, squeezing it for reassurance, imagining she could still hear her grandmother's voice telling stories of the countryside far away.

Home had become a confusing word. The small, cramped apartment on Kimball Avenue was filled with the familiar smells of Korean food—spicy kimchi and steamed rice—but beyond those walls, the city felt like a foreign landscape. Her father worked long hours at the steel mill in South Chicago, coming home late with his hands calloused and stained. Her mother took in sewing work from their neighbors, sitting up late into the night as the sewing machine clicked steadily, stitching together small pieces of their income. They spoke in low voices, shielding Yoon-Ji from their worries, but she could see the lines deepening on their faces.

Tommy Carter, a 12-year-old boy with freckles and unruly brown hair, was one of the kids who seemed to know every alley and street corner in Albany Park. He could often be found running errands for his mother or helping out at his uncle's hardware store on Montrose Avenue. The neighborhood had changed since the war began. His older brother was stationed in Korea, and his mother spent hours each night listening to the crackling radio, hoping for news. Tommy had grown accustomed to the look of worry etched into the faces of the people he passed every day.

But Tommy wasn't the type to sit still with his worries. One evening, as he walked past the dimly lit storefronts, an idea took root in his mind. He decided to start a toy drive, collecting toys for the kids in the neighborhood whose families were struggling this Christmas. He knew it wouldn't solve everything, but maybe it could bring a little light back into their lives, if only for a moment.

The next day at school, he told his best friend Billy about the idea while they sat on the steps outside the school building, their breath visible in the frigid air. Billy, always up for a project, was enthusiastic right away. But when they mentioned it to a few other kids, the reaction was mixed.

"Who's going to give away toys this year?" one girl asked. "Nobody has any money."

"Doesn't have to be new toys," Tommy said, determined. "We can collect the ones we don't use anymore, fix them up, wrap them nice. It's not about getting something new—it's about making sure every kid has something to open on Christmas."

Tommy and Billy got to work immediately, making posters to hang in the windows of the hardware store and the bakery. The signs were simple, drawn in colored pencil: "Toy Drive for Christmas—Donate What You Can!" They spent the weekend knocking on doors up and down the blocks of Albany Park, explaining their plan to neighbors. Some offered warm smiles and promised to look for old toys in their attics. Others were less enthusiastic.

"Times are hard, son," an old man said gruffly, waving them away. "People have bigger worries than toys."

Tommy thanked him and moved on without missing a beat. By Sunday night, the first few donations had trickled in: a ragged teddy bear with a missing ear, a metal truck with a dented hood, and a small stack of well-worn books. It wasn't much, but it was a beginning.

The toy drive had started small, but it was driven by a deep, quiet hope. Tommy couldn't yet see how his simple idea would ripple out into the neighborhood, or how it might bring a smile to a girl he'd never even noticed before—a girl named Yoon-Ji, standing at the edge of the playground, clutching a worn doll and wishing for a piece of home in a city that felt cold and distant.

The Forgotten Toy Drive

The posters had gone up all over Albany Park—in the windows of the bakery on Lawrence Avenue, tacked to the bulletin board at St. Edward's Church, and taped beside the register at the corner grocery store. Each sign was simple, just a hand-drawn picture of a teddy bear and a plea for donations: "Toy Drive for Christmas—Donate What You Can!" The message spread quickly through the neighborhood, carried by word of mouth and the curiosity of children who tugged at their parents' sleeves, asking if they had any old toys to give.

At first, the response was mixed. Some families welcomed the idea, eager to help in any small way they could. The neighbors on the second floor of the Kims' apartment building, a Polish couple with a daughter about Yoon-Ji's age, brought down a stack of picture books, their spines frayed from years of reading. Mrs. Lanowski from the bakery donated a few handmade rag dolls, her fingers stiff from kneading dough but warmed by the thought of children's smiles.

Others were indifferent. "We've got our own problems," muttered Mr. O'Malley, the owner of the hardware store, when Tommy asked if he had any toys to spare. He shook his head, grumbling about the price of goods and the latest news from Korea. Some people even scoffed at the effort, saying it was foolish to focus on toys when so many families were struggling just to put food on the table.

"Kids need more than toys," one man said as Tommy and Billy knocked on his door. "They need their fathers back."

Tommy nodded respectfully, not arguing, but the comment stayed with him. He knew the man wasn't entirely wrong, but he also knew the power of a small act of kindness, how a single toy could bring a flicker of joy to a child who hadn't smiled in weeks. He kept going, knocking on door after door, gathering what he could.

Yoon-Ji and her mother saw one of the posters taped to the window of the grocery store as they walked home one evening. Her mother paused, tilting her head as she read the words slowly, tracing the letters with her eyes. Yoon-Ji couldn't fully understand the message either, but she caught the picture of the teddy bear and the word "Christmas," written in bright red crayon.

"Toy drive," her mother said softly, turning to Yoon-Ji. "They are collecting gifts for the children."

Yoon-Ji shrugged, not sure what it meant for her. Her family had nothing extra to give—no old toys lying around in the cramped apartment, only the few precious items they'd managed to bring with them from Korea. She clutched the doll in her pocket, feeling its familiar shape and wondering if other kids would be getting new toys while she had only this old one.

Her mother, however, seemed to understand something more. That night, after dinner, she took out a small piece of cloth she had saved, one of the few remnants from their life before. She worked quietly by the light of the lamp, her needle moving in precise, practiced stitches. Yoon-Ji watched, puzzled, as her mother cut and sewed, fashioning a tiny stuffed bird—a crane, like the ones in the stories her grandmother used to tell.

In the morning, her mother wrapped the little crane in plain brown paper and tied it with a piece of string. "For the toy drive," she said, handing it to Yoon-Ji. "It is small, but it is something from us. We must be part of this place, even if we have little to give."

Yoon-Ji took the package, her heart swelling with a mix of pride and sadness. She didn't say it, but she wished they could keep the crane, a piece of home they couldn't replace. Still, she nodded and slipped the gift into her school bag.

At school, the buzz of the toy drive was inescapable. Kids chattered excitedly in the hallways, swapping stories about the toys they hoped to receive or what they planned to donate. Yoon-Ji tried to follow the conversations, but the words slipped past her, like pebbles skipping across a pond. She sat at the back of the classroom, listening to the laughter and feeling the familiar ache of being an outsider.

Miss Reynolds, her teacher, noticed. She had been keeping an eye on Yoon-Ji since the first day of school, sensing the girl's struggle to fit in. During recess, while the other kids raced out to the playground, Miss Reynolds called Yoon-Ji to her desk.

"Yoon-Ji," she said gently, pulling out one of the toy drive posters. "Do you know about this?"

Yoon-Ji nodded slightly, but her face was blank.

Miss Reynolds smiled and pointed to the picture of the teddy bear. "The children are bringing toys to share. For families who might not have gifts this year."

Yoon-Ji's eyes widened, and she looked down at her bag, where the little package her mother had made was tucked safely away. She didn't trust her English enough to explain, but she pulled it out and handed it to Miss Reynolds.

Miss Reynolds unwrapped it slowly, revealing the tiny crane. Her eyes softened as she held it up, turning it gently in her fingers. "This is beautiful, Yoon-Ji. Did you make this?"

"My… mother," Yoon-Ji managed to say, her voice small but steady.

Miss Reynolds nodded; her smile warm. "Your mother made a very special gift. Thank you for sharing this."

Yoon-Ji felt a swell of pride, a small spark of connection that warmed her in a way she hadn't felt since arriving in this new country.

The toy sorting took place at the Albany Park Community Hall, a large, drafty room filled with folding tables and mismatched chairs. Tommy, Billy, and a handful of other kids gathered there on a Saturday morning, sorting through the pile of donations. The air was filled with the excited buzz of their voices as they unpacked each toy, some new, many well-loved and showing signs of wear.

There were stuffed animals missing eyes, board games with taped-up boxes, and a few shiny, untouched toy cars. Tommy's hands were busy sorting when he came across a small, brown-wrapped package tied with simple string. He picked it up and noticed the delicate Korean writing on the edge.

"What's this?" Billy asked, peering over his shoulder.

Tommy turned the package over, unable to read the characters. "I don't know. It looks like it's from someone new in the neighborhood."

A few of the other kids laughed, pointing out the unfamiliar label. "Probably doesn't belong here," one boy said, sneering.

Tommy shook his head firmly. "No, it does. Every gift matters, no matter where it's from." He placed the package carefully on the table, setting it with the rest of the toys.

The kids continued sorting, but the little crane remained in Tommy's mind—a small, delicate offering from a family he hadn't yet noticed, a reminder of the quiet generosity that often went unseen. As the morning sun filtered through the dusty windows, the pile of toys grew, a testament to the spirit of a neighborhood that, despite its struggles, still found ways to come together.

For Tommy, it was a start. For Yoon-Ji, though she didn't yet realize it, this small act would be the first step toward feeling like she belonged in this vast, unfamiliar city.

The air was crisp and sharp on Christmas Eve as Tommy Carter and a few volunteers, including Miss Reynolds, bundled up in scarves and heavy coats to make their deliveries. The streets of Albany Park were quieter than usual, blanketed in a fresh layer of snow that softened the edges of the city. Tommy and his friends pushed a red wagon piled high with wrapped packages through the neighborhood, stopping at doors and knocking with mittened hands.

At each stop, they handed out gifts—carefully chosen and wrapped, each one matched to the children they knew lived there. A little girl on Sawyer Avenue clapped her hands when she received a stuffed rabbit missing an ear. A boy on Kimball Avenue beamed when he unwrapped a shiny, red toy truck. Parents nodded their thanks, their eyes filled with a mix of gratitude and relief, knowing their children would have something special on this night.

Miss Reynolds carried a clipboard, keeping track of the families on their list. "Just one more stop," she said, glancing at Tommy as they turned onto a narrow side street lined with brick apartments. "The Kims' place."

Tommy hesitated, looking down at the small, neatly wrapped package he'd set aside in his coat pocket. The brown paper and delicate Korean script stood out from the other gifts. He hadn't been sure whether to bring it, unsure how it would be received. He took a deep breath and nodded, following Miss Reynolds up the icy steps.

The door opened to the smell of steaming rice and the soft murmur of voices. Yoon-Ji's mother stood in the doorway; her face lit by the warm glow of the kitchen behind her. She was surprised to see them there, blinking as if she couldn't quite believe they had come.

"Merry Christmas," Miss Reynolds said gently, handing over a couple of wrapped gifts. "These are for your family."

Tommy stepped forward, pulling the small package from his pocket. He held it out to Yoon-Ji, who had come to the door, peeking out shyly from behind her mother. For a moment, he wasn't sure what to say. He simply offered it to her, his own hand trembling slightly in the cold.

Yoon-Ji's eyes widened as she took the package. Her hands were small and delicate, fingers brushing against the rough paper. She looked up at Tommy, her expression a mixture of wonder and disbelief. Tears welled up in her eyes, but she smiled—small, hesitant, but real.

"Thank you," she whispered, her voice barely audible.

Her mother placed a hand on Yoon-Ji's shoulder and nodded at Tommy. "Thank you," she said, her English broken but clear, the gratitude in her voice unmistakable.

Tommy nodded, feeling a warmth spread through his chest, a sense of relief and joy he hadn't expected. He realized, in that moment, how much this small gesture meant. He turned back to the group, giving Yoon-Ji one last smile before they moved on, leaving the family to their Christmas Eve.

At home, Yoon-Ji unwrapped the package slowly, savoring the moment, her fingers gently peeling back the tape. Inside, nestled in a piece of soft cloth, was a small doll—a tiny figure dressed in a bright hanbok, just like the one she'd lost during the long journey from Korea. The doll's hair was made of black yarn, tied with a red ribbon, and its face was stitched with a gentle smile.

Yoon-Ji stared at the doll, her breath catching in her throat. It was almost identical to the one she had carried in her pocket for years, the one that had slipped from her hands when they boarded the ship. She hugged the doll tightly, pressing it against her cheek as tears spilled over her lashes. It was as if a piece of her past, a fragment of her old life, had found its way back to her.

For the first time since arriving in America, she felt a spark of true joy— a deep, unspoken connection that bridged the gap between this new world and the one she had left behind. The loneliness that had weighed on her every day seemed to lift, just a little, replaced by a quiet, glowing warmth.

The first day back at school after the holiday break, the playground was alive with chatter and laughter. Children swapped stories about their Christmas presents, showing off new toys and trading bits of candy. Yoon-Ji stood at the edge, holding her new doll, her fingers tracing the red ribbon tied around its hair.

She watched the other kids, her usual shyness creeping in, but today felt different. Today, she had something to share, something that made her feel like she belonged, if only a little. Gathering her courage, she stepped forward, her heart pounding.

Tommy was standing with Billy by the swings, talking about the toy drive's success. When he saw Yoon-Ji approaching, he broke into a smile. She held out the doll for him to see, her eyes shining with gratitude.

"Thank you," she said, louder this time, her voice clear despite her thick accent.

Tommy nodded, understanding more than her words. He gave her a thumbs-up and then gently patted the doll's head, as if greeting an old friend. "You're welcome," he said softly. He didn't need to say more.

Yoon-Ji took a deep breath, feeling a new sense of confidence. She turned back toward the playground, where a few girls had noticed her doll and were already coming over, curiosity lighting up their faces. One of them asked to see it, and Yoon-Ji nodded, holding it out for them to touch.

They gathered around her, asking questions, and for the first time, Yoon-Ji found herself in the center of the circle instead of standing on the outside looking in. She wasn't sure she could answer all their questions, but she didn't need to. The simple act of showing her doll, of being included, was enough.

The sun peeked out from behind a cloud, casting a pale light over the playground. As the laughter of the children echoed across the snow-covered yard, Yoon-Ji looked up, feeling the warmth of the day seep into her bones. She wasn't entirely alone anymore. She had found a friend, and she had been given a gift far more valuable than a toy—she had found a place where she belonged.

THE THANKSGIVING VISITOR

The Lonely Life of Abner Whittaker

Abner Whittaker lived alone in a small, creaky house perched on the edge of a quiet neighborhood in St. Clairsville, Ohio. The house, with its peeling paint and sagging roofline, seemed to exhale with each gust of the November wind, whispering the stories of the years it had endured. The wood floors groaned beneath his feet as if sighing in sympathy with the old man who shuffled through its dimly lit rooms. The place was a museum of memories, filled with sepia-toned photographs of faces long gone. His late wife's smiling portrait watched from the mantle, her laughter now only an echo in the silence that filled the space between these four walls.

It was 1967, a year thick with the scent of change that Abner didn't quite understand. He'd wake each morning to the soft hum of the radio, where the melodies of the Beatles drifted in, singing about strange new worlds. He'd flip the dial, preferring the comfort of the newsreader's voice discussing the escalating conflict in Vietnam, even though it only reminded him of the senseless losses he knew too well. Thanksgiving was approaching, and the town was preparing—windows filled with pumpkin displays, and families chattering in the distance about gatherings and feasts. But for Abner, it was just another reminder of the emptiness that had settled into his bones.

The front room held the heart of his solitude—a threadbare armchair facing a window overlooking his small, neglected garden. The flowers had long withered, and the vegetable patch was now a tangle of brittle stems and leaves left to rot in the cold. He'd sit there, day after day, grumbling under his breath as he watched the world go by. The children from the neighborhood ran past, their laughter piercing through his thin patience. "Too loud," he'd mutter, shaking his head. "No respect for the peace of an old man."

Yet, despite his cantankerous exterior, there were moments when his softer side peeked through. He'd quietly set out a dish of milk for the stray cat that frequented his porch—a skinny tabby with a patch of missing fur. The cat had no name, and Abner pretended he didn't care, but he'd watch the creature lap up the milk, a small smile tugging at the corner of his lips as if the tiny visitor brought a fleeting comfort he could not admit.

One cold afternoon, as he sat in his usual spot, squinting out the window at the weak November sun, the sound of children's voices cut through the stillness. He scowled, muttering about the noise. A small red ball came bouncing into his yard, rolling to a stop against the steps of his porch. Abner leaned forward, peering at it as if it were some foreign object dropped from the sky. Before he could react, a little girl appeared—a thin, brave thing with wild curls and a splash of freckles across her nose. She hesitated only for a moment, then darted forward to retrieve the ball, her bright eyes meeting Abner's stern gaze.

"Sorry, Mister," she said, clutching the ball to her chest. Her voice was clear and innocent, carrying a note of kindness that cut through his gruff demeanor.

"You ought to be more careful," Abner grumbled, his voice rough as the wind rustling the bare branches overhead.

The girl didn't flinch. Instead, she offered a smile that seemed to warm the cold air between them. "You should come to dinner," she blurted out suddenly. "My family's having a big Thanksgiving feast, and you're invited."

Abner stared at her, stunned into silence. He couldn't remember the last time anyone had invited him to anything, let alone a family dinner. He opened his mouth to respond, but the words tangled in his throat. He simply nodded, once, as the girl gave a small wave and skipped away, leaving him there on the porch, bewildered and, for the first time in years, feeling something he couldn't quite name—something like hope.

The Invitation and the Decision

Abner Whittaker shut the front door behind him with a thud, the echo hanging in the quiet room like the lingering aftertaste of an unfamiliar kindness. He muttered to himself as he settled back into his armchair, replaying the moment with the little girl in his mind. He convinced himself it was nothing—a child's innocent remark, nothing more. He wouldn't fit in at a bustling Thanksgiving dinner full of strangers, and he had long since accepted his place at the edge of things, alone and unseen.

But that night, as the moon cast its pale light across the cracked ceiling, Abner lay awake, staring at the shadows. He could almost smell the roasting turkey, hear the laughter of his children, see his wife's kind eyes catching his across the table. The last Thanksgiving he shared with his family came rushing back in vivid detail, unbidden and bittersweet.

It had been years ago, but the memory was sharp and clear, like the first frost on an autumn morning. The table had been filled with the laughter of his two sons, their wives, and his grandkids. His wife, Mary, had worn her favorite apron with little embroidered pumpkins. She'd carved the turkey with her usual precision, insisting that everyone take a moment to share what they were thankful for before digging in. Abner had felt a warmth then, a contentment he thought would last forever. But forever was a fragile thing, easily shattered by time's relentless march. That had been the last Thanksgiving before Mary fell ill, before the house fell silent, before the children moved away and his world grew smaller and smaller.

James, his oldest son, moved away to pursue a career on the West Coast in the late 1950s, chasing opportunities in California's booming aerospace industry. Despite early closeness, the demands of his career and a strained relationship with his father led to infrequent visits and, eventually, to silence. The last time Abner saw James was at Mary's funeral. James couldn't bear the grief, and they exchanged words that left both men wounded, creating a rift that was never bridged.

His younger son Michael was drafted into the military during the early years of the Vietnam War. He was eager to serve and saw it as a way to make a difference, but the war took a heavy toll. He returned home changed— haunted, distant, and struggling with what we would now recognize as PTSD. The experience fractured his relationship with his family. He left St. Clairsville soon after returning, seeking solace in a small town in New Mexico where he could be alone with his thoughts. Letters from Michael stopped arriving years ago, leaving Abner with only memories and the hope that his son found some measure of peace.

He pushed the memory aside and clenched his jaw. It was easier to be angry, easier to turn away. He wouldn't fit in at a noisy family table anymore. They wouldn't want an old man like him—a grumbling, brittle relic of a past they didn't know.

The next day, as Abner made his way to the mailbox, the sound of footsteps approached from behind. He turned to see a small group of children—Lily was there, her curly hair bouncing as she ran up, joined by her brother Tommy and two of their friends. They carried a piece of construction paper decorated with bright scribbles and glitter, the words *"You*

Are Invited!" written in large, uneven letters.

Lily stepped forward, holding out the invitation like an offering. "We really want you to come," she said, her voice sincere and full of a sweetness that pierced through Abner's well-worn defenses.

Tommy chimed in, shuffling his feet a bit. "Mom and Dad said it would be great if you could join us. They remember you from the Methodist Church."

Abner blinked, taken aback. He hadn't set foot in that church in years, not since the funerals, not since he couldn't bear the pitying looks and the whispered condolences. He cleared his throat, feeling the old, familiar armor of his pride trying to protect him. "I—I don't think I'd be much fun at a family gathering," he muttered, trying to sound gruff.

Lily looked up at him, her eyes wide and honest. "But it won't be the same without you," she said simply, as if it were the most obvious truth in the world.

The children handed him the paper, then scampered off, waving and shouting, "See you on Thanksgiving, Mr. Whittaker!" before he could protest.

Abner held the invitation in his hands for a long time, staring down at the colorful mess of crayon and glitter. He felt a pang deep in his chest, a sensation that was almost painful, like the thawing of something long frozen. He placed the paper carefully on the kitchen table, where it sat like a tiny, hopeful spark in the middle of his otherwise empty home.

The following morning, Thanksgiving Day, dawned cold and clear. Abner awoke to the sun streaming through his curtains and the sound of birds chattering in the bare branches outside. He shuffled to the front door to retrieve the newspaper, only to find something unexpected on his doorstep: a small wicker basket lined with a red-checkered cloth. Inside were a dozen cookies, each one clumsily decorated with swirls of icing, and a folded piece of paper.

He picked it up, feeling the rough texture of the construction paper between his fingers. The note was written in large, uneven letters: "We hope to see you today!" At the bottom, a child's drawing depicted Abner, with his silver hair and round glasses, standing alongside a group of smiling kids. They had drawn him taller than all of them, with a big, lopsided smile on his face.

Abner felt the sudden sting of tears at the corners of his eyes. He hadn't cried in years, and the sensation was foreign and uncomfortable. He wiped his eyes with the back of his hand, clearing his throat as if to push the emotion away. He looked back at the basket, at the cookies made with tiny hands, at the note filled with earnest, hopeful scrawls.

For a moment, he stood there in the doorway, the cold November air nipping at his face. He could feel the pull, the gentle insistence of something that had been missing from his life for so long. It was terrifying, this feeling of being wanted, of being needed, even if only for a single meal.

He took a deep breath, the kind that reaches down into the lungs and brings up something deep and old, something almost forgotten. He set the basket on the kitchen table and turned away, his heart pounding as though he were standing on the edge of a great, invisible cliff.

And then, slowly, he walked to the closet, pulled out his best suit—the one he hadn't worn in years, the one Mary had once loved. He ran his fingers over the fabric, smoothing out the wrinkles. He put it on, buttoning each button with a kind of reverence, as if preparing for something sacred.

As he adjusted his tie in the cracked mirror, he almost didn't recognize the man staring back at him. There was something different in his eyes—a softness, a lightness he hadn't seen in decades.

With one last look around the house, Abner stepped out into the morning sun, the crunch of frost beneath his shoes mingling with the sound of children's laughter carried on the wind. He headed down the road toward Lily's house, toward the warmth and noise of a family Thanksgiving he never expected to be a part of.

And for the first time in years, Abner Whittaker felt like he was walking toward something, rather than away.

A Thanksgiving to Remember

The front door opened before Abner could even raise his hand to knock. Lily stood there, beaming, her curls bouncing as she pulled him inside. "You came!" she cried, her small hand warm in his cold one as she led him through the doorway. The smell of roasting turkey and spiced cider wrapped around him like a comforting blanket, filling the house with a warmth that felt like a forgotten dream.

"Look, everyone!" she called, her voice echoing through the bustling rooms. "Mr. Whittaker is here!"

Heads turned, and a chorus of welcomes rose from the family gathered in the cozy, crowded living room. Abner shifted uncomfortably, his old suit feeling tight around the collar, but the smiles that met him were genuine, softening the nervous tension in his chest.

Lily's mother approached, wiping her hands on a festive apron. She had a kind face, her eyes crinkling at the corners as she extended her hand. "You must be Mr. Whittaker," she said warmly. "We're so glad you could join us. I'm Margaret, Lily's mother."

"Thank you… thank you for having me," Abner replied, his voice rough but steady.

"Nonsense," Margaret replied, patting his arm. "There's always room for one more at our table. Besides," she added with a playful wink, "we've heard so much about you from Lily, it feels like you're already part of the family."

Abner's face flushed, and he looked down, touched and embarrassed by the thought of being remembered, being talked about. "I'm… I'm glad to be here," he managed, glancing around at the gathering. There were cousins and grandparents, babies squealing in laps, aunts laughing over a shared secret—faces bright with love and laughter.

"Come, sit by me!" Lily tugged him toward the long, crowded table, where plates and platters filled every available space. The food was laid out like a feast from a storybook—golden-brown turkey, buttery mashed potatoes, cranberry sauce glistening like jewels, and warm rolls stacked high in a basket.

He settled into his chair, feeling the gentle weight of eyes on him, not with judgment but with curiosity and kindness. He wasn't sure what to say, so he folded his hands, his gaze tracing the pattern of the tablecloth, embroidered with autumn leaves and acorns.

As everyone took their places, Margaret raised her glass. "Before we eat, I'd like us all to go around the table and share something we're thankful for." She glanced at Abner, her smile encouraging. "It's a tradition of ours."

One by one, they spoke—some shy, some bold, voices young and old blending together in a soft symphony of gratitude. A young mother gave thanks for her new baby, a teenage boy expressed his gratitude for passing his math test, and an elderly man chuckled as he said he was thankful for his "new knees." Laughter rippled around the table, and Abner felt himself relax, bit by bit.

Finally, all eyes turned to him. He cleared his throat, shifting in his chair, searching for words that felt right. "I'm… well, I'm thankful to be here," he said slowly, his voice quiet but full. "It's been a long time since I've been around a table like this." His eyes grew distant, his gaze unfocusing as he allowed himself, for just a moment, to remember. "I lost my family a while ago, you see. My wife, Mary, and my boys…" His voice caught, and he paused, feeling a swell of emotion rise.

Lily reached out, slipping her small hand into his, her touch grounding him. He gave her a soft smile, continuing, "But tonight… tonight, I feel like I'm part of something again. So, thank you. Truly."

Silence followed his words, the kind that holds weight and warmth rather than discomfort. Margaret raised her glass again, her voice gentle. "To Abner. And to family—chosen and found."

Glasses clinked around the table, and Abner's eyes misted as he lifted his own glass, feeling a warmth that wasn't just from the cider he sipped.

The meal began, a happy cacophony of clinking forks, passing plates, and voices overlapping in conversation. Abner found himself laughing at the children's antics, joining in the family's teasing banter, letting himself melt into the easy rhythm of their togetherness. Tommy asked him about the "old days," eyes wide as Abner shared stories of growing up, of Thanksgivings past and games played in open fields.

At one point, Lily reached for the wishbone and held it out to him, her eyes sparkling with excitement. "Let's make a wish together, Mr. Whittaker!"

He hesitated, then took the other end, feeling the delicate bone in his fingers. They pulled, the bone snapping with a soft crack, and Lily cheered, clutching her half. "I won!" she exclaimed, laughing as she pressed her wish into her heart.

"What'd you wish for?" he asked, smiling, feeling light in a way he hadn't in years.

She leaned close, whispering so only he could hear. "That you'll come back next Thanksgiving."

Abner's heart tightened, a smile spreading across his face as he whispered back, "I think that can be arranged."

As the evening wore on, the family began clearing plates, moving to the living room where a fire crackled in the hearth. Abner found himself drawn to an armchair by the fire, Lily climbing onto his lap with a contented sigh. Around him, voices drifted in gentle conversation, laughter echoing softly in the warm glow.

In that moment, surrounded by the quiet hum of life, he felt something he hadn't felt in years—a sense of belonging, of having found, even if just for tonight, a place where he fit.

When it was finally time to leave, Margaret walked him to the door, her hand resting gently on his shoulder. "You're welcome here anytime, Mr. Whittaker," she said softly, her voice full of genuine warmth. "You're family now."

He nodded, swallowing the lump in his throat. "Thank you," he whispered, his voice choked with emotion. He glanced back one last time at the room filled with laughter, with light, with life—a room that had, just for a while, made him feel whole.

As he stepped out into the night, the cold air met him, but it no longer felt harsh. He walked home under the November stars, his heart fuller than it had been in a long, long time. He knew that Thanksgiving would never be the same, that he'd never be quite the same, for he'd been given a gift he hadn't expected—a chance to be part of something, to love and be loved.

And as he reached his small, quiet house, he paused, looking back down the road toward the warm glow of the house he'd just left behind. A promise lingered in the night air—a promise of next Thanksgiving, and the one after that, and perhaps even more to come.

Abner Whittaker smiled, his heart light as he stepped inside, finally home.

THE LANTERN PARADE

New Beginnings in a Town of Shadows

The train rolled into Benwood, West Virginia, with a groaning sigh, as though it, too, felt the weight of the times. Richard Barrett leaned against the window, his breath fogging the glass as he peered out at the unfamiliar landscape. The town lay spread out below a gray sky, the once-busy factories now silent giants, their smokestacks like broken fingers pointing to nothing. He could see clusters of men standing idle by the train tracks, their faces worn and hollow, eyes searching for any sign of work. The Great Depression had drained the life from this place, just as it had from the cities they'd left behind.

"Richard, help your brother with the bags," his mother's voice came, soft but tinged with a weariness he'd noticed more and more lately. He turned to see her standing there, one hand resting protectively on the shoulder of his little sister, Mary, who clutched her ragged doll like a lifeline. Brady, his younger brother, stared wide-eyed at the scene outside, too young to fully understand the quiet despair that seemed to hang in the air like smoke.

"Yes, Mama," Richard said, sliding off his seat. He hoisted the worn suitcase; its handle frayed from years of use and followed his family onto the platform. His father stood a few steps ahead, shoulders hunched under the weight of his coat, which seemed far too thin for the December chill. He was a tall man, once strong and broad-shouldered, but the months of worry had left him gaunt, like a tree stripped of its leaves.

"This is home now," his father said, almost to himself, as he looked out over the town. He turned to Richard with a small, tight smile. "It's hard work, son. But it's honest work, and it keeps us together."

Richard nodded, trying to mirror his father's stoic expression, but he could feel the unease settling in his stomach. The coal mines had taken the place of the factory job his father lost back in Pittsburgh. He knew what that meant—long hours underground, the black dust clinging to his father's skin like a second layer. It was dangerous work, the kind that swallowed men whole, but it was the only chance they had to keep food on the table.

The Barrett family made their way to the small, rundown apartment they would now call home. It was nothing more than a few rooms above a boarded-up shop, the walls thin and drafty. Their belongings, few as they were, sat in a neat pile on the floor—a patchwork quilt, a tin of old photographs, a couple of chipped plates. Richard watched as his mother unpacked, humming an old Irish lullaby under her breath, her voice soft and wavering like the flame of a candle fighting the wind.

"Come on, Mary," she said gently, smoothing the girl's hair. "Sing with me, darling. Let's show your brothers how we used to sing back home."

Mary's thin, sweet voice joined in, but the song faltered when Tommy tried to join, his voice breaking into a childish giggle. Richard smiled despite himself, the sound like a tiny ray of sunshine breaking through the gray.

Later that afternoon, while his parents were busy settling in, Richard slipped outside. The cold air bit at his cheeks, but he didn't mind. He needed to see the town; to understand this place they were now a part of. He walked slowly, his boots crunching on the thin layer of snow that covered the ground, his breath puffing out in small white clouds.

He hadn't gone far when he spotted a man hunched over a pile of rags, carefully picking through them. The man's clothes were little more than patched-together scraps, and his fingers were blue with cold, but his eyes were kind when he looked up and met Richard's gaze.

"Morning, kid," the man said with a nod. "Name's John, but folks around here call me the Rag Picker."

Richard hesitated, then stepped closer. "I'm Richard," he said, offering a small, shy smile.

John straightened, pulling a bit of bread from his pocket. He tore off a piece and handed it to Richard, who took it gratefully, surprised by the gesture. "Hard times don't take away our stories, kid," John said, his voice low and gravelly. "They give us new ones to tell. Remember that."

Richard nodded, tucking the bread into his coat pocket. "I'll remember," he promised, feeling a strange sense of connection to this man who seemed to carry the whole town's history in his worn, weathered hands.

He continued, wandering deeper into the heart of Benwood. The streets were narrow and lined with old brick buildings, many of them boarded up. The air was filled with the smell of coal smoke, sharp and acrid, mingling with the faint sweetness of chestnuts roasting on a vendor's cart. He spotted a man hauling a block of ice from the back of a horse-drawn wagon, his muscles straining as he heaved it into a cart.

The iceman caught Richard watching and flashed a quick, tired grin. "Cold enough for you, boy?" he called out, wiping the sweat from his brow with a gloved hand.

Richard laughed. "Cold enough," he replied.

The man stepped closer, holding out a sliver of ice. "Here, take this. It's a treat, even if it doesn't look like much," he said with a wink. Richard took it, pressing the icy shard to his lips, feeling the sharp, clean cold melt on his tongue.

"Keep your head up, boy," the iceman said quietly. "Even ice melts in the warmth of a good story."

As the sun began to sink behind the hills, casting long shadows over the town, Richard made his way toward the streetcar stop. The conductor, a large man with a red face and a booming laugh, leaned out of the window and waved him over.

"Need a lift, son?" he asked, his voice as cheerful as the ringing bell of the streetcar.

"I don't have any money," Richard admitted, shuffling his feet.

The conductor waved his hand dismissively. "Nonsense! Hop on. This ride's on me."

Richard climbed aboard, taking a seat near the front. The streetcar lurched forward, and the conductor began to talk, filling the air with stories of the town's better days. He spoke of crowded cars filled with factory workers singing their way home, of Christmas parades and fireworks lighting up the sky.

"Things were different back then," the conductor said wistfully. "But who knows? Maybe they'll be that way again someday. Maybe a boy like you will help remind us how."

Richard felt a flicker of something deep inside—something that felt like hope. He nodded, watching the lights of the town blur past as the streetcar carried him back home.

When he returned to the apartment, his family was gathered around the small kitchen table. His mother had managed to make a simple stew, and the room was filled with the comforting smell of onions and potatoes. Richard's father looked up as he entered, a tired smile on his face.

"Did you meet anyone interesting?" his father asked.

Richard grinned, pulling out the sliver of ice and holding it up. "I think I made some new friends," he said.

His father's smile widened, a spark of pride in his eyes. "That's my boy," he said quietly. "That's how we'll make it through—together, and with a good story to tell."

Richard's Stories and the Seeds of Hope

The first few weeks in Benwood passed in a blur of gray mornings and long, cold nights. Richard could feel the heaviness of the town pressing down on him, a kind of silent sorrow that seemed to seep from the boarded-up windows and empty storefronts. The streets were quiet, except for the shuffling of tired feet and the hollow sound of the wind whipping through the alleyways. It was a place stuck in a slow, unending winter, where even the sun seemed reluctant to shine.

But Richard wasn't one to give in to gloom easily. He knew the power of stories—the way they could lift people up, make them laugh, or help them remember the good times when everything else seemed dark. He decided that if there was any way he could help bring some light to Benwood, it would be through the tales he carried with him like treasures in his mind.

One day after school, Richard found himself on the playground, sitting on the edge of a frozen puddle while the other kids huddled in small groups, their eyes darting to him now and then, wary and curious. He spotted a few of the boys who had bullied him earlier—Johnny and Pete, rough-looking kids with dirt smudged on their faces and anger in their eyes, like they were searching for someone to blame for their empty bellies.

"Hey, Patchy!" Johnny called out; his voice harsh. "What are you doing over there by yourself? Making up some fancy story about being a king?"

Richard felt the sting of the words but held his ground. "Maybe I am," he replied with a smile that caught them off guard. "Or maybe I'm just thinking about the time I met the Rag Picker. He told me a secret, you know."

Pete's sneer faltered. "A secret? What kind of secret?"

Richard's eyes twinkled. He could see he had their attention now, even if they didn't want to admit it. "He said that this town is full of hidden treasures," Richard continued. "Stories buried deeper than coal, and all we have to do is dig them up."

The other kids drew closer, despite themselves. One of the younger girls, Kata, who spoke with a thick Hungarian accent, piped up. "Tell us a story,

Richard. Please?"

Richard leaned back, feeling the ice cold against his hands, but the warmth of the children's eager faces was enough to keep him going. He started with a tale his mother had told him, about an Irish fiddler who could make the very air dance with his music. As he spoke, the kids gathered around, forming a tight circle, their laughter mingling with the wind. Even Johnny and Pete sat quietly, their expressions softening.

Richard's stories became a small beacon for the neighborhood kids. Each afternoon, they'd gather, waiting for the next tale—a Hungarian legend about a wolf that turned into a man, or a Greek fable of a young boy who brought light to his village with a lantern made of moonlight. He mixed their traditions together, weaving a tapestry of words that made them feel connected, as if they all shared the same roots, stretching deep into the earth beneath the crumbling streets.

One gray December day, as Richard sat with his small group of listeners, he noticed Niko, a boy with wild black hair and a serious face, standing on the edge of the playground, watching but not approaching. Richard raised his hand in a wave. "Come on, Niko," he called. "We're just about to start."

Niko hesitated, then walked over, shoving his hands into his coat pockets. "I'm Greek," he said bluntly. "I don't know your stories."

Richard smiled gently. "Then why don't you tell us yours?"

Niko blinked, as if the thought had never occurred to him. Slowly, he began to speak, his voice low but growing stronger as he told them about the lantern parades his grandmother used to describe, back in their village by the sea. He spoke of the golden glow that lit up the streets, of the songs that filled the air, and the way the lanterns seemed to chase away the dark.

"That's it!" Richard shouted, jumping to his feet. The sudden movement startled the kids, who stared at him in confusion. "That's what we need here. A lantern parade!"

Johnny frowned. "A parade? In this town? You're crazy."

"No," Richard said firmly, his eyes bright with excitement. "Think about it! All of us together, each carrying a lantern we make ourselves. We'll bring light to this whole place. We'll remind everyone of what it was like before… before everything turned so dark."

There was a moment of silence, the kind that crackles with possibility. Kata was the first to smile, her cheeks rosy in the cold. "My grandmother used to make lanterns out of tin cans," she said softly. "We could do that."

Niko's face lit up. "I can show you the designs my yia-yia taught me. We could carve stars and moons, like the ones from the old country."

The other kids began to nod, the idea taking shape in their minds. Even Johnny looked intrigued, though he tried to hide it with a scowl. "We don't have much to make them with," he muttered.

Richard's smile didn't falter. "We don't need much. Just scraps and light… and a little bit of hope."

The Gathering of Scraps and the First Lanterns

The next week was a flurry of activity. The children scoured the alleys and backyards, gathering anything they could use—old tin cans, bits of broken glass, scraps of colored paper. Richard showed them how to punch holes in the cans to let the light shine through, creating patterns that would dance when the candles flickered inside.

They met in the empty lot near the tracks, huddled together in the cold, their breath misting in the air as they worked. The rag picker stopped by one evening, watching with a quiet smile as the kids decorated their lanterns.

"You've started something here, boy," he said, crouching down beside Richard. He handed him a small, polished piece of glass, smooth and blue like the summer sky. "Use this. It'll make your lantern shine brighter."

Richard took the glass, feeling its cool weight in his hand. "Thank you," he whispered.

The iceman came by, too, on his way home after a long day. He paused, wiping his brow, and looked at the children with a grin. "Well, would you look at that," he said. "Looks like you're bringing back a bit of Christmas magic."

Richard beamed up at him. "Will you come to the parade?"

The iceman's eyes softened, and he nodded. "Wouldn't miss it for the world, kid."

Turning Point: A Setback and a Spark of Resilience

Just as the lanterns were starting to take shape, disaster struck. One evening, as the children were finishing their work, a group of older boys stormed into the lot, sneering and shouting. They knocked over the lanterns, smashing the tin cans and tearing the delicate paper designs.

Johnny was the first to jump up, fists clenched. "Hey! Stop it!" he yelled, but he was shoved to the ground, his anger turning quickly to tears.

Richard stood in the center of the wreckage, staring at the pieces of their hard work scattered across the ground. He felt a hot wave of despair, but then he took a deep breath, letting it out slowly. "We can fix it," he said softly. "We can make new ones. They can break the lanterns, but they can't break the light."

The children gathered around him, nodding. They began to pick up the scraps, their fingers numb with cold but their spirits unbroken.

Richard held up the blue piece of glass the rag picker had given him, catching the last rays of the setting sun. "We still have this," he said, his voice clear. "And we have each other."

The children cheered, their voices rising into the twilight, a promise that the parade would go on.

As the children worked to rebuild the lanterns, the bitter cold seeped into their hands, but they didn't let it stop them. Richard moved from one child to the next, encouraging them with quiet words of determination. "We're not just making lanterns," he said. "We're making something bigger. Something they can't take away." His words spread like the warmth of a fire, igniting the resolve of his friends.

Johnny, his cheeks streaked with dried tears, held up a bent wire frame. "This one's not too far gone. I can fix it," he said, his voice quivering but steady. Mary Ellen, the youngest in the group, carefully smoothed out a torn piece of paper, her little fingers pressing it back into place. Even the older boys, who had once dismissed the project as silly, joined in, bringing extra tools and supplies to help repair the damage.

By the end of the evening, the lot was transformed into a bustling hive of creativity and camaraderie. The children's laughter mixed with the sound of scissors cutting paper and the clink of tin cans being shaped into new lanterns. As the first stars appeared in the dark winter sky, Richard held up the nearly completed lantern with the blue glass at its center. The glass caught the light from the fire, casting a shimmering, otherworldly glow over the group.

"We're doing more than fixing lanterns," Richard said, his voice firm. "We're showing them we won't give up. This parade isn't just for us. It's for everyone in Benwood who needs to remember that the light is still there, even when everything feels dark."

The next day, news of the children's determination spread through the town. The blacksmith offered to create stronger wire frames for the lanterns, while the grocer donated a roll of colorful paper to replace the torn designs.

Neighbors who had been strangers just days before arrived at the lot, bringing scraps of tin, paint, and even hot cocoa to keep the children warm as they worked. For the first time in what felt like forever, the town was united by a common purpose—bringing back the light.

On the night of the parade, the streets of Benwood glistened with fresh snow. The children, bundled in scarves and mittens, lined up with their lanterns, each one a masterpiece of resilience and creativity. As the procession began, the blue-glass lantern led the way, its light piercing through the cold night air. Families gathered on porches and sidewalks; their faces illuminated by the warm glow. For a moment, the weight of the Great Depression seemed to lift, replaced by the joy of seeing the children's vision come to life.

Among the spectators, Mr. Caldwell, the rag picker who had gifted Richard the blue glass, stood silently, his face a mix of pride and awe. He tipped his hat to Richard as the boy walked by, their eyes meeting in a moment of shared understanding. This wasn't just a parade; it was a declaration. The light had returned, and with it, the promise of better days ahead.

The children's voices rose in song, carrying over the rooftops of Benwood and into the starry night. It was a melody of hope, resilience, and the unbreakable bond of community. For Richard, it wasn't just the culmination of their hard work—it was the beginning of something far greater.

Epilogue: The Light That Endures

Years passed, and the town of Benwood changed in many ways. The factories roared back to life, the smokestacks once again filling the sky with plumes of black smoke. The coal mines thrummed with the sounds of drills and pickaxes, and the streets bustled with laughter, chatter, and the clanging of streetcars. The Great Depression slowly faded into memory, but the night of the lantern parade remained etched in the hearts of the townsfolk—a beacon of light in their shared story.

Every Christmas Eve, the children of Benwood would gather in the town square, their lanterns swaying gently in the cold winter air. New faces joined the old ones—children who had never known the darkness of those hard times but who carried the tradition as a gift from the past, a reminder of the resilience and unity that had brought them through.

Richard Barrett, now a grown man with children of his own, stood at the edge of the square, watching the parade with a smile. He saw echoes of his younger self in the bright faces of the children leading the procession, their voices lifted in song. His daughter, a spirited girl with his same twinkling eyes, held her lantern high, the blue glass from the rag picker still nestled at its center, casting its familiar glow.

As the parade wound down, she ran to him, her cheeks pink with the cold, her breath a puff of white in the air. "Papa, did you really start the first lantern parade?" she asked, her voice full of wonder.

Richard knelt down to her level, his eyes softening as he took her small hand in his. "I didn't do it alone," he said gently. "It was all of us, together. That's what made the light shine so brightly."

His daughter squeezed his hand, looking up at him with a smile that reminded him so much of the hope he'd felt all those years ago. "Then I'll make sure to carry it on," she said proudly. "Just like you did."

Richard hugged her close, feeling the warmth of her tiny lantern against his chest. "That's my girl," he whispered. "As long as there's a story to tell and a light to share, we'll never be in the dark."

The crowd began to disperse, families heading home to their Christmas feasts, but the lanterns still glowed in the fading light, casting long, golden shadows on the snow-covered ground. Richard watched as the last of the lanterns disappeared into the night, leaving behind a trail of hope that seemed to stretch far beyond the town, into the future.

And as he stood there, the cold wind tousling his hair, he knew that the light of that first parade—born from scraps and stories, from the hope of a young boy—would burn on, carried forward by the hearts of those who believed in its magic.

Benwood would always remember the night the children brought back the light, and the lanterns would continue to shine, a promise that no matter how dark the times, there would always be a spark to guide them home.

THE LAST SLEIGH RIDE

The Call of the Journey

The December air in Tolerance, Iowa felt off this year. Normally, by now, the town and surrounding fields would be blanketed in snow—thick, white drifts that softened every edge and muffled the sounds of the small town. But today, the ground was bare. The sky hung low and gray, pressing down like a heavy quilt, while an unseasonal warmth drifted through the streets, unsettling the townsfolk. They went about their daily routines, but a murmur of disquiet threaded through their conversations. It was as if Tolerance itself held its breath, waiting for something that wasn't coming.

In the old farmhouse on the outskirts of town, Enoch Lightfoot stood by the window, staring out at the barren landscape. The trees were stripped of their leaves, their skeletal branches reaching up like pleading hands. Enoch's eyes drifted to the barn, where his horse-drawn sleigh sat in the shadows, gathering dust. He could almost see it as it once was—painted bright red, its runners gleaming silver against the crisp snow. But that was years ago. Now, the sleigh was just an old relic, a ghost of winters past.

He sighed, pressing his hand against the cold glass. It had been a long time since he'd taken the sleigh out. Retirement had come slowly, like the creeping aches in his joints, and he wasn't sure he had another ride left in him. He missed the snow-covered streets, the children's shouts of joy when they saw him coming, the way the town felt alive and connected during those holiday deliveries. He missed the purpose it gave him.

The sound of soft footsteps interrupted his reverie. Beatrice entered the room, humming a tune under her breath. She was still beautiful to him—her auburn hair now streaked with silver, her eyes bright and quick despite the lines etched by time and laughter. She carried the scent of cinnamon from the kitchen, a warm contrast to the chill outside.

"Still brooding over that old sleigh, are you?" Beatrice teased, slipping her arms around Enoch's waist. He chuckled, leaning into her embrace.

"Just thinking, that's all," he replied. "Hard to imagine a Christmas without snow."

"Hard to imagine a Christmas without you complaining about the snow," she shot back with a grin, giving him a playful squeeze.

He turned to face her, a smile tugging at the corners of his mouth. "You know me too well, Bea."

"I'd be worried if I didn't after all these years," she said, her voice softening. "Maybe it's a sign, though. No snow, but people still need their Christmas cheer. And who better to deliver it than Enoch Lightfoot?"

He raised an eyebrow. "You're not serious. I'm too old for this."

"You're not too old," Beatrice countered, brushing a strand of hair from his forehead. "You're just rusty. Besides, the town could use a little magic. And so could you."

Before Enoch could respond, there was a knock at the door. He frowned, glancing at Beatrice. "Expecting company?"

"No," she said, moving to open the door. "But maybe it's a visitor from the North Pole, here to tell you to get that sleigh ready."

The door swung open, revealing Lena, the neighbor's daughter. She was a bright spark of energy, her cheeks flushed pink from the cold, despite the unseasonal warmth. She held a large bundle of letters and packages, almost too big for her small frame.

"Hi, Mr. Lightfoot! Hi, Mrs. Lightfoot!" Lena chirped; her voice as bright as the bells that once jingled on Enoch's sleigh. "The post office is a mess this year. They asked me to bring these over—said they didn't have enough people to get everything delivered before Christmas."

Enoch took the bundle from her, his fingers brushing against a familiar blue envelope. He paused. It had no return address, and the handwriting seemed almost hesitant, as if the sender had second thoughts before sealing it.

"What's this?" he asked, holding up the letter.

Lena shifted on her feet, suddenly looking unsure. "I don't know. It was just in the pile. It feels… different, though, doesn't it?"

Enoch nodded slowly; his curiosity piqued. He glanced at Beatrice, who was watching him with that knowing smile she always wore when she was a step ahead of him.

"Maybe it's a Christmas mystery," Beatrice said lightly. "And who better to solve it than you?"

He shook his head, but he couldn't help the grin that crept onto his face. "You're pushing me, Bea."

"You need a push sometimes, old man," she laughed, her eyes twinkling. "And I think you want this as much as I do."

Enoch turned back to Lena. "Well, you've certainly brought us something interesting today. Thank you, Lena."

She beamed, bouncing on her toes. "Are you really going to take the sleigh out, Mr. Lightfoot? Even without snow?"

Beatrice leaned in close to Enoch, her voice a warm whisper. "Go on, Enoch. One last ride. For the town. For us."

He felt the familiar thrill of adventure stir in his chest, mingled with the ache of old memories. He thought of all the winters past, the children's faces, the warmth of the hearths he'd glimpsed through frosted windows. And then he looked at Beatrice, her face so full of hope and love.

"Alright," he said finally, his voice steady. "Alright, I'll do it. But only because you two won't give me any peace if I don't."

Beatrice clapped her hands, laughing. "I knew it! Enoch Lightfoot, back in action!"

Lena cheered, her eyes sparkling. "This is going to be the best Christmas ever, Mr. Lightfoot!"

Enoch glanced out the window one last time, at the barn where the sleigh waited, as if it had been expecting him all along. He felt the weight of the mysterious letter in his hand, the promise of the unknown tugging at him.

"Come on, then," he said, grabbing his old coat from the hook by the door. "Let's get Willow harnessed up. The sun's rising, and we've got a town to visit."

The sky lightened as they stepped outside, a pale wash of gold breaking through the clouds. For a moment, it felt like the whole world held its breath, waiting for the sound of sleigh bells that hadn't rung in years.

And as the first flakes of snow began to fall, Enoch Lightfoot took the reins once more, ready to deliver the unexpected gifts this strange December had brought.

The Unfolding Mysteries

Enoch snapped the reins gently, and Willow began to pull the sleigh through the streets of Tolerance. The runners scraped against the frozen ground with an odd, metallic whisper. It wasn't the smooth glide he remembered from snowy winters past; instead, it felt as if the town itself resisted the sleigh's movement, like the old traditions had become strangers in this snowless December. He kept one hand close to the pocket of his coat where the mysterious letter rested, its corners crumpled slightly from his fingers. He'd ask Beatrice about it later—she had a knack for unearthing the truth hidden in the smallest of details.

The first stop was the Petersons' house, a white clapboard structure with sagging eaves. The yard, usually dotted with snowmen this time of year, was bare. Enoch climbed down from the sleigh, the stiffness in his knees making him wince. He knocked on the door, feeling the cold seeping into his bones.

Mrs. Peterson answered, looking more fragile than he remembered. Her hair, once a vibrant chestnut, was now wispy and gray, and her eyes, once so full of life, seemed dulled by exhaustion.

"Enoch," she said with a smile that didn't reach her eyes. "It's good to see you. I didn't think you'd be out this year, what with the weather and all."

"I wasn't planning to," Enoch replied, handing her a small parcel wrapped in faded red paper. "But I figured the town could use a little old-fashioned spirit, snow or no snow."

She nodded, her gaze drifting over the sleigh. "It's been a strange year, hasn't it? Almost feels like we're all waiting for something that never comes."

Enoch hesitated, sensing a deeper sadness in her voice. "Is everything alright, Betty?"

She looked away, blinking quickly. "Oh, you know how it is. Just the usual troubles. The kids are busy with their own lives, and the house feels too quiet these days." Her eyes flicked back to his, as if she wanted to say more but couldn't find the words.

He gave her hand a gentle squeeze. "You take care now. And if you need anything, you know where to find us."

As he climbed back into the sleigh, he couldn't shake the feeling that something was left unsaid, something lingering in the space between their words. He tapped Willow's reins, and they moved on, the sleigh's runners scraping out a tune of uncertainty.

The next few stops were much the same. Old Mr. Doyle, once the town's most talkative gossip, barely muttered a "thank you" as he took his package. The new family in the yellow house—he hadn't learned their names yet—accepted their letters with polite, tight smiles. Even the Jenkins boys, who usually chased the sleigh down the street, shouting for candy canes, stood silently by their gate, watching Enoch pass with somber eyes.

It was as if a gray veil had settled over the town, dulling the colors and muffling the sounds. The usual laughter and cheer seemed to be missing, replaced by an unspoken tension that Enoch couldn't quite place.

He made his way toward the old church at the edge of town, where the children's choir was practicing. The sound of their voices, pure and clear, cut through the heavy air like sunlight piercing through clouds. He paused, letting the music wash over him. It was a Christmas hymn, one he recognized from years of deliveries past, but today it held a haunting, melancholy quality that made his chest ache.

Just as he was about to continue, Jacey emerged from the church. She was bundled in a too-large coat, her dark curls poking out from under a knitted hat. She spotted Enoch and broke into a run, her boots slapping against the hard ground.

"Mr. Lightfoot!" she called out, breathless but smiling. "Wait!"

He pulled the reins to stop Willow, looking down at the girl as she approached. Her cheeks were flushed, and her eyes sparkled with a mix of excitement and something else—something he couldn't quite read.

"I'm glad I caught you," Jacey said, holding out an envelope. "I meant to mail this weeks ago, but I never got the chance. Could you deliver it for me?"

Enoch took the letter, feeling its weight in his hand. The handwriting was uneven, as if written in a hurry. "Who's it for, Jacey?" he asked gently.

She bit her lip, glancing around as if she were worried someone might overhear. "It's for… someone I haven't seen in a long time," she whispered. "I don't know if it'll even reach them, but I wanted to try."

Enoch's heart softened. "I'll make sure it gets where it needs to go," he promised, tucking the envelope into his coat pocket, right next to the mysterious letter from earlier.

"Thank you," Jacey said, her voice almost a whisper. She looked up at him, her eyes filled with a mix of hope and secrecy that made Enoch's chest tighten. "You're the best, Mr. Lightfoot."

He watched her run back into the church, her small figure disappearing behind the heavy wooden doors. The choir's voices rose again, but now they sounded like a plea, echoing off the stone walls and into the quiet town.

Enoch took a deep breath and gave Willow a gentle nudge. They continued down the main road, the sun starting its slow descent, casting a soft pink light across the sky. He fished out his old flip phone from his coat pocket—Beatrice had bought it for him years ago as a joke, but he'd grown fond of it. He dialed her number, listening to the familiar ring.

"Calling me from your grand adventure already?" Beatrice answered, her voice warm and teasing.

"You could say that," Enoch replied. "Picked up a couple of letters today that feel... different. One from Jacey, and another with no return address. I'm not sure what to make of them."

Beatrice's laugh was light, a sweet sound that made the cold air feel warmer. "Enoch Lightfoot turned detective. I knew this sleigh ride would be more than just a delivery route. You've always had a way of finding the stories hidden in plain sight."

"Well, you know me," he said, smiling into the phone. "Can't help but dig a little deeper when something feels off."

"Don't take too long out there," Beatrice said softly. "The sun's setting, and you'll need your strength for whatever mystery you're unraveling."

"I'll be home soon," he promised, though he felt a pang of reluctance as he said it. There was something about these letters that pulled at him, as if they were trying to tell him something important, something that needed to be uncovered before the night was through.

He clicked the phone shut, tucking it back into his pocket, and looked up at the sky. The clouds were tinged with the soft pink and gold of twilight. It was beautiful, but fleeting, like a moment he knew he couldn't hold onto.

Enoch guided Willow down the last stretch of road, feeling the weight of the letters against his chest. The sun dipped lower, casting long shadows across the town. He glanced back once, at the small figures moving inside their homes, the lights flickering on one by one. It was as if Tolerance itself had become a patchwork of secrets, each window a small, untold story.

And as the first star blinked into the darkening sky, Enoch realized he was no longer just delivering mail. He was carrying pieces of the town's heart, bound up in paper and ink, waiting to be read.

Revelations and Reunions

Snow began to fall gently as Enoch arrived home, the first flakes swirling down in lazy spirals. It was as if the sky had finally granted the town of Tolerance the gift it had been waiting for all season. The sleigh's runners made a soft, hissing sound as he pulled into the barn, where the scent of hay and old wood filled the air. He unhitched Willow, patting her neck with a murmured thank you, and then made his way inside, brushing snow from his coat.

Beatrice was waiting for him, curled up in her favorite chair by the fire, the flames casting a golden glow across the room. The smell of cocoa simmering on the stove was rich and comforting, wrapping around him like a warm embrace.

"You look like a man who's seen a ghost," she teased, setting down her knitting. "Did the sleigh ride turn you into a Christmas spirit?"

Enoch chuckled, settling into the chair next to her. "Not quite. But I did bring home a couple of surprises." He pulled out the two letters from his coat pocket, laying them on the small table between them.

Beatrice picked up the first one—Jacey's—and unfolded it with care. She read aloud, her voice gentle:

"Dear Grandpa,

I know we haven't seen each other in a long time. Mom says it's because of something that happened before I was born, but I don't care about that. I just want you to come back. It's almost Christmas, and I asked Santa for just one thing this year—for you to be with us again. I promise we'll be good and make you cookies, and I'll even give you my favorite book to read. Please come back. I miss you, even though I've never met you.

Love, Jacey."

Beatrice's voice faltered as she finished reading, and she pressed the letter to her chest. "Oh, Enoch. This poor girl. She's never even met her grandfather, and yet her heart is so full of love for him."

Enoch nodded; his throat tight with emotion. "It's the kind of love that doesn't come from knowing—it comes from feeling what's missing. She knows there's a piece of her family that's lost, and she's trying to bring it back."

They sat in silence for a moment, the weight of the child's plea hanging between them. Beatrice's eyes were misty as she folded the letter carefully. "We can't let her down, Enoch. We must find him."

Enoch reached for the second letter, his hands trembling slightly. "There's more. This one's addressed to you, Bea."

She looked at him, surprised, and took the envelope. Her fingers moved slowly, almost reverently, as she broke the seal. As she read, her expression shifted from curiosity to shock, and then to a deep, wistful sadness.

"It's from Helen," she whispered. "My old friend, the one who disappeared all those years ago."

"Helen?" Enoch leaned forward; his brow furrowed. "The one who left Tolerance without a word? I thought she'd never come back."

Beatrice nodded, staring down at the letter as if it held a piece of her own past. "Listen to this," she said, her voice shaky:

"Dear Bea,

It's been too long, and I have no right to ask this, but I'm coming back to Tolerance. I've carried the weight of my choices all these years, and I can't do it any longer. I need to make things right—with you, with the town, and with the family I left behind.

If you're reading this, it means I've found the courage to return. I hope there's still a place for me in your heart and in the place we once called home.

Yours,

Helen."

Beatrice's hand shook as she folded the letter. "I kept her secret, Enoch. All these years, I promised her I wouldn't tell anyone where she went. She needed to escape, to heal. I never thought I'd hear from her again."

Enoch took her hand in his. "And now she's coming back. Maybe it's time for old wounds to be healed, Bea."

Beatrice's eyes softened. "Maybe it is. But first, we need to deliver Jacey's letter. That little girl deserves her Christmas wish."

They held each other's gaze, a shared understanding passing between them. They knew this was more than just a delivery—it was a chance to mend the broken threads of the town's tapestry, to bring people back together after years of silence and separation.

A Journey Through the Snow

The next morning, they set out together, bundled against the cold. The sleigh glided smoothly over the fresh snow, making a soft shushing sound that seemed to hush the world around them. The town was blanketed in white now, the rooftops and trees draped in glistening snow, as if Tolerance itself had been reborn overnight.

They stopped at the small diner on Main Street. Through the frosted glass, Enoch spotted an old man sitting alone at a table, staring out at the snow with a distant, sorrowful look. It was Jacey's grandfather—Enoch recognized him from years ago, though the man looked older, wearier, as if time had worn him thin.

Beatrice gave Enoch a gentle nudge. "Go on," she said softly. "He needs to hear it from you."

Enoch approached the man slowly, his boots crunching in the snow. He pulled out Jacey's letter and laid it gently on the table. "Sir," he said, his voice kind but firm. "This is for you. It's from your granddaughter, Jacey."

The man's hand trembled as he took the letter. He read it silently, his eyes welling up with tears that spilled over and ran down his cheeks. He pressed a hand to his mouth, struggling to hold back a sob.

"I didn't think anyone wanted me back," he whispered, his voice broken.

"Jacey does," Enoch replied, placing a comforting hand on his shoulder. "And maybe that's enough to start with."

The old man stood, clutching the letter to his chest like a lifeline. He looked at Enoch with a tearful, grateful smile. "I need to see her," he said. "I need to go home."

Enoch nodded. "You do that. And take your time. There's no rush today."

The Return of an Old Friend

Leaving the diner, Enoch and Beatrice continued toward the outskirts of town. The snow fell in fat, lazy flakes, settling over the fields and the old stone bridge that marked the boundary of Tolerance. There, waiting by the bridge, was a woman wrapped in a dark coat, her hood pulled low.

Beatrice knew it was Helen before she even saw her face. She stepped down from the sleigh, her breath catching in her throat. "Helen," she called softly.

Helen turned, her face lined with years of sorrow and regret, but her eyes held a glimmer of hope. She took a hesitant step forward, then another, until she was standing before Beatrice. They looked at each other for a long moment, the silence filled with everything they couldn't say.

"I'm so sorry," Helen whispered, her voice cracking. "I should have never left like that. I was so lost, and I didn't know how to come back."

Beatrice pulled her into a tight embrace. "You're here now," she said, her voice thick with emotion. "That's all that matters."

Helen clung to her, tears streaming down her cheeks. "Do you think they'll forgive me? The people I left behind?"

Beatrice pulled back, cupping her friend's face in her hands. "You've already been forgiven. Now you just need to forgive yourself."

They stood together, wrapped in the quiet understanding that comes only from shared history and deep love. Enoch watched from the sleigh, feeling a deep, quiet satisfaction in his chest. The snow fell around them, blanketing the town in a peace that only the season could bring.

The Last Gift of the Season

They rode home together, the three of them, the sleigh gliding smoothly through the snow. The town of Tolerance was hushed and still, the lights in the windows casting a warm glow into the night. As they approached the barn, Enoch slowed the sleigh and glanced back at Helen, who was smiling softly, her face alight with hope for the first time in years.

Beatrice squeezed Enoch's hand as they stepped inside, closing the barn door behind them. The sleigh sat in the shadows, now covered in a fresh layer of snow—a silent witness to the unexpected gifts of the day.

They guided the sleigh back to the barn, where Enoch unhitched Willow and gave her a gentle pat. The snow-covered sleigh sat quietly in the shadows, a silent witness to the unexpected gifts of the day.

Beatrice took Enoch's hand as they stepped out of the barn and into the night air. The soft glow of their home's windows welcomed them just a few steps away, casting a warm light across the snow-covered yard. They entered the house together, closing the door behind them, feeling the magic of the season settle around them.

THE PUMPKIN WAGON

The Journey Begins

The sun hung low over the central Kansas plains, casting long shadows across the barren fields. Dust swirled in small, restless spirals, carried by a dry wind that sang its hollow song through the brittle stalks of what was once a thriving cornfield. It was mid-October 1912. The earth, cracked and parched, stretched out like a sea of sorrow, a silent testament to the years of drought that had stripped the land of its life.

Pa stood by the wagon, a weathered man whose face bore the lines of countless harvests. His hands, rough from years of toil, cradled a large, misshapen pumpkin, the very last from a crop that had once promised so much. He set it gently into the wagon, where it joined the others, a collection of sunburned and scarred pumpkins—imperfect, but full of the last remnants of hope.

Ma watched from the doorway of their small, clapboard house, her apron fluttering in the wind like a faded flag. Clara and Billy stood beside her, their eyes wide with a mix of excitement and uncertainty. It had been years since they'd seen a proper Halloween, the kind with carved jack-o'-lanterns and laughter filling the air. The drought had stolen more than just crops; it had taken away their joy, too.

Pa turned to them; his voice rough but warm. "We're taking these to the townsfolk," he announced, wiping sweat from his brow. "Let's give the children something to smile about again."

Clara, her brown hair tied back with a strip of frayed cloth, stepped forward. "Will there be enough for everyone, Pa?"

He gave a small, tight smile, more a stretch of the lips than an expression of joy. "There'll be enough," he replied. "Because it's not the size of the gift that matters—it's the spirit behind it."

Billy, still young enough to believe in magic, clapped his hands together. "I'll help carve them!" he exclaimed, his eyes sparkling.

"Good boy," Pa chuckled, ruffling his hair. "Now help me hitch up the wagon."

As they made their final preparations, the sky began to shift, the pale blue deepening into shades of purple and gold. It was then that they saw him—a small figure standing at the edge of the field, almost blending into the landscape. Maka "Mac" Redbird, a 12-year-old Lakota Sioux boy, watched them with quiet, thoughtful eyes. He was barefoot, the hem of his trousers dusted with dirt, and in his hands, he held a small carved wooden pumpkin.

Pa raised a hand in greeting. "Mac! What brings you here, son?"

Mac stepped closer, his movements graceful and deliberate. He glanced at the wagon, then back at Pa. "I heard you were leaving with pumpkins," he said softly. "I'd like to come with you."

Ma stepped forward, wiping her hands on her apron. "Oh, Mac," she said, her voice gentle. "We'd be glad to have you. But it's a long journey, and we might not have much to share."

Mac smiled, a quiet smile that seemed to hold secrets of the earth itself. He held up the wooden pumpkin. "I bring my own," he said. "And I bring a story."

Clara and Billy exchanged glances; their curiosity piqued. "A story?" Clara asked, stepping closer. "What kind of story?"

Mac looked at her, then out across the field, where the wind was beginning to pick up again, carrying the scent of dry leaves and distant smoke. "A story from my people," he said. "About the harvest, and why we must share what we have, no matter how little."

Pa nodded, understanding something deeper than words could express. He gestured to the back of the wagon. "Well then," he said, his voice thick with emotion. "Climb aboard, Mac. We've got a lot of road ahead of us."

As Mac hoisted himself up into the wagon, Billy leaned over to get a closer look at the wooden pumpkin. "Did you carve this?" he asked, his small fingers tracing the smooth lines of the carving.

Mac nodded. "Yes," he said simply. "It's a symbol of the harvest. It reminds us that even in the hardest of times, we must give thanks."

Clara's eyes softened. "It's beautiful," she whispered.

The family fell into a comfortable silence as Pa took the reins, giving the horses a gentle nudge. The wagon creaked and groaned as it rolled forward, kicking up small clouds of dust. The sun dipped lower, casting long, golden beams that seemed to light the path ahead.

They were on their way, the farmer's family and the quiet boy from the reservation, bound together by a wagon full of pumpkins and a shared hope that perhaps, just perhaps, they could bring a bit of light back into the world.

As they rolled down the winding dirt road, Mac began to speak, his voice soft but clear, carrying the melody of ancient winds. "My people tell the story of the Great Pumpkin Spirit," he began. "A guardian of the harvest, who watches over the fields and blesses those who share their bounty, no matter how small."

Billy and Clara leaned in closer, their eyes wide, as the landscape stretched out before them—an endless canvas of dry, golden grass swaying under the deepening sky. The journey had begun, and with it, a new story, one filled with pumpkins, laughter, and the promise of brighter days ahead.

The Road of Trials

The wagon rattled and groaned as it rolled over the cracked earth, the wooden wheels kicking up small clouds of dust that swirled like ghosts in the dry autumn air. The sun burned a fierce orange overhead, casting long, jagged shadows across the plains. Mac sat at the back of the wagon, his carved wooden pumpkin resting in his lap. Clara and Billy sat beside him, their legs dangling over the edge, bare feet swinging as they bumped along the uneven road.

Billy's eyes widened as he pointed to the horizon. "Look, Clara! It's another dust storm!" He squinted at the dark, roiling cloud in the distance, like a monstrous wave ready to crash over the land.

Pa tugged on the reins, slowing the horses. "Hold on tight, everyone!" he called, his voice stern but steady. "We need to take cover."

Ma, sitting beside him on the front bench, turned to the children. "Get inside the canvas, quick!" She glanced back at Mac, who hadn't moved. "Mac, do you know a safe spot nearby?"

Mac nodded, his eyes scanning the landscape with an ancient familiarity. "There's a dry creek bed just over that rise," he said calmly, pointing with his free hand. "It'll shelter us from the worst of it."

Pa didn't hesitate. "Good eyes, Mac," he said, urging the horses forward. They veered off the road, the wagon bouncing and jostling over the rough ground until they reached the shallow dip of the creek bed.

As the wind picked up, carrying the first gusts of stinging sand, the family ducked beneath the canvas cover. The air filled with the sharp, metallic scent of dust, and the world outside turned a murky brown as the storm engulfed them.

Clara huddled close to Mac, her small hand clutching his arm. "I'm scared," she whispered, her voice trembling.

Mac patted her hand reassuringly. "It's okay, Clara," he said, his voice low and soothing. "The storm will pass. My grandmother used to say that the wind is just the earth's way of singing. It's loud, but it can't harm us here."

Billy peeked out from under the canvas, watching the swirling dust. "Does the earth sing in your stories, Mac?"

Mac nodded, a small smile playing at his lips. "Yes," he replied. "In our stories, everything sings. The trees, the rivers, even the stones. They all have voices if you listen."

Pa leaned in, wiping the sweat and dust from his brow. "Mac," he said, his voice full of gratitude, "I don't know what we'd do without you. You've guided us through more than just this storm."

Ma nodded in agreement. "You've brought us more than we could ever give back," she said softly.

Mac looked down at his wooden pumpkin, tracing the smooth lines of the carving with his thumb. "My grandmother always said that when you share what little you have, you never go without," he said. "I'm just following her wisdom."

The storm raged on outside, but inside the canvas, a quiet warmth filled the space, like the glow of a hearth in a dark room. Clara and Billy listened intently as Mac began to tell another story.

"Long ago," Mac began, his voice taking on a rhythmic cadence, "the buffalo spirit walked among my people. He was a giant, with eyes like the deepest lakes and a coat as thick as the winter snow. He watched over the plains and brought us good harvests. One year, the earth dried up, just like it has now. The rivers turned to dust, and the corn wouldn't grow. The people were afraid."

Clara leaned closer; her eyes wide. "What happened then, Mac?"

Mac continued; his eyes distant as if he could see the story playing out in the dust outside. "The buffalo spirit told the people to carve pumpkins and place them at the edge of the village, to show gratitude for what they still had. It wasn't much, but it was enough. That night, the pumpkins glowed brighter than the moon, and the next morning, the rains came."

Billy's mouth dropped open. "Is that true?" his voice filled with wonder.

Mac shrugged, a twinkle in his eye. "It's true if you believe it," he said simply. "Sometimes believing is the hardest part."

The dust storm began to subside, the roaring wind quieting into a gentle breeze. Pa peeked out from under the canvas and gave a nod. "Storm's passed," he said, his voice filled with relief. "Let's get back on the road."

They emerged from their shelter, shaking off the dust like old memories. The sun was lower now, casting a soft golden light across the plains. As they climbed back into the wagon, Mac glanced back toward the road they'd left behind.

"There's a town up ahead," he said. "I think we should stop there tonight."

Pa nodded. "You're right, Mac. Let's see if we can bring a bit of Halloween cheer."

The Town of Ash Creek

They arrived at Ash Creek just as the sun dipped below the horizon, casting long shadows that danced like specters between the empty buildings. The town was eerily quiet, the only sound the creak of the wagon wheels and the distant, hollow clatter of a wind-blown shutter.

Clara shivered. "It feels like a ghost town," she whispered.

Billy hopped down from the wagon, clutching one of the smaller pumpkins. "Do you think the kids here will want to carve pumpkins, Pa?"

Before Pa could answer, a small face appeared in the window of a dilapidated building. A girl, no older than Billy, peeked out, her eyes wide with curiosity. Slowly, more faces emerged—children, their cheeks smudged with dirt, eyes hollow with hunger but glimmering with a spark of something long forgotten.

Pa lifted a pumpkin high above his head. "Gather 'round, folks!" he called, his voice carrying over the empty street. "We've brought pumpkins! Let's carve some jack-o'-lanterns and bring back a bit of Halloween!"

At first, there was only silence, a hesitation that spoke of long years of disappointment. But then Mac stepped forward, holding his wooden pumpkin. He knelt down and offered it to the little girl from the window.

"This is for you," he said, his voice gentle. "It's a gift, from my people to yours. Let's carve together, and I'll tell you a story of the buffalo spirit who blesses those who share."

The girl took the wooden pumpkin, cradling it as if it were made of gold. She looked up at Mac with a smile that seemed to light up the entire street.

"Can we make the face scary?" she asked, her voice small but eager.

Mac grinned. "The scarier, the better."

And so, they carved. Pa handed out pumpkins to the children, while Ma helped the littlest ones scrape out the seeds. Clara and Billy showed the other kids how to cut triangle eyes and jagged mouths. Mac told stories, his voice rising and falling with the rhythm of the knife scraping the pumpkin flesh. He spoke of the Great Pumpkin Spirit and the songs of the earth, stories that made the children laugh and gasp in wonder.

As the sun set and the first stars blinked into the night sky, the town square filled with the warm, flickering light of jack-o'-lanterns. It was a small miracle—a moment of laughter and light in the darkness of the Dust Bowl.

Pa stood back, watching the children dance around the glowing pumpkins. He felt a lump in his throat, a feeling he couldn't quite name. He turned to Mac, his voice choked with emotion. "Thank you, Mac," he said. "For everything."

Mac simply nodded, his eyes reflecting the light of the jack-o'-lanterns. "We're all part of the same harvest," he said quietly. "We share what we have, and the earth sings a little louder."

The Celebration of Light

The wagon rolled into the heart of the town of Tatum Creek just as twilight settled, casting a deep purple glow over the empty streets. The air was cool now, a welcome respite from the relentless sun. Pa guided the horses slowly, their hooves clopping softly on the packed dirt road. The buildings, worn and sagging, looked like weary travelers themselves, leaning into the shadows for support.

Mac hopped down from the wagon, his moccasin-shod feet landing softly on the ground. He looked around, his sharp eyes taking in the details—a swing swaying in the wind, its ropes frayed; a tattered banner from a long-past harvest festival; a small pumpkin left to rot on a porch, its face barely visible through the cracks.

"This town's seen better days," Pa muttered, shaking his head.

Ma nodded, clutching her shawl tighter around her shoulders. "We have enough pumpkins for one last stop," she said. "Let's make it count."

Clara and Billy jumped down eagerly, each grabbing a pumpkin. "Let's find the children!" Clara called, her voice echoing down the empty street.

Mac raised a hand, signaling for quiet. "Wait," he said softly. He closed his eyes for a moment, listening. "They're here," he murmured. "They're just hiding."

Pa frowned. "Hiding?"

Mac pointed to the edges of the square, where the darkness gathered thick like smoke. "They're afraid," he explained. "They've forgotten what it's like to trust strangers."

Without a word, Mac stepped forward into the middle of the square, holding his carved wooden pumpkin high. He looked into the shadows, his voice calm and inviting. "Come out," he called. "We've brought stories, pumpkins, and light. We've come to share what we have."

For a long moment, nothing happened. The wind picked up, rustling the dry leaves that skittered across the ground. Then, slowly, a small figure emerged from the darkness—a boy, about Billy's age, with dirt-smudged cheeks and hollow eyes. He looked at Mac's wooden pumpkin, his expression a mix of fear and longing.

"What is that?" the boy asked, his voice barely more than a whisper.

Mac knelt down to meet the boy's gaze. "This," he said gently, "is a pumpkin carved with a story. It's a gift, and it's here to remind us that even in hard times, there's still light to be shared."

The boy stepped closer, drawn to Mac's calm presence. He reached out a tentative hand, brushing his fingers against the smooth wood. "Can we carve one too?" he asked, glancing at the wagon where the other pumpkins lay.

Clara grinned, holding out a small, lopsided pumpkin. "Of course!" she said, her voice bright. "Come help us! We'll make the best jack-o'-lanterns this town has ever seen."

With that, the spell of silence broke. Children began to pour out from the shadows—dozens of them, many barefoot and hungry-looking, but with eyes that sparkled in the fading light. They gathered around the wagon, their hands reaching out eagerly for the pumpkins.

Pa and Ma exchanged a glance, their eyes welling up with tears. "We did it," Ma whispered, squeezing Pa's hand. "We really did it."

As the children set to work carving, Mac sat with a small group of them, telling his stories in a voice that wrapped around them like a warm blanket.

"There's an old tale my people tell," Mac began, using his knife to carve a careful, smiling mouth into a pumpkin. "Long ago, before the first frost, the Great Pumpkin Spirit would walk the fields at night. He'd touch each pumpkin, filling it with a light so bright that it could chase away the darkest shadows."

A girl with tangled hair looked up at him, her hands sticky with pumpkin seeds. "What happened to the spirit?" she asked, her voice full of wonder.

Mac paused, his hands still as he looked up at the sky, where the first stars had begun to peek through. "Some say he's still out there," he said softly. "Watching over the harvest. And when people share what they have—like we're doing tonight—that's when he appears."

The girl's eyes widened. "Do you think he'll come tonight?"

Mac smiled, a secretive, knowing smile. "Maybe," he said. "If we believe."

As the children finished carving, Pa and Ma began placing the jack-o'-lanterns all around the square. The flickering candles inside made the pumpkins glow like small, golden suns. The whole town seemed to come alive in that light—doors creaked open, and more townsfolk stepped out, drawn by the laughter and the glow of the pumpkins.

An old man shuffled forward; his face lined with the wrinkles of a thousand hardships. He looked at the jack-o'-lanterns, then at Pa. "We haven't seen anything like this in years," he said, his voice choked with emotion. "You brought Halloween back to us."

Pa shook his head. "It wasn't just us," he said, placing a hand on Mac's shoulder. "It was Mac who brought the stories and the spirit."

The old man turned to Mac, his eyes misting over. "Thank you, son," he said quietly. "You've given us something we thought we'd lost forever."

Mac simply nodded. He took a step back, looking out over the sea of glowing pumpkins, his expression peaceful and content.

Just then, a gust of wind blew through the square, carrying the scent of rain. The children stopped, their heads tilting up as the first drops began to fall—soft and cool, kissing the dry earth. The old man's eyes widened, and he threw his arms up to the sky, laughing. "It's rain!" he shouted. "It's finally raining!"

The townsfolk lifted their faces to the sky, their cheers mingling with the sound of the falling rain. It wasn't a downpour, just a gentle, steady shower, but it was enough. The earth drank it up eagerly, the dust settling as the water soaked into the cracks.

Pa pulled Ma into his arms, spinning her around in a dance. Clara and Billy whooped with joy, their bare feet splashing in the growing puddles. Mac stood in the middle of it all, his face upturned, eyes closed, as if he were listening to a song only he could hear.

The rain fell, washing away the dust, the sorrow, and the silence. In its place, there was laughter, light, and the promise of new life.

As the rain slowed, the townsfolk gathered around Mac one last time. Pa stepped forward, holding out the last pumpkin—a small, bright orange one, untouched by knife or hand. "This one's for you, Mac," he said. "To take with you, wherever your journey leads."

Mac took the pumpkin, cradling it as if it were the most precious thing in the world. "Thank you," he said softly. He looked at the faces around him, the faces of people who had been strangers only hours before, now friends connected by shared stories and a shared night.

With a final wave, Mac turned and walked away, his silhouette disappearing into the dark horizon, the carved wooden pumpkin tucked under his arm. The family and the townsfolk watched him go, standing together in the glow of the jack-o'-lanterns.

"He'll be back," Billy said confidently, looking up at Clara. "Won't he?"

Clara smiled, wiping a tear from her cheek. "Maybe," she said, hugging her little brother. "If we believe."

The wagon rolled out of town the next morning, empty of pumpkins but full of something far more valuable. The sun rose, casting a golden light over the plains, and for the first time in a long time, the earth sang with the promise of a new harvest.

THE SWING OF HOPE

A New Arrival in Wilbur

The town of Wilbur, nestled in southcentral Ohio, could have easily been mistaken for any other midwestern small town in the early 1950s. The streets were lined with elm trees, their branches stretching across the narrow roads like outstretched arms, offering shade on warm summer days. A single main street ran through the center of town, dotted with a diner, bakery, general store, gas station, hardware store, and a modest post office where neighbors exchanged pleasantries and gossip alike. On Sundays, families filled the pews of the Baptist church at the corner, and on weekdays, children raced along the sidewalks, trailing the scent of fresh-baked pies wafting from open kitchen windows.

But beneath the surface, Wilbur was a town set in its ways. Quiet prejudices whispered through the streets, carried on the wind like secrets shared behind closed doors. The people of Wilbur were kind enough, but their smiles sometimes came with a hint of suspicion when they encountered someone different, someone new.

The Washington family arrived in Wilbur on a sticky July afternoon. They traveled north from Mississippi, their old Ford creaking under the weight of all they owned, piled high and tied down with fraying rope. The Great Migration had called to them, promising better opportunities, a chance to escape the suffocating grip of Jim Crow laws. They pulled into their new home, a modest clapboard house on Maple Street, and stepped out into the unfamiliar air of a northern summer.

"Home sweet home," Mr. Washington said, trying to muster a smile for his wife. He squeezed her hand, and she returned the gesture, though her eyes darted around the neighborhood warily.

Mrs. Washington sighed, wiping sweat from her brow with a handkerchief. "Let's get settled, Henry," she said softly. "Inez, come help us unload."

From the back seat, a small girl hopped out, her feet landing with a soft thud on the gravel driveway. Inez Washington was ten years old, small for her age, but with a spirit that seemed to take up more space than her little body allowed. Her dark hair was tied back with a faded blue ribbon, and her bright eyes sparkled with curiosity as she looked around at her new home.

"This is it?" Inez asked, her voice tinged with both excitement and trepidation. She could already feel the difference in the air, a certain heaviness that had nothing to do with the summer heat.

"This is it," her mother replied, trying to sound cheerful. "We're gonna make it nice, you'll see."

The First Walk in the Park

A week later, Inez found herself standing at the edge of the neighborhood park. She had begged her mother to let her go exploring on her own, promising she wouldn't wander too far. The park was small, just a patch of green with a rusty slide, a couple of benches, and a sandbox filled with sun-bleached toys. In the center, there was an old oak tree, its branches thick and gnarled, perfect for climbing or, Inez thought, for hanging a swing.

A group of children played near the sandbox, their laughter ringing out across the park. Inez hesitated, watching them from a distance. She recognized a few of them from the street where they lived, but she hadn't spoken to any of them yet. Her heart pounded in her chest, a mix of hope and fear. Would they accept her? She took a deep breath and stepped forward.

As soon as they saw her, the children paused. Their play slowed, and they turned to stare, the way children do when they encounter something unfamiliar. Inez felt their eyes on her, felt the weight of their silence. She smiled shyly and gave a small wave.

"Hi," she said, her voice soft but steady.

The oldest of the group, a boy about eleven with a mop of sandy hair, stepped forward. His name was Tommy. He had seen Inez once or twice on the street and had been curious about her. He squinted at her now, as if trying to solve a puzzle.

"You're new here," Tommy said, more a statement than a question.

Inez nodded. "We just moved in on Maple Street."

Tommy nodded back slowly. "I'm Tommy. That's Mary and Bobby." He pointed to a tall girl with freckles and a boy clutching a toy truck.

Inez offered a small smile. "I'm Inez."

Mary frowned, crossing her arms over her chest. "Where are you from?"

she asked bluntly.

"Corinth, Mississippi," Inez replied.

Bobby's eyes widened. "That's down south," he said. "A long way from here."

Inez nodded again. "My dad got a job at the factory," she explained. "We came up here to start fresh."

The children exchanged glances. They had heard the quiet talk from their parents about "the new Negro family on Maple Street." But standing there in front of them, Inez didn't seem so different. Just a girl, like them, who wanted to play.

"What do you like to do?" Tommy asked, breaking the silence.

Inez's eyes lit up. She pointed to the old oak tree in the center of the park. "I love swings," she said, her voice brightening. "I used to swing so high; I felt like I could touch the sky."

Tommy glanced at the tree, then back at Inez. "There isn't a swing here," he said.

"I know," Inez said wistfully. "But if there was one, I'd be the first to try it."

Tommy's face broke into a grin. "Well then," he said, glancing at the others, "maybe we should build one."

The suggestion hung in the air like a challenge. Mary looked uncertain, and Bobby shifted on his feet, frowning.

"My dad won't like it," Bobby muttered, half to himself.

Tommy ignored him. He turned back to Inez. "What do you say? You want a swing?"

Inez's smile was small but genuine. "I'd like that," she said. "I'd like that very much."

The Decision to Build

The children gathered under the oak tree, the shadow of its branches stretching long in the late afternoon sun. They huddled close, sharing their plans. Inez sat quietly, listening to their excited chatter, feeling a warmth spread through her chest. It was the first time since they moved to Wilbur that she felt like she might belong.

"We'll need rope," Mary said decisively. "And something for the seat."

"I can get rope from my dad's shed," Tommy offered. "But we'll have to keep it quiet. He doesn't like us playing with his tools."

Bobby frowned, looking over at Inez. "Why are we even doing this?" he asked. "She's not like us."

Silence fell over the group. Inez looked at Bobby, her gaze steady. "I'm not so different," she said softly. "I just want to swing, like any of you."

Tommy stepped closer to Bobby and put a hand on his shoulder. "Maybe that's enough," he said quietly. "Maybe we all just want to swing."

The tension melted away, replaced by a tentative understanding. The children nodded, one by one. Together, they set off to gather what they needed, a small army united by the simple, shared dream of building something beautiful.

The stage was set, and the work had begun. The swing was no longer just a project—it was a promise. A promise of new beginnings, of friendships that defied the quiet prejudices of the town. And at the heart of it all was Inez Washington, a little girl who dared to dream of flying high, even when the world tried to keep her on the ground.

Building Bridges

The sun dipped lower in the sky as the children returned to the park, their arms laden with supplies scavenged from sheds, garages, and forgotten corners of their homes. There was a sense of excitement in the air, mixed with a subtle tension. The old oak tree stood tall and unyielding, its thick branches stretching out like the strong arms of a protector, ready to cradle the swing they were about to build.

Inez watched as Tommy and Mary laid the pieces on the grass—a long, sturdy rope, a worn-out plank for the seat, and a handful of rusty nails. She glanced at Bobby, who lingered at the edge of the group, his arms crossed tightly over his chest. He seemed torn between wanting to help and the words his father had breathed in his ear the night before.

"Remember, son," his father had said, lowering his voice as if he feared being overheard, "people like them are different. You stay away from that new girl, you hear?"

Bobby swallowed hard, the memory pressing down on him like a weight. He kicked at the dirt, watching the dust rise and settle. He knew what his father thought, but looking at Inez, he didn't see a stranger. He saw a girl who wanted to swing just like anyone else.

Tommy clapped his hands, breaking the silence. "All right, team," he said, trying to sound like a coach, "let's get to work."

Mary knelt by the rope, running her fingers along its coarse surface. "This rope is pretty old," she said. "Do you think it'll hold?"

Inez stepped forward, surprising everyone by her sudden confidence. "It'll hold," she said quietly. "I used to have a swing just like this back home. The rope was older than this, and it never broke."

The children exchanged glances. There was something about the way Inez spoke—calm, assured—that made them believe her.

"Well then," Tommy said with a grin, "let's get this thing tied up."

Tensions Rise

As the children worked, the sun cast long shadows across the park, the light turning golden and soft. They laughed and bickered, their voices filling the air with the sound of summer. Tommy clambered up the tree, gripping the thick branch as he looped the rope around it. Mary held the seat steady, while Inez tied knots with nimble fingers, her face set in concentration.

Bobby, however, stood apart, his eyes darting from the swing to the street beyond the park. He thought he saw a shadow moving near the edge of the trees. He squinted, his heart pounding as the figure stepped into the light.

It was Mr. Thompson, Bobby's father, his face twisted into a scowl. He stood with his arms crossed, watching the group with narrowed eyes.

"Bobby!" Mr. Thompson's voice cut through the children's laughter like a cold wind. "What are you doing?"

The laughter stopped abruptly. The children turned to see the tall, imposing figure of Bobby's father striding toward them. He looked like a storm rolling in, dark and full of fury.

Bobby's face paled, and he glanced at Tommy and Mary, who stared back at him, wide-eyed. Inez remained still, her small hands gripping the rope tightly as she looked up at Mr. Thompson. She knew this moment would come—had felt it building like a gathering cloud. But she was determined not to show fear.

"What's going on here?" Mr. Thompson demanded, his gaze flicking to the swing and then landing squarely on Inez. He seemed to tower over her, a giant casting a long, dark shadow.

"We're building a swing," Tommy said, his voice shaky but defiant. "It's for all of us."

Mr. Thompson snorted. "For all of you, huh?" He pointed a finger at Inez. "Even her?"

Tommy's jaw clenched. He nodded. "Yes, sir. Even her."

A tense silence fell over the park, broken only by the rustle of leaves in the breeze. The other children shifted uncomfortably, their eyes darting between Mr. Thompson and Inez.

Inez looked up at Mr. Thompson, meeting his harsh gaze with her own calm, steady eyes. "I'm not here to cause trouble," she said softly. "I just want to swing."

Mr. Thompson's lips curled into a sneer. "Swinging won't change anything," he spat. "You don't belong here."

Bobby's face crumpled. He felt a hot, shameful tear slide down his cheek, and he quickly wiped it away. "Dad, please," he whispered. "She's just a kid."

Mr. Thompson's eyes flashed, and he grabbed Bobby's arm roughly. "Come on," he said through gritted teeth. "You're coming home. Now."

Tommy stepped forward; his fists clenched. "It's not fair," he blurted out. "We all worked on this swing. Inez helped, too."

Mary nodded, stepping beside Tommy. "She tied the knots better than any of us could," she said, her voice small but resolute.

Mr. Thompson glared at them, his face growing red. "You think this changes anything?" he snapped. "You're fooling yourselves if you do."

He yanked Bobby away, dragging him back toward the street. Bobby looked over his shoulder, his face twisted in a mix of regret and fear. "I'm sorry," he mouthed to Inez.

Inez stood still, the swing seat hanging limply from her hands. The other children watched Mr. Thompson's retreating back, their faces pale and troubled. The joyful excitement of the afternoon had evaporated, leaving behind a bitter chill.

A Glimmer of Hope

Tommy turned to Inez; his face crumpled in frustration. "I'm sorry, Inez," he said. "I didn't think it would be like this."

Inez offered him a small, sad smile. "It's not your fault," she said quietly. "It's just the way things are. But I still want to swing."

Her words hung in the air, filled with a simple, unyielding determination. The other children exchanged glances. Mary stepped forward and put her hand on the swing seat.

"Then let's finish it," she said, her voice stronger now. "If Inez wants to swing, we'll make sure she gets her chance."

Tommy nodded, a fierce look in his eyes. He climbed back up the tree and tightened the knot, yanking it hard to make sure it would hold. Inez took a deep breath and stepped up to the swing. She felt a strange flutter in her chest—not fear, but a feeling she hadn't had since she left Mississippi. It felt like hope.

From the edge of the park, a shadow lingered, watching. Mr. Thompson had stopped to see what would happen next. He frowned, but something in his eyes softened as he watched the little girl swing higher and higher, her face lit up with pure happiness.

Maybe, he thought, just maybe, they had built more than a swing that day.

The First Flight

The sun had dipped behind the treetops, casting the park in a dusky, golden light. The swing, finished and sturdy, hung from the old oak like a promise fulfilled. Inez stood by, looking at it with a mixture of awe and disbelief. It was real, and it was hers—built by children who decided to see her for who she was, not what others thought she should be.

Tommy clapped Inez on the back, his grin wide. "Well, go on," he urged. "You're the first to try it out."

Inez's heart beat fast. It wasn't just about swinging anymore. It was about proving that she belonged here, in this park, in this town. She stepped forward, her small hand brushing the rough, frayed rope. For a moment, she hesitated, feeling all the eyes on her—Tommy's and Mary's, filled with encouragement; Bobby's, filled with regret; and from the shadows beyond the park, the eyes of the adults who watched, waiting for her to falter.

Taking a deep breath, Inez sat on the wooden seat. The children gathered around, holding their breath as if the world had paused just for this moment.

The First Push

Tommy stepped behind her, giving a light push. The swing moved slowly at first, creaking on the rope, then picked up speed. The wind rushed past Inez's ears, and she felt herself rise higher and higher. She closed her eyes and let the sensation wash over her, the joy bubbling up in her chest like a laugh she couldn't hold back.

The children cheered, clapping and shouting her name. Inez laughed, a sound so pure and free that it seemed to cut through the tension in the air, carrying away the whispers of prejudice that had clung to the park like smoke.

From the edge of the park, Mr. Thompson watched, his face hard but unreadable. He had brought Bobby home, but the boy had run back to see what would happen. Now, Bobby stood beside his father, looking up at him with pleading eyes.

"Dad, look at her," Bobby said softly. "She's just a kid, like us."

Mr. Thompson's jaw clenched, the muscles ticking under his skin. "You don't understand," he muttered. "This isn't how things are done."

Bobby's face twisted in frustration. "Maybe it's time things change," he said, his voice daring, filled with a courage he didn't know he had.

A Storm Approaching

As Inez swung higher, dark clouds began to gather in the sky. The wind picked up, rustling the leaves of the old oak, sending a shiver through the park. It was as if the weather itself sensed the tension, the storm brewing not just in the sky but among the people watching.

Tommy turned his face up to the clouds. "We'd better get going soon," he said, a nervous edge to his voice. "A storm's coming."

But Inez didn't want to stop. She pushed off harder, pumping her legs, determined to swing as high as she could, as if she could fly away from all the ugliness that had followed her north. She felt the raindrops on her cheeks, mixing with her tears of joy.

From the other side of the park, a group of men had gathered—fathers, storekeepers, neighbors. They murmured among themselves, glancing at Inez and then at each other, their faces pinched and disapproving. The children felt their stares like the sting of a cold wind. Mary's eyes darted to Tommy, filled with fear.

"Tommy," she whispered, "we need to go. They don't look happy."

Tommy squared his shoulders, a defiant set to his jaw. "I don't care," he said. "This is our swing. We built it together. It belongs to all of us."

One of the men stepped forward. It was Mr. Jenkins, the owner of the general store, a man whose voice carried weight in the town. "This needs to stop," he called out, loud enough for everyone to hear. "You can't have her here like this."

Inez slowed her swinging, her feet brushing the ground as she came to a stop. She looked at the group of men, her eyes wide but unafraid. "Why?" she asked quietly. "Why can't I be here?"

Mr. Jenkins shifted uncomfortably, not expecting her to challenge him.

"It's just the way things are, girl," he said. "You don't belong."

A crack of thunder split the sky, the first roll of the storm announcing itself. The children flinched, but Inez didn't move. She stood up from the swing, stepping forward until she was in front of the group of men. She was small, dwarfed by their height, but in that moment, she seemed taller than any of them.

"I belong," Inez said, her voice steady and clear. "I belong because I'm here, and because my friends built this swing for me. It's not your swing. It's ours."

The rain started to fall, hard and fast, soaking the ground, but no one moved. The children gathered behind Inez, standing with her—Tommy, Mary, even Bobby, who broke away from his father's side to join them.

"We built it together," Tommy said, stepping up beside Inez. "It's for all of us. You can't take it away."

The Moment of Change

The men stood there, frozen, as if they didn't know what to do next. They hadn't expected this—a united front, children standing together against the old rules, the unspoken laws of segregation that had kept their world divided. The rain poured down, drenching everyone, washing away the dirt and sweat of the long day.

Mr. Thompson looked at his son, then at Inez. His face softened, the lines of anger smoothing into something that looked almost like sadness. He took a step back, then another, lowering his head.

"Let's go," he said quietly to the men around him. "There's nothing we can do here."

The men hesitated, then slowly turned away, defeated not by force but by the quiet strength of a little girl who refused to be told she didn't belong. One by one, they disappeared into the rain, leaving the children standing alone under the old oak tree.

Inez turned back to the swing, her hands trembling as she gripped the rope. She looked at Tommy, Mary, and Bobby, her eyes shining. "Thank you," she whispered. "For standing with me."

Tommy grinned, wiping the rain from his face. "You don't have to thank us," he said. "We're friends, aren't we?"

Inez nodded; her heart full. "Yes," she said. "We are."

A Seed Planted

As the rain began to lighten, the children stood in a small, soaked circle under the old oak tree, their clothes clinging to their skin and their faces still flushed with emotion. The swing swayed gently in the wind, dripping water as though it too had joined in the catharsis of the moment.

Inez touched the rope one last time, her fingers lingering on the rough texture as if memorizing the feeling. Her heart was still racing, but it wasn't fear anymore—it was triumph. For the first time since arriving in Wilbur, she didn't feel like an outsider. She felt seen. She felt valued.

Tommy, brushing rain from his face, looked at her with a grin that spoke more than words. "You really showed them," he said.

Inez smiled back, her spirit soaring higher than the swing ever could. "We showed them," she corrected. "I couldn't have done it without all of you."

Behind them, the park began to empty as the adults dispersed. Mr. Thompson lingered the longest, standing near the tree line, his figure shadowed but still visible. He watched as the children laughed, their defiance softened into joy, and something inside him began to shift. For years, he had clung to the beliefs he had been taught, never questioning them, never seeing a reason to. But tonight, as he saw his son stand beside that little girl, drenched but proud, he felt the first twinges of doubt.

"Bobby," he called, his voice quieter now.

Bobby turned, his face expectant but cautious. "Yes, sir?"

Mr. Thompson hesitated. He didn't know how to say what he felt, didn't even fully understand it himself. Finally, he nodded toward the swing. "You did good," he said gruffly before turning and walking away.

The words weren't much, but to Bobby, they felt like an olive branch. His shoulders relaxed, and he turned back to Inez and the others with a small smile.

As the rain tapered to a drizzle, the children made their way home. The park, now quiet except for the occasional drip of water from the tree, seemed transformed. The swing hung motionless, a testament to what had happened, a reminder of what could be.

Ripples in the Community

In the days that followed, word of the swing and the events at the park spread through Wilbur. Some whispered about it disapprovingly, clucking their tongues and muttering that "things were changing too fast." Others, however, found themselves intrigued, their curiosity outpacing their prejudice.

Mrs. Grady, who ran the diner on Main Street, asked Inez's mother about her pie recipes after church one Sunday. Mr. Jenkins, though still stern and set in his ways, nodded curtly at the Washingtons when he saw them on the street. Small gestures, barely perceptible, but each one carried the weight of a world beginning to turn.

At school, Inez found herself the subject of cautious but genuine attention. Mary invited her to sit together during lunch, and Tommy, always the leader, insisted she join their kickball game during recess. Even Bobby, though quieter than the others, gave her a shy smile every now and then.

The swing became a gathering spot. Children who might never have spoken to Inez before lined up for their turn, laughing and joking as they pushed each other higher and higher. The oak tree, once just a feature of the park, became a silent witness to the slow but steady unraveling of barriers.

A Glimpse of Tomorrow

One evening, months later, Inez and her parents sat on their porch, the warm glow of the setting sun casting long shadows across Maple Street. The air was cool, carrying the scent of fall leaves and chimney smoke. Inez hugged her knees to her chest, staring out at the park in the distance.

"Do you think it'll always be this hard?" she asked softly.

Her father looked up from his newspaper, his gaze steady and thoughtful. "Change is never easy," he said. "But every step you take makes the next one a little lighter—for you and for those who come after."

Her mother reached over, brushing a strand of hair from Inez's face. "And you've already taken some mighty big steps," she added with a proud smile.

Inez let their words settle in her heart. She thought of the swing, still hanging from the oak tree, and the friends who had stood by her side. She thought of Tommy's grin, Mary's courage, and even Bobby's quiet apology. They were small moments, but they felt like the start of something bigger—something worth believing in.

As the first stars began to twinkle in the sky, Inez whispered a quiet promise to herself. "I'll keep swinging," her voice firm. "No matter what."

And in that moment, the park, the swing, and the little town of Wilbur seemed to hold their breath, as if they too were waiting to see how far she could fly.

THE CEREMONIAL WIND CHIME

The Preparations for New Year's Eve

The morning sun crept over the ridges of the Appalachian mountains, casting a pale, wintry light across Tinker Creek. The small town was tucked away in a valley, hidden between steep, snow-covered hills and dense forests of pine and oak. Smoke rose lazily from the chimneys of old miner's cottages, twisting into the blue sky. It was late December, and a thick silence blanketed the landscape, broken only by the occasional call of a crow or the crunch of frost underfoot.

At the edge of the forest stood the Rainwater cabin, a simple wooden structure with a roof weathered gray by years of mountain storms. It was small but sturdy, built by Roscoe's great-grandfather, who had come down from Cherokee lands to settle here long before the coal mines scarred the hills. Smoke curled from the stone chimney, carrying the scent of burning hickory and pine, a familiar smell that felt like home.

Roscoe Rainwater stepped outside, his breath puffing out in little clouds as he looked up at the sky, clear and bright. He was seventeen, tall and lean, with deep-set eyes that seemed to hold the stories of those who had come before him. His dark hair was tied back loosely, and his hands were rough from work, but there was a gentleness in the way he moved, as if he could feel the pulse of the earth beneath his feet.

He knelt by the edge of the woods, gathering bits of bark, fallen branches, and smooth stones worn by the creek. He worked slowly, selecting each piece with care. His grandmother's words drifted through his memory, as soft as the rustle of leaves. "They carry the voices of the past, child," she had told him. "Each note is a message from our ancestors."

Roscoe's hands paused over a piece of driftwood; its surface polished smooth by years in the creek. He could almost see his grandmother's face in his mind—her dark eyes wise and kind, framed by silver hair that fell like a waterfall down her back. She had passed three winters ago, but her spirit was still here, woven into the fabric of the land and the wind that sang through the trees.

He tucked the driftwood into his bag and stood, looking out at the mountains. Snow dusted the peaks like powdered sugar on a cake, and the cold air was crisp and clean. He could see the town below, the tiny church steeple poking up through the trees, the old coal tipple standing dark against the sky. Tinker Creek was a small town, held together by the grit of the miners who had carved out a living here and the traditions that ran as deep as the veins of coal beneath the earth.

Family Background and Heritage

Roscoe turned back toward the cabin, where his mother was standing on the porch, her arms wrapped tightly around herself against the cold. She was a tall woman, with a strong, angular face softened by years of laughter and hard work. Her hair, streaked with gray, was tied up under a worn kerchief. She had the look of the mountain folk, descended from generations of settlers who had lived and died by the rhythms of the land.

His father, on the other hand, had the dark, sharp features of his Cherokee ancestors. He rarely spoke of the Trail of Tears, the forced march that had driven their people from their homes, but the pain of it lingered in his eyes, like a shadow that never fully faded. He was a quiet man, reserved but kind, who carried the weight of their family's history in the lines etched deep into his face.

Together, the Rainwaters had created a home that honored both parts of their heritage. Every New Year's Eve, they made a wind chime as a tribute to the loved ones they had lost—a tradition passed down from Roscoe's Cherokee ancestors but adapted with the materials and customs of the Appalachian mountains. The chime was made from natural elements found in the forest: bones, shells, feathers, and stones, all tied with strands of colored yarn.

Roscoe stepped inside the cabin, where the warm glow of the fire welcomed him. His mother was at the stove, stirring a pot of stew, the scent of onions and smoked meat filling the room. His father sat at the table, whittling a piece of bone with his hunting knife, carving tiny patterns into its surface. The rhythmic scrape of the knife was the only sound, a comforting background to their quiet work.

"Got enough for the chime?" his mother asked, without looking up from the pot.

Roscoe nodded, emptying his bag onto the table. The pieces clattered softly against the wood—driftwood, stones, a few small bones, and the hollow shell of a bird's egg.

His father glanced at the pile and gave a small nod of approval. "That'll do," he said in his low, gravelly voice. He handed Roscoe the carved bone, its surface etched with tiny, swirling patterns. "This one's for your grandmother," he said softly.

Roscoe took the bone in his hand, running his fingers over the delicate carvings. He could feel the weight of his father's grief, still heavy even after all these years. He tied it carefully to a strand of red yarn—the color for his grandmother, who had loved red wildflowers and always wore a crimson shawl.

As they worked, the room filled with a quiet reverence.

The Importance of the Chime

"Do you remember the first time we made one of these?" his mother asked, her voice light but tinged with nostalgia. "You were just a boy, no taller than the table."

Roscoe smiled, glancing up at her. "Grandma had me tie the knots," he said. "She said my fingers were good for it."

"She was right," his father added, a rare smile tugging at his lips. "You've got her hands."

Roscoe felt a swell of pride, but also a pang of sadness. He missed his grandmother more than words could say. Making the chime was a way to keep her close, to honor the wisdom she had passed down to him.

They worked in silence for a while longer, each lost in their own thoughts. The chime was nearly complete now, a beautiful, delicate creation that seemed to hum with a life of its own. Roscoe held it up, letting it catch the light. The stones glimmered, the feathers fluttered, and the bones clinked together softly, like the first notes of a song.

His father took a deep breath, his eyes shining with unshed tears. "It's good," he said. "She would have loved it."

Roscoe nodded, feeling a lump form in his throat. He stepped to the window, looking out at the snow-covered forest. The sun was starting to set, casting long shadows across the ground. The sky was turning a deep, rich blue, like the color of his grandmother's favorite shawl.

"Tomorrow, we'll hang it in the clearing," "And we'll listen."

His mother came up behind him, resting a hand on his shoulder. "Yes," she said. "We'll listen. And they'll sing for us, like they always do."

Roscoe closed his eyes for a moment, letting the warmth of her touch and the memory of his grandmother wash over him. The chime in his hand felt light, but it carried the weight of so many voices—voices that would soon be carried on the wind, whispering their stories into the night.

The Crafting of the Wind Chime

Evening settled slowly over Tinker Creek, casting long shadows across the snow-covered ground. The Rainwater family gathered in their small kitchen, the warm glow of the fireplace dancing off the rough wooden walls. The scent of pine logs burning filled the room, mingling with the rich aroma of the stew simmering on the stove. It was a quiet, reverent time as they prepared for their annual tradition.

Roscoe sat at the table, the pieces he had collected spread out before him: driftwood, smooth stones, small animal bones, and delicate feathers. He moved with a careful, practiced touch, threading yarn through holes drilled in the bones, knotting each piece into place. His fingers, though rough and calloused from work, moved with a gentleness that seemed to carry the memory of his grandmother's hands guiding him long ago.

His mother, Leah Rainwater, stood beside him, braiding colorful strands of yarn. The colors held special meanings—red for his grandmother, blue for his uncle who had drowned in the swollen creek, and green for his cousin who had died in a cave-in at the coal mines. Her fingers worked swiftly, the yarn twisting together into a strong, intricate braid.

"Make sure those knots are tight, Roscoe," she said without looking up. Her voice was soft but carried the authority of years spent teaching him the old ways. "The wind has a way of testing everything."

Roscoe nodded, pulling the yarn tighter. He glanced over at his father, Samuel Rainwater, who was sitting across from him, carving patterns into a piece of hollow bone with his hunting knife. Samuel was a quiet man, his face lined with the hardships of a coal miner's life. He had the look of the Cherokee elders, with high cheekbones and dark, knowing eyes that seemed to see through the veil of time itself.

Samuel finished carving the bone and handed it to Roscoe. "This one's for your uncle," he said in his deep, gravelly voice. The bone was etched with tiny swirling designs, symbols of water and waves, a tribute to the uncle who had drowned when the creek flooded one spring.

Roscoe took the bone with both hands, nodding solemnly. He tied it to a strand of blue yarn and added it to the growing chime, the pieces clinking softly together. The sound was delicate, like the first sigh of the wind through the pines, and it filled the room with a quiet, soothing melody.

A Moment of Storytelling

As they worked, Leah began to speak, her voice taking on the rhythmic cadence of a storyteller. "I remember the first time we made one of these chimes," she said, smiling at the memory. "You were just a little boy then, Roscoe. Barely old enough to tie your shoes, but you tied the knots just right. Your grandmother was so proud."

Roscoe smiled, his eyes glinting with nostalgia. "She said I had the hands for it," he murmured. "Said the spirits liked it when the knots were tight and even."

Leah nodded, her face softening at the memory of her mother-in-law. "She knew the old ways better than anyone," she said. "She could hear the voices in the wind, like the hushed words from our ancestors."

Samuel looked up from his carving, a rare smile tugging at the corners of his mouth. "Your grandmother had a gift," he agreed. "She knew things, things that most people wouldn't understand."

Leah chuckled, shaking her head. "Do you remember the time she told the weather before it happened? Said a big storm was coming, even though the sky was clear as a bell. Everyone laughed at her, but she was right. We had the worst thunderstorm I've ever seen that night."

Roscoe laughed softly, feeling a warmth spread through his chest. Talking about his grandmother like this made him feel close to her again, as if she were still sitting at the table with them, her wrinkled hands working the yarn alongside his own.

Tension in the Air

As the chime neared completion, a knock sounded at the door, loud and unexpected in the quiet of the evening. The Rainwater family exchanged glances, a flicker of uncertainty passing between them. Visitors were rare, especially on a cold night like this.

Samuel rose slowly, wiping his hands on a cloth before crossing the room to answer the door. He pulled it open to reveal Mr. Tucker, one of the older men from the town. Tucker was a tall, wiry man with a face that looked as though it had been carved from the very rocks of the mountains. He had a reputation for being gruff, a man of few words who kept to himself.

"Tucker," Samuel greeted him with a nod. "What brings you out here tonight?"

Tucker stepped inside, rubbing his hands together for warmth. "Saw the smoke from your chimney," he said. "Figured you'd be doing your New Year's tradition."

Leah gave him a small smile, though there was a note of caution in her eyes. "We are," she said. "You're welcome to join us if you'd like."

Tucker shifted uncomfortably, glancing at the wind chime on the table. "I lost my brother this year," he muttered, his voice softer now. "Thought maybe... maybe the chime could sing for him too."

Roscoe looked up in surprise, his hands freezing in place. He had never known Tucker to show much interest in their traditions before. The older man had always seemed skeptical, dismissive even. But tonight, there was something different in his eyes—something softer, almost vulnerable.

Samuel nodded slowly, stepping aside to let Tucker into the circle around the table. "Of course," he said. "The chime sings for all who listen."

Tucker nodded, swallowing hard as he took his place beside Leah. He reached out a calloused hand, tracing the feathers with his fingertips. "My brother loved these hills," he said quietly. "I like to think he's still out there somewhere, running through the pines."

Finishing the Chime

Roscoe tied the last piece onto the chime, a small bird's egg that his mother had found in the forest that morning. It was delicate and white, a symbol of new beginnings and the fragile beauty of life. He held the chime up, letting it sway gently in the air. The stones clinked softly against the bones, the feathers fluttering as if caught in an unseen breeze.

Leah stepped back; her hands pressed together as if in prayer. "It's ready," she said softly.

Roscoe felt a lump rise in his throat as he looked at the finished chime. It was beautiful, but it was more than that—it was a song, a story, a piece of his family's history woven together with love and loss. He could feel the presence of his grandmother beside him, hear her whispering on the wind.

Samuel laid a hand on Roscoe's shoulder, squeezing gently. "You did good, son," he said, his voice rough with emotion. "She'd be proud."

Roscoe nodded, unable to speak. He took a deep breath, closing his eyes for a moment. He could almost hear the chime's song already, carrying their memories into the night, calling out to the spirits of those they had lost.

"Tomorrow," he said quietly, "we'll take it to the clearing."

Tucker nodded; his face somber. "I'd like to be there," he said simply. "To hear it sing."

Leah smiled; her eyes bright with unshed tears. "You will," she promised. "We all will."

Outside, the wind picked up, rustling the branches of the pines and carrying a faint, ghostly whisper through the air. It sounded almost like a song, a melody that danced just out of reach, waiting for the chime to join in.

The Rainwater family stood together, the chime swaying gently between them, a delicate creation filled with the weight of their love, their grief, and the unbreakable thread of their shared history.

The stage was set for the ceremony, and the night held its breath, waiting.

The Ceremony in the Forest

The sky was a deep, rich blue, the color of twilight just before nightfall, as the Rainwater family made their way along the narrow path that cut through the woods. Snow crunched beneath their boots, and their breath puffed out in frosty clouds. The forest was silent except for the occasional call of an owl echoing through the trees. The clearing lay ahead, a sacred place where the family had gathered for as long as Roscoe could remember.

Roscoe led the way, the wind chime held carefully in his hands. It was heavier now, not because of its materials but because of the weight of their memories, their prayers, and the stories that it carried. Behind him walked his mother, Leah, her face serene but her eyes glistening with unshed tears. His father, Samuel, followed in silence, his expression stoic yet softened by a deep, quiet sorrow. And at the edge of the group, a step behind, walked Mr. Tucker, his hands shoved deep into his coat pockets, his head bowed.

The wind picked up, rustling the bare branches above them, and Roscoe felt a shiver run down his spine. He knew it wasn't just the cold. There was something in the air tonight—something electric, like the moments just before a storm. He glanced back at Tucker, who gave him a small nod of encouragement. It was strange having the old man here, but it felt right somehow, like they were all part of something bigger than themselves.

They reached the clearing, a small, open space surrounded by ancient pine trees that towered over them like silent guardians. The snow lay untouched here, a pristine blanket reflecting the pale light of the rising moon. In the center of the clearing stood a tall, twisted pine, its branches bare but still strong. It was here that they hung a new wind chime every year, a tribute to those who had passed on.

Roscoe stepped forward, feeling the eyes of his family and Mr. Tucker on him. He lifted the chime, the strands of yarn trailing in the wind like ribbons. He tied it to a low branch, securing it with knots his grandmother had taught him, knots that were tight and even, meant to withstand the strongest gusts.

As he stepped back, the chime swayed gently, the bones, stones, and feathers clinking together in a soft, melodic sound. It was barely audible at first, just a faint tinkling, but then the wind picked up again, and the song grew louder. The notes were clear and pure, like the voice of the forest itself, calling out into the night.

A Sacred Song

Leah closed her eyes, lifting her face to the sky. She began to hum a low, haunting melody, a tune passed down through generations. It was a song of remembrance, of love and loss, sung in both Cherokee and the old mountain dialect of her Appalachian ancestors. The sound was deep and resonant, filling the clearing with a palpable sense of grief and grace.

Samuel joined in, his deep voice blending with Leah's, creating a harmony that echoed through the trees. Roscoe felt the song vibrate through his chest, stirring something deep inside him. He had heard this song every year, but tonight it felt different—more powerful, more urgent.

He closed his eyes and began to sing too, his voice carrying the names of those he wished to remember: his grandmother, his uncle, his cousin. The names slipped from his lips like prayers, carried away by the wind to wherever their spirits might be listening.

Mr. Tucker stood at the edge of the circle, his eyes wide and shining in the moonlight. He looked as though he wanted to speak but couldn't find the words. Instead, he took a step closer, lifting his hand to touch the chime. It clinked softly under his fingertips, the sound gentle and forgiving.

"I never understood this before," Tucker murmured, his voice barely more than a whisper. "But now... it feels like I can almost hear them."

Leah stepped beside him, placing a hand on his shoulder. "That's because you're listening with your heart," she said softly. "The chime sings for all of us, not just for our family. It carries every voice, every memory, if you're willing to hear it."

Tucker nodded, a tear slipping down his weathered cheek. "I lost my brother this year," he said, his voice breaking. "He was all I had left."

Roscoe met Tucker's gaze, seeing the raw pain there, the kind that only comes from losing someone who was part of your very soul. Without a word, Roscoe reached out and took Tucker's hand, squeezing it tightly.

"You can share our song," Roscoe said. "It's for everyone who needs it."

Tucker's face crumpled, and he nodded, stepping fully into the circle. He stood beside Leah and Samuel, his head bowed, listening as the chime's song rose higher, carried on the wind like a prayer sent to the heavens.

The Spirits Speak

Suddenly, a gust of wind rushed through the clearing, strong enough to shake the branches of the trees. The chime sang out, a bright, clear sound that seemed to pierce the stillness of the night. The notes were high and haunting, like voices calling from far away. The sound sent a shiver down Roscoe's spine, and he felt the hair on the back of his neck stand up.

He looked up, and for a moment, he thought he saw something—a flicker of movement among the trees, a shadow that wasn't quite solid. It was gone as quickly as it had come, but it left behind a feeling, a presence that he couldn't shake.

"Did you see that?" he asked his mother.

Leah nodded, her eyes wide and glistening. "I felt it," she said. "They're here with us tonight."

Samuel took a deep breath, looking up at the chime. "It's a good sign," he said quietly. "They've accepted our tribute."

The wind calmed, and the chime fell silent, swaying gently on its branch. The clearing was still again, but it felt different now—warmer, filled with a sense of peace that hadn't been there before.

Roscoe stepped forward, reaching up to touch the chime one last time. He closed his eyes and whispered, "Thank you," feeling the words carried away on the wind.

A New Year's Gift

As they turned to leave, Mr. Tucker hesitated. He looked at Roscoe, then back at the chime, a strange, almost hopeful expression on his face. "I'd like to hang one next year," he said quietly. "If you'll have me."

Roscoe's heart swelled with emotion, and he nodded. "We'd be honored," he said. "You're part of this now."

Tucker gave a small, grateful smile, the first genuine smile Roscoe had ever seen on the man's face. "Thank you," he said. "For letting me listen."

The Rainwater family and Mr. Tucker walked back together, their footsteps mingling in the snow. The night was quiet again, but the song of the chime lingered in the air, echoing through the forest, a reminder of the love and memories they had shared.

As they reached the edge of the forest, the first snowflakes of the new year began to fall, drifting softly down like tiny, frozen stars. Roscoe tilted his head back, catching one on his tongue, and laughed.

"Happy New Year," Leah said softly, looking at each of them in turn.

"Happy New Year," they all echoed, their voices blending, warm and strong.

Roscoe looked back once, seeing the chime swaying gently in the clearing, a small, bright beacon in the darkness. He knew that it would sing on the wind all night, carrying their memories into the new year, a song that would never truly fade.

And as they walked home, he felt lighter, the weight of grief lifted, replaced by something stronger—hope.

THE CIVIL WAR DRUM

The Discovery of the Drum

The early morning mist hung low over the battlefield, curling around the broken fences and rusted cannons like ghostly tendrils. It was June 1865, just weeks after the Civil War had ended, but the scars of the conflict remained etched into the Virginia countryside. The land bore its wounds—charred trees, splintered wagons, and patches of earth churned to mud by countless boots and hooves. The air was heavy with silence, a quiet so profound it felt as though the battlefield itself was holding its breath.

For most, this was a place to avoid, a grim reminder of lives lost and battles fought. But for eleven-year-old Jasper Cooperrider, the field was a place of fascination. Jasper had grown up hearing his father's stories of the war—the tales of bravery, sacrifice, and tragedy that had shaped the very ground he now walked on. The boy was drawn here, unable to resist the pull of the past, even though his mother had warned him time and time again to stay away.

"Jasper Reynard Cooperrider!" she had shouted after him that morning, her voice sharp as a whip. "You hear me, boy? That battlefield's no place for you. It's full of ghosts and sorrow. Stay away!"

"I'll just look around," Jasper had replied, his sandy hair falling into his eyes as he dashed out the door. "I won't go far, Ma, I promise!"

Now, as he trudged through the mist with his hands stuffed into his pockets, Jasper couldn't help but feel a thrill of curiosity. The air smelled of damp earth and something else—something faintly metallic, like the lingering echo of gunpowder. He stopped beside a crumbling stone wall, crouching down to examine a dented canteen lying half-buried in the dirt. His fingers brushed the cool metal, and he imagined a soldier once gripping it tightly, his hands shaking as bullets whizzed overhead.

Jasper stood and scanned the field. In his mind's eye, he could see it as it must have been months ago—soldiers shouting, horses rearing, cannon fire shaking the ground. He shivered, not from the chill but from the strange, electric energy that seemed to hum through the air. It was as if the land itself was alive, whispering its secrets to anyone willing to listen.

He took a few steps forward, and that's when he saw it. A flash of red and blue caught his eye, half-hidden beneath the mud. Jasper's heart thudded in his chest as he knelt down, brushing away the dirt with trembling hands. Slowly, the shape of a drum emerged—a Union drum, its paint faded and chipped, but still intact. The leather straps were frayed, and the emblem of the Union Army was barely visible beneath the grime, but Jasper could tell this was no ordinary relic.

"A drummer's drum," he whispered, his voice barely audible. His father had told him about the drummer boys of the Civil War, boys not much older than him who had marched alongside soldiers, their drumbeats guiding the troops into battle. Jasper's fingers traced the rim of the drum, and a strange sensation washed over him—a feeling of warmth, like sunlight breaking through a storm cloud.

For a moment, he hesitated. The drum felt important, sacred even, and a small voice in the back of his mind told him to leave it where it lay. But his curiosity burned brighter than his fear. With a deep breath, he lifted the drum from the mud, its weight surprising him. He cradled it in his arms, staring at it as if it might suddenly speak.

And then he heard it—a faint, rhythmic tapping. It was so soft at first that he thought he might be imagining it, but the sound grew louder, steadier, like the distant beat of a marching army. Jasper froze, his heart pounding. He turned his head, scanning the empty field. The mist swirled around him, thick and heavy, but there was no one in sight.

"Hello?" Jasper called out, his voice cracking in the cold morning air. There was no answer, only the tapping, growing fainter now, as though it was retreating into the mist. A shiver ran down his spine, and he clutched the drum tighter. He wasn't sure if he should run or stay, but his legs felt rooted to the ground.

Then, at the edge of the field, he saw it. A figure stood in the distance, barely visible through the fog. The man wore a Union uniform, his kepi hat tilted low over his brow. He was motionless, his hands clasped in front of him, his posture solemn. Jasper squinted, his breath catching in his throat. The figure didn't move, but Jasper felt its gaze fixed on him, heavy and unyielding.

"Who's there?" Jasper called, his voice shaking. The figure raised a hand in a slow, deliberate salute. For a moment, the world seemed to stand still. Then, as suddenly as it had appeared, the figure melted into the mist, leaving

Jasper alone on the battlefield.

The drum in his arms felt heavier now, almost as if it was pulling him toward the ground. He turned in a slow circle, his eyes darting to every shadow, every movement of the fog. But the field was empty. Only the faint memory of the drumbeat remained, echoing in his ears like a heartbeat.

Jasper took a deep breath and started walking, his boots crunching against the frosted grass. He didn't know what he had seen—if it was a ghost, a trick of the light, or something else entirely—but he couldn't shake the feeling that the drum had been waiting for him. As he left the battlefield behind, the mist closed in, erasing his footprints and swallowing the land in silence once more.

As Jasper walked away, he glanced over his shoulder one last time, half-expecting to see the figure again. The field was empty, but the air felt charged with something unseen. The drum in his arms let out one faint, ghostly tap before falling silent, leaving Jasper to wonder what secrets it carried—and what they would demand of him.

The Drum's Secrets

The drum sat on the kitchen table, its battered surface catching the flickering light of the oil lamp. Jasper Cooperrider stared at it, his fingers twitching at his sides. His mother had scolded him the moment he walked through the door, covered in mud and clutching the relic like a treasure.

"Jasper Cooperrider! What did I tell you about that battlefield?" she had said, wagging a finger at him. "It's not a playground, and that… that thing shouldn't be in this house."

"But Ma," Jasper had protested, his voice filled with urgency, "it's not just any drum. It belonged to someone—someone important. I can feel it."

Her lips pressed into a thin line, and she had shaken her head before storming off to the other room, muttering about boys and their foolishness. Now, Jasper sat alone with the drum, its presence as heavy as the questions swirling in his mind.

He reached out and ran his fingers over the rim. The paint was chipped, the leather frayed, but it felt alive, as though it had soaked up the essence of the soldier who had once carried it. The memory of the shadowy figure in the mist sent a shiver down his spine. Who was he? And why did Jasper feel like the drum had been meant for him?

A Father's Story

The sound of boots scuffing on the wooden floor pulled Jasper from his thoughts. His father, Henry Cooperrider, entered the room, wiping his hands on a rag. A historian by nature and a farmer by necessity, Henry had always carried himself with a quiet, thoughtful demeanor. He stopped short when he saw the drum, his brows furrowing.

"Where'd you find that?" he asked, his voice low but steady.

"Out on the battlefield," Jasper replied, sitting up a little straighter. "It was buried in the mud, but it's still in one piece."

Henry approached the table slowly, his gaze fixed on the drum as though it were something sacred. He reached out and placed a hand on its surface, his fingers lingering for a moment before pulling away. "This belonged to a Union drummer," he said softly. "A boy, not much older than you."

Jasper's heart quickened. "How do you know?"

"I've seen one like it before," Henry said, his voice tinged with a mix of awe and sorrow. "There was a young man—a freedman—who carried a drum just like this one. His name was Elijah Freeman. He was a drummer for the 54th Massachusetts, one of the first Black regiments to fight in the war. I met him once, during a campaign. He had a way of making that drum speak, like it wasn't just an instrument but a voice for the whole regiment."

"What happened to him?" Jasper asked, leaning forward.

Henry hesitated, his jaw tightening. "He died in battle. They said he never stopped drumming, even when the enemy charged. He kept the rhythm strong, gave the soldiers something to hold onto when everything else was falling apart." He paused, his eyes growing distant. "Some say his spirit stayed with his drum, keeping watch over the battlefield."

Jasper swallowed hard, his hands tightening into fists. "Do you think this is his drum?"

Henry's eyes flicked to the drum, and he gave a small nod. "It might be. If it is, you've found something more than an artifact, son. You've found a piece of history."

The Drum Speaks

Later that night, long after the house had gone quiet, Jasper sat in his room with the drum resting on his lap. Moonlight spilled through the window, casting a silvery glow across the worn leather. He felt a pull, a need to understand what made this drum so different. Slowly, he picked up a pair of wooden spoons from his bedside table and began to tap a rhythm—soft and steady, like a heartbeat.

At first, the sound was ordinary. The hollow thump of the drum echoed faintly in the room. But then something changed. A chill swept through the air, and the drum seemed to vibrate in his hands, the sound deepening, resonating in a way that made his chest tighten. It was no longer just a drumbeat—it was a voice.

Whispers filled the room, faint and indistinct. Jasper froze, his hands hovering over the drum. The voices grew louder, more distinct. They weren't words, exactly, but fragments of emotion: courage, fear, determination. He could feel them pressing against him, wrapping around him like a cloak.

And then, in the distance, he heard it—a single, clear note, high and piercing, like a trumpet's call. Jasper's breath hitched as his surroundings began to blur. The walls of his room melted away, replaced by the misty expanse of the battlefield. He was there again, but it was different this time. The field was alive with movement. Soldiers in Union blue marched in formation, their faces set with grim determination. Smoke curled from cannons, and the sharp crack of musket fire rang in the air.

At the center of it all was a young Black man, standing tall despite the chaos around him. He held a drum against his chest, his hands moving with practiced precision as he beat out a rhythm that cut through the noise like a beacon. His face was streaked with sweat and dirt, but his eyes burned with unyielding resolve.

"Elijah," Jasper whispered, the name falling from his lips without him realizing.

The drummer's gaze flicked toward him, and for a moment, their eyes locked. Jasper felt a jolt, like a lightning strike, and the vision dissolved. He was back in his room, the drum sitting silent and still in his lap. His chest heaved as he struggled to catch his breath.

A Haunting Realization

Jasper stared at the drum, his mind racing. It wasn't just an object. It was a vessel, a bridge to the past. Elijah's spirit—his story—was trapped inside, waiting for someone to listen, to carry it forward.

He clenched his fists, his jaw setting with determination. He couldn't leave the drum to gather dust or sit forgotten in the shadows. Elijah's bravery deserved to be remembered; his sacrifice honored. Jasper didn't know how, but he felt certain the drum had found him for a reason.

He stood, the drum still in his hands, and made his way to the window. The moon hung high in the sky, its light bathing the battlefield in a pale glow. The air was still, but Jasper swore he could hear it—the faint echo of a drumbeat, steady and relentless, like the march of time itself.

Jasper leaned out the window, his eyes scanning the field. For a fleeting moment, he thought he saw a figure standing at the edge of the trees—a man in a Union uniform, watching him. When he blinked, the figure was gone, but the beat of the drum lingered in his ears, pulling him toward a destiny he didn't yet understand.

The Final Tribute

The battlefield was shrouded in the pale light of early dawn, the mist curling around the broken earth like a veil. Jasper Cooperrider stood at its edge; the drum strapped tightly to his back. He had told no one about his plan, not even his father. Something deep inside him said that this was a journey he needed to take alone. The drum had called to him in the dead of night, its silent weight a constant reminder of Elijah Freeman and the untold stories it carried.

As Jasper stepped into the field, the world seemed to shift around him. The air grew colder, heavier, as though the earth itself was watching. His boots sank into the damp soil, and he paused, glancing over his shoulder. The outline of his small town had disappeared, swallowed by the morning fog. He was alone, surrounded only by the echoes of a war that had ended, but had never truly left.

A Walk Through Memory

Jasper moved forward, his heart hammering in his chest. Every step felt deliberate, as though the battlefield itself was guiding him. He passed rusted bayonets stuck in the ground, torn fragments of uniforms tangled in the brush, and the rotting remains of wooden carts. This was no longer just a field; it was a graveyard, a place where courage and fear had collided in equal measure.

The drum pressed against his back, its presence both comforting and unnerving. He felt its pull, as if it were urging him onward, toward the very heart of the field. Jasper clutched the straps tightly, his breath clouding in the chill air.

A sound stopped him in his tracks. It was faint at first, almost indistinguishable from the breeze, but it grew louder with each passing second—a drumbeat, steady and rhythmic. Jasper's pulse quickened as he scanned the empty field, his eyes darting to every shadow and flicker of movement. There was no one in sight, but the sound persisted, surrounding him, pulling him forward.

"Elijah," he whispered, his voice trembling. "Is that you?"

The drumbeat grew louder in response, its rhythm sharp and commanding. Jasper swallowed hard and quickened his pace, the mist thickening around him. The battlefield seemed alive now, the silence broken by distant echoes—murmured voices, the clatter of swords, the faint cry of a bugle. Jasper felt as though he had stepped back in time, the present slipping away with every step.

The Soldiers' Procession

He reached the center of the field, a spot marked by a gnarled, half-burned tree. Jasper stopped and unstrapped the drum, setting it gently on the ground. He knelt beside it, his hands trembling as he adjusted the frayed straps. The air around him was charged, humming with an energy he couldn't explain. He felt as though he was being watched, the weight of unseen eyes pressing down on him.

Taking a deep breath, Jasper picked up his drumsticks and began to play. The rhythm started slow, a mournful beat that echoed across the empty field. The sound was heavy, filled with sorrow and longing, but as he played, it began to change. The beat grew stronger, faster, a cadence that spoke of resilience and hope.

And then they appeared.

At first, it was just shadows, faint and indistinct, moving through the mist. But as the drumbeat grew louder, the figures took shape—soldiers in Union blue, their faces pale and their uniforms torn. They marched in perfect formation, their eyes fixed ahead, their movements silent but purposeful. Jasper's breath caught in his throat as he watched them pass, their presence both haunting and awe-inspiring.

At the head of the procession was Elijah Freeman, his drum slung across his chest. He was tall and proud, his face set with a calm determination. His eyes, dark and piercing, met Jasper's, and for a moment, the boy felt as though the world had stopped. Elijah raised his drumsticks and began to play, his rhythm blending seamlessly with Jasper's.

The two drummers played together, their beats echoing across the field like thunder. The soldiers raised their hands in salute, their ghostly forms illuminated by the first rays of sunlight breaking through the mist. Jasper felt tears streaming down his face, but he didn't stop. The drum was no longer just an object—it was a voice, a bridge between the living and the dead.

A Final Goodbye

As the last of the soldiers passed, Elijah stepped forward, his drum silent now. He stood before Jasper, his expression one of gratitude and peace. Slowly, he reached out and placed a hand on the boy's shoulder. Jasper felt a warmth spread through him, a sense of reassurance that he couldn't put into words.

"Elijah," Jasper whispered, his voice barely audible. "I'll remember you. I'll tell your story."

Elijah nodded, a faint smile playing at the corners of his lips. He lifted his drumsticks in a final salute, then turned and walked away, his form dissolving into the mist. The drumbeats faded, the echoes growing softer until they disappeared entirely. The field was quiet again, the soldiers gone, but the air was lighter now, the weight of the past lifted.

Jasper knelt by the drum, his chest heaving as he tried to process what he had just witnessed. He ran a hand over its surface, the once-battered leather now smooth and whole, as though it had been restored by the spirits who had carried it.

The Walk Home

The sun was fully up by the time Jasper made his way back to the edge of the battlefield. The mist had cleared, revealing the familiar outline of his town in the distance. He paused at the top of a hill, looking back one last time. The field stretched out before him, quiet and unassuming, but he knew its secrets now. He knew the stories it held, the lives that had been lost and the courage that had endured.

Jasper strapped the drum to his back and started down the hill, his steps lighter than they had been in days. He didn't know what the future held, but he was certain of one thing: Elijah Freeman's story would not be forgotten. The drum would speak for him, and Jasper would make sure the world listened.

As he reached the edge of town, a breeze swept past him, carrying with it a faint, familiar sound—the steady beat of a drum. Jasper smiled, his heart full, and walked on, the rhythm guiding him home.

CLEVELAND LIGHTS WINTER FESTIVAL

The Idea Takes Shape

It was early December 1956. Cleveland's Tremont neighborhood sparkled under a blanket of fresh snow, the kind that made everything look clean and soft—even the blackened smokestacks of the Republic Strip Mill rising in the distance. Twelve-year-old Zebulon "Zeb" Kostas leaned on the chain-link fence at the corner of West 11th Street, his breath puffing out in white clouds. He squinted down University Road, the steep hill that cut through Tremont and rolled straight toward the Flats where the mills roared. To Zeb, it wasn't just a hill. It was the perfect starting line for greatness.

"Zeb," Danny O'Malley muttered, his freckled nose red from the cold, "I don't know if this is a good idea. You know how your ma gets when she thinks you're up to something."

Zeb grinned, his dark eyes gleaming with mischief. "Danny, this isn't just a good idea—it's the best idea. You see that hill? That's our ticket to the Cleveland Lights Winter Festival. We build the fastest sled Tremont's ever seen, and by next week, we'll be legends."

Danny stuffed his hands deeper into the pockets of his patched coat and kicked at a chunk of ice. "Yeah, but how are we supposed to build a sled outta nothing? You think I got a hardware store in my basement?"

Before Zeb could answer, a voice called out behind them. "You boys better not be planning anything dumb."

Ania Kaminski trudged through the snow toward them, a heavy sketchbook tucked under her arm. Her black braids peeked out from under her knit cap, and her breath came in short puffs. She fixed them with a look that could cut steel. "I saw you two standing here, scheming. What's the plan this time?"

Zeb threw an arm around her shoulders, ignoring the fact that she rolled her eyes. "Ania, my brilliant engineer, I was just telling Danny here that we're gonna build the fastest sled Cleveland's ever seen. The kind of sled that wins races and makes the front page of the *Cleveland Press.*"

Ania raised an eyebrow and opened her sketchbook, flipping to a page filled with half-finished drawings of sled designs. "Well, I hate to break it to you, Zeb, but a dream sled needs more than dreams to run. What's the plan for materials?"

Zeb hesitated, but Danny cut in, his voice dripping with sarcasm. "Oh, I'm sure Zeb's got it all figured out. He's probably got a deal with Santa for some extra reindeer parts."

"Very funny," Zeb shot back, rolling his eyes. "I've got a plan, alright? My dad's been bringing home scrap metal from the mill for years. I'll get some of that. Danny, your uncle's got that old wagon in his garage—don't tell me he's still using it."

Danny groaned. "You're really gonna make me dig that thing out? It's more rust than wood at this point."

"And you, Ania," Zeb said, spinning to face her. "You've got the brains for this. Your designs are genius. We'll need your dad's tools, too."

Ania gave him a long, skeptical look. "You're lucky I like a challenge, Zeb. But if we're doing this, we're doing it my way. No shortcuts, no slapping a few wheels on and calling it done."

Zeb held up his hands in mock surrender. "Fine, fine. You're the boss of the blueprints. But I'm the boss of speed."

The Winter Festival Announcement

As the trio walked back toward Zeb's house, they passed one of the bright posters announcing the Cleveland Lights Winter Festival. The glossy paper shimmered under the weak winter sunlight, showing a colorful drawing of the sled race with kids laughing as they hurtled downhill. The race was the crown jewel of the festival, drawing kids from every corner of Cleveland to compete.

"We've got one week," Zeb said, his voice filled with determination. "One week to build something that'll leave every other sled in the dust."

"You mean snow," Ania corrected, smirking. "And that's if we even finish in time."

Danny sighed, his breath fogging the air. "If we crash, I'm blaming you, Zeb. Just so we're clear."

"Crash?" Zeb said, laughing. "Danny, when have we ever failed? This sled's gonna fly. You just wait."

The First Hurdle – Gathering Materials

The next few days were a blur of planning and scavenging. After school, the trio met in Zeb's snowy backyard to discuss their progress. The cold bit at their fingers, but their excitement burned bright enough to keep them moving.

"I got the metal," Zeb announced, dropping a bundle of scrap pieces onto the ground with a loud clang. "Told my dad I needed it for a school project. He didn't even ask questions."

Danny dragged over a wheel he'd pulled from his uncle's ancient wagon, its edges caked with grime. "This was the best one. The others looked like they'd fall apart if you sneezed on 'em."

Ania spread her sketches on the ground, weighing the corners with rocks. "This could work," she muttered, chewing on her lip. "We'll need to reinforce the frame with crossbars. Otherwise, it'll break on the first bump."

Zeb slapped a hand on Danny's shoulder. "See? She's got it all figured out. We're unstoppable."

Trouble at the Mill

Late one night, with the snow crunching underfoot and their breath hanging in the air like smoke, Zeb led Danny and Ania to the Republic Strip Mill yard. The towering fences loomed above them, their tops laced with barbed wire.

"This is crazy," Danny whispered. "If we get caught, they'll send us straight to juvie."

"Relax," Zeb hissed, glancing back at them. "We're just here to grab a few pieces of scrap. No one's even gonna notice."

They climbed through a gap in the fence and darted across the yard, the piles of rusted metal casting long shadows in the moonlight. Zeb crouched by a heap of discarded pipes, motioning for the others to help. They worked quickly, the silence of the night broken only by the sound of metal scraping against metal.

Then a flashlight beam cut through the dark.

"Hey! What are you kids doing here?"

They froze as the voice of the security guard boomed through the yard. Zeb's heart thundered in his chest, but he forced himself to stand, the pipes clutched in his arms.

"We're, uh… we're building a sled," he stammered. "For the festival. We just needed a little extra… you know… metal."

The guard stared at them for a long moment, then shook his head. "You kids are lucky I've got a soft spot for dreamers. Take what you need—but don't let me catch you here again."

As they slipped back through the fence, their arms full of scrap, Zeb couldn't help but grin. "I told you it'd work."

"Yeah," Danny muttered, shaking his head. "Next time, you're doing the talking alone."

The following morning, the snowy streets of Tremont glistened under the pale winter sun, but the real action was happening in Danny O'Malley's garage. The trio had transformed the dusty, cluttered space into their personal workshop. The air was filled with the sound of clanging metal, the whir of an old hand drill, and the occasional burst of laughter as they worked on their sled, now affectionately nicknamed The Silver Arrow.

The Workshop Comes to Life

Ania crouched over a large sheet of paper spread across the workbench, her pencil flying as she sketched out their final design. "We'll use the wagon frame for the base," she explained, her voice steady with confidence. "But the runners need to be reinforced with those steel strips Zeb 'borrowed' from the mill. Otherwise, they'll buckle under the weight."

Danny, already elbow-deep in grease, nodded from his corner of the garage. He was working on sanding down the salvaged wheels, muttering to himself about rust and friction. "These things are older than my uncle's dentures," he grumbled. "But give me a little time, and they'll be smoother than a sheet of ice."

Zeb leaned against the wall, watching his friends with a grin. "See? I told you we could do this. We're like a well-oiled machine."

Ania didn't even look up from her sketches. "Less talking, more helping, Zeb. Grab that saw and start trimming the wood panels for the sides. And don't mess up—I measured those pieces exactly."

"Yes, ma'am," Zeb said with a mock salute, grabbing the saw. "You're the boss."

Conflict in the Ranks

As the afternoon wore on, the garage grew colder, and the group's energy began to wane. Tensions bubbled to the surface as the deadline for the festival loomed closer.

"Zeb, you're cutting that panel all wrong," Ania snapped, pointing at the jagged edge of the wood he had just sawed. "It's supposed to fit flush with the frame, not look like a beaver chewed it."

Zeb frowned, his cheeks flushing. "It's fine, Ania. No one's gonna care about a few rough edges when we're flying down that hill at lightning speed."

"They'll care if we crash!" Ania shot back, her voice rising. "This isn't just about speed—it's about balance and control. If we don't get it right, all your big dreams are going to end in a pile of splinters."

Danny looked up from his corner, grease smeared across his forehead. "Alright, alright, cool it, you two. We're all tired, and we've got a lot to do. Let's just focus on finishing this thing, okay?"

Ania huffed but turned back to her plans. Zeb muttered under his breath as he picked up the saw again. The garage fell into a tense silence, broken only by the sound of tools scraping and clanging.

A Spark of Community

Word of their project began to spread through the neighborhood. By the next day, neighbors started showing up, offering small but meaningful contributions.

Old Mr. Novak from down the street stopped by with a can of silver paint. "Figured your sled could use a little shine," he said, his wrinkled face breaking into a grin. "Make it look like something out of a fairy tale."

Ania's father arrived with a tray of steaming pastries from the bakery. "You kids need fuel if you're gonna win that race," he said, setting the tray down on the workbench. "And Ania—don't forget to wear your gloves. Your mother will have my head if you catch a cold."

Even old Mrs. Petrov, who rarely left her house, sent over a bundle of thick yarn for lashing the runners to the frame. "It's strong," she said in her thick accent. "Will hold better than those fancy bolts."

The trio's spirits lifted as the community rallied around them. The sled began to take shape, its sleek frame gleaming under Ania's careful design and Danny's meticulous repairs. Zeb, ever the dreamer, painted bold silver stripes along the sides, imagining the gasps of the crowd as they flew down University Road.

The Test Run

By Friday afternoon, the sled was ready for its first test run. The trio hauled it to Lincoln Park, where a small hill offered a safe trial before the big race. The snow sparkled under the weak winter sun, and their breath puffed in the frigid air as they lined the sled up at the top of the slope.

"Alright, here's the plan," Zeb said, climbing into the front to steer. "I'll handle the speed. Danny, you're in the middle to shift the weight, and Ania, you keep an eye on balance from the back. Got it?"

"Got it," Ania and Danny said in unison, though Ania shot Zeb a warning look. "Just don't get us killed, okay?"

"Relax," Zeb said with a grin. "This is gonna be amazing."

He gave the sled a push, and they began to slide. At first, it was exhilarating—the cold wind whipping past their faces, the sled picking up speed as it raced down the hill. But halfway down, they hit a patch of ice, and the sled wobbled dangerously.

"Lean left!" Ania shouted, gripping the sides.

Danny shifted his weight, but it wasn't enough. The sled veered sharply to the right and tipped over, sending all three of them tumbling into the snow. They lay there for a moment, breathless and covered in frost, before Zeb groaned and sat up.

"Well," he said, brushing snow off his coat, "that could've gone better."

"Better?" Ania snapped, inspecting the broken runner. "We just wrecked the sled! How are we supposed to fix this before the race?"

"We'll fix it," Danny said, sitting up and wiping his nose on his sleeve. "We have to. I mean, we've come this far, right?"

Zeb stood and helped Ania to her feet. "Danny's right. We can fix this. We've got one night to pull it together—and I know we can do it."

Ania stared at the sled, her lips pressed into a thin line. Finally, she nodded. "Fine. But we're doing it my way this time."

A Snowstorm Rolls In

As they hauled the sled back to Danny's garage, the sky began to darken, and the wind picked up. By the time they reached Tremont, snow was falling in thick, heavy flakes.

"Great," Danny muttered, glancing at the sky. "If this storm keeps up, there won't even be a race tomorrow."

Zeb tightened his grip on the sled's frame, his jaw set. "Then we'll be ready anyway. Storm or no storm, The Silver Arrow is going to fly."

The trio disappeared into the garage, the storm raging outside as they worked late into the night, determined to bring their dream to life.

The Race and the Lights

By the time the sun rose over Tremont, the storm had passed, leaving the neighborhood blanketed in a pristine layer of snow. The streets were alive with activity as families made their way to the top of University Road, where the Cleveland Lights Winter Festival's sled race would soon begin. The air was crisp, filled with the mingling scents of roasted chestnuts and hot cocoa. Children tugged their parents along, their excitement spilling over into laughter that echoed through the chilly morning.

In Danny's garage, Zeb Kostas, Ania Kaminski, and Danny O'Malley stood in a circle around The Silver Arrow, their sled gleaming under the soft light of a single hanging bulb. The night's work had paid off—every joint reinforced, every surface polished to perfection. The sled looked better than ever, its silver stripes shimmering like streaks of lightning against the dark wood.

"Well," Danny said, wiping his hands on his coat, "if we crash this time, at least we'll look good doing it."

"We're not crashing," Ania said firmly, tucking her sketches back into her satchel. "I triple-checked everything. This sled is solid. Right, Zeb?"

Zeb grinned, his confidence infectious. "Right. This is it, you two. Today, we're gonna show Cleveland what we're made of."

The Starting Line

At the top of University Road, the crowd buzzed with anticipation as teams lined up their sleds. The hill was a sharp, unforgiving incline, cutting down toward the Flats, where the steel mills loomed in the distance. It was the kind of slope that demanded skill, guts, and maybe a little bit of luck.

The Silver Arrow sat at the starting line, drawing curious glances from the other competitors. It stood out from the patchwork sleds around it, its sleek design and polished runners a testament to the trio's hard work.

"Next up," the announcer's voice boomed over the loudspeaker, "we've got Kostas, Kaminski, and O'Malley with their sled… The Silver Arrow!"

The crowd erupted in cheers, with neighbors shouting words of encouragement. Ania's father waved from the sidelines, holding up a fresh pastry in triumph. Mr. Novak tipped his hat, and Mrs. Petrov clapped enthusiastically, her scarf fluttering in the wind.

Zeb climbed into the front of the sled, gripping the rope tightly. Danny settled in behind him, shifting his weight to find the perfect balance, while Ania took her place at the back, her sharp eyes scanning the course.

"This is it," Zeb said, his voice steady despite the adrenaline pumping through his veins. "You two ready?"

"Ready," Ania and Danny said in unison.

The announcer's voice rang out: "On your marks… get set… go!"

The Race Begins

The Silver Arrow shot forward, its polished runners slicing through the snow with ease. The wind whipped past their faces, cold and biting, but exhilarating. Zeb leaned forward, his gloved hands gripping the rope as he steered them down the hill. The world blurred around them, the snow-covered trees and cheering crowd melting into streaks of color.

"Left turn coming up!" Ania shouted over the roar of the wind.

"I see it!" Zeb yelled back, pulling the rope to guide the sled into a sharp turn. The sled tilted dangerously, the runners skidding over the ice, but Danny shifted his weight just in time to steady them.

Behind them, the other teams struggled to keep up. Sleds spun out on patches of ice, or tipped over on the tight turns, their drivers tumbling into the snowbanks. But The Silver Arrow held its course, gliding down the hill with precision.

"Straightaway!" Danny called out. "This is where we make up speed!"

Zeb tightened his grip and leaned forward, urging the sled faster. The Silver Arrow flew down the hill, the wind howling in their ears. But as they neared the final stretch, the course took an unexpected turn—literally.

Disaster Strikes

A jagged patch of ice gleamed in the sunlight, right in their path. Zeb's heart lurched. "Hold on!" he shouted, yanking the rope to steer them away.

The sled wobbled, its runners catching on the uneven ice. Ania threw her weight to the left, trying to stabilize them, while Danny braced himself against the sides.

"We're gonna tip!" Danny yelled.

"Not on my watch!" Zeb growled, his muscles straining as he fought to regain control. The sled tilted precariously, the right runner lifting off the ground for a heart-stopping moment. The crowd gasped as The Silver Arrow teetered on the brink of disaster.

And then, miraculously, it leveled out. The runners found their grip, and the sled shot forward like a silver bullet, hurtling toward the finish line.

The Finish Line

The Silver Arrow crossed the finish line in second place, just behind the leading sled. The crowd erupted into cheers, the air filled with applause and shouts of encouragement.

Zeb let out a whoop of triumph, throwing his arms in the air. "We did it! We actually did it!"

Danny collapsed onto the sled, laughing breathlessly. "I thought we were goners back there. Did you see that ice patch?"

"I saw it," Ania said, grinning from ear to ear. "And I saw you two save it. That was teamwork."

As they climbed out of the sled, their neighbors rushed forward to congratulate them. Ania's father hugged her tightly, while Danny's uncle slapped him on the back with pride. Even Zeb's mother, who had initially frowned upon the whole idea, smiled as she wiped a tear from her cheek.

"You kids did good," she said softly, ruffling Zeb's hair.

The Lights Ceremony

That evening, as the sun dipped below the horizon, the Cleveland Lights Winter Festival's namesake event began. Strings of twinkling lights illuminated the neighborhood, casting a warm glow over the snow-covered streets. The trio stood together in the town square, The Silver Arrow parked beside them, its silver paint catching the light like a beacon.

Cleveland Mayor Celebrezze stepped forward to present a special award. "Tonight, we celebrate not just the winners of the race, but the spirit of determination and teamwork that makes our community strong. Kostas, Kaminski, and O'Malley—your sled is a symbol of what Tremont stands for. Congratulations."

As the crowd cheered, Zeb looked at his friends, his heart swelling with pride. "We didn't take first," he said, "but we built something unforgettable. And this is just the beginning."

Ania smirked. "Next year, we'll win."

Danny chuckled. "As long as Zeb doesn't steer us into a snowbank, I'm in."

They laughed together, their voices mingling with the carolers' songs and the hum of the lights. Above them, the Cleveland lights shone bright, a reminder of the dreams they had built together.

REDEMPTION

The Rise and Fall

The streets of Wheeling, West Virginia, carried the echoes of a proud industrial past. By 1969, the steel mills still operated, but they were struggling against mounting foreign competition and the rise of automation. For the working families of Wheeling, the air was thick with both the soot of the mills and the unspoken fear that the foundations of their way of life were beginning to crumble.

For 18-year-old Peter Di Lonzo, Wheeling was both home and a place he yearned to escape. A star running back at Wheeling Central Catholic High School, he was the town's golden boy, someone the community could rally around. Yet Peter felt a restlessness that no amount of touchdowns or accolades could quell.

"Peter, you're gonna be late again," Anita Di Lonzo called from the kitchen, her tone exasperated but warm.

"I'm coming, Mom," Peter replied, stuffing a notebook into his bag as he grabbed his jacket.

He'd spent the last fifteen minutes staring out the window at the steel-gray sky, his mind drifting between the game that night and the uncertain future waiting just over the horizon.

Anita stood at the stove, flipping sausage links in a cast-iron skillet. The small kitchen was filled with the comforting smell of coffee and sizzling meat. She glanced over her shoulder, her expression softening as Peter entered the room.

"The coach called last night. Wants to make sure you're ready for tonight's game," she said, sliding the sausages onto a plate. "Big one, huh? Wheeling High?"

"Yeah," Peter said, leaning against the doorframe. "Biggest game of the season. Packed house for sure."

Anita placed the plate on the table and smirked. "You score a touchdown tonight, don't forget to thank God. Or at least your mother."

Peter chuckled, his grin momentarily chasing away the weight in his chest. "Always do, Mom," he said, kissing her cheek before digging into his breakfast.

His father, Giuseppe, entered the kitchen just as Peter was finishing. The elder Di Lonzo's face was etched with years of labor at the steel mill, his calloused hands a testament to a lifetime of hard work.

"Make us proud out there, son," Giuseppe said, clapping a heavy hand on Peter's shoulder.

Peter nodded, meeting his father's steady gaze. "I will, Dad."

Game Night

The Wheeling High Stadium buzzed with excitement, the stands packed with fans wrapped in scarves and coats against the autumn chill. The field glowed under the bright stadium lights, casting long shadows over the turf. Wheeling High versus Wheeling Central wasn't just a football game; it was a community event, a clash of rivalries and pride.

Peter jogged onto the field with his teammates, his breath visible in the cold night air. The roar of the crowd washed over him, a mix of cheers and taunts from the opposing side. He could see banners waving in the stands, the faces of classmates and neighbors filled with expectation.

The first half was a grueling battle. Wheeling High's defense was relentless, meeting Peter at every turn. But Peter was relentless too. With every play, he pushed harder, his focus narrowing to the ball, the field, and the end zone. Late in the second quarter, he broke through the line of scrimmage, weaving past defenders with a speed and agility that left the crowd breathless.

"Touchdown, Di Lonzo!" the announcer's voice boomed as Peter crossed into the end zone. The stands erupted in cheers, and Peter allowed himself a small smile as his teammates surrounded him in celebration.

By the end of the game, Peter had scored three touchdowns, leading Wheeling Central to a narrow 36-33 victory. As the final whistle blew, the field was a blur of movement and noise. Coaches congratulated players, fans cheered, and the opposing team trudged off in defeat.

Angela Marciano was waiting for him by the bleachers, leaning against a post with her hands tucked into her jacket pockets. Her dark eyes sparkled in the stadium lights, her smile teasing.

"Another big night for the great Peter Di Lonzo," she said as he approached, tossing his helmet into his duffel bag.

"Had to keep it interesting," Peter replied, his grin widening.

Angela stepped closer, the crisp air turning her breath into visible puffs. "So, this is it, huh? The season's over. You're leaving Wheeling next fall."

Peter hesitated, the weight of her words sinking in. "That's the plan," he said, his voice quieter than he'd intended.

"Ohio University, right? I heard Coach talking about the scouts."

"Yeah," Peter said, though the certainty he once felt was beginning to waver. "Athletic scholarship. If I don't screw it up."

Angela tilted her head, studying him. "You ever think you might miss this place? The people?"

Peter shrugged, his gaze drifting back to the emptying field. "Not much to miss."

Angela punched him lightly on the arm. "You're such a liar. You'll miss it, even if you won't admit it."

Peter smirked, but her words lingered as they walked to the parking lot together.

College Dreams

The fall 1969 arrived. Ohio University was supposed to be Peter's ticket out of Wheeling, his chance to carve out a future beyond the mills. The rolling hills of Athens, Ohio, offered a fresh start, and for a time, Peter thrived. On the field, he was unstoppable, his speed and skill earning the admiration of teammates and the attention of scouts.

But the discipline required off the field proved more difficult. Classes felt like an uphill battle, and Peter's restlessness returned with a vengeance. Late nights at the campus pool hall became a habit, and his grades began to slip.

"Di Lonzo, wake up!" Coach Patterson barked during a film session one morning. "You think the pros are gonna draft a kid who can't keep his eyes open in a film room?"

Peter muttered an apology, rubbing his eyes as the other players chuckled. He knew he was on thin ice, but pulling himself together felt impossible.

Claire Montgomery, a junior studying education, noticed his struggles. "Peter, if you spent half as much time studying as you do at that damn pool table, you might actually pass calculus," she said one afternoon, tossing a textbook onto the library table where he sat slouched.

"You sound like my mom," Peter replied with a grin, though his smile didn't reach his eyes.

"Your mom sounds like a smart woman," Claire shot back, her tone sharp but kind.

Her wit and encouragement drew Peter in, and for a time, he felt like he had someone who believed in him. But when he lost his scholarship after his sophomore year, their relationship began to unravel.

"You could've done better," Claire said during a walk across campus, her voice tinged with frustration.

"I tried, Claire. Football was my ticket out, and now it's gone."

"It wasn't just football, Peter. You could've cared more about everything else."

Her words stung, but Peter couldn't argue. When Claire walked away, he let her go, unable to face the truth she had seen in him.

Peter's early years in Wheeling and his struggles in Athens were the foundations of his eventual fall. But even as the cracks in his life began to show, Peter's story was far from over.

Redemption, though distant, would come to define him in ways he couldn't yet imagine.

The Fall in Pittsburgh

By 1973, Peter had traded his cleats for steel-toed boots, working as a shipping manager at Edgar Thomson Mill in nearby Braddock. The city was a haze of smog and ambition, its once-booming industry showing the first signs of decline. Peter's days were spent scheduling freight and managing unionized workers, a far cry from the glory of the football field. The nights, however, belonged to the smoky bars and pool halls where he sought solace in bourbon and the thrill of gambling.

One such night, he met Sofia Benedetti. She was perched at the end of the bar, her dark curls tumbling over her shoulders and a cigarette balanced delicately between her fingers. Her laugh cut through the clinking glasses and the low hum of conversation, and Peter was drawn to her like a moth to flame.

"You look like you've lost more bets than you've won," she said, sliding onto the stool beside him.

Peter smirked, swirling the amber liquid in his glass. "Depends on who's asking."

Sofia tilted her head, studying him with an amused glint in her eye. "You don't strike me as the type to win gracefully."

Peter laughed, the sound deep and warm. "And what type do I look like?"

"The kind who bets on long shots," Sofia replied, exhaling a plume of smoke.

Over the next few months, Sofia became a fixture in Peter's life. She was sharp, confident, and unapologetically herself, qualities that both intimidated and intrigued him. She introduced him to her family, a tight-knit Italian-American clan who welcomed Peter with open arms. For a while, he felt like he'd found something steady, something good.

But his gambling spiraled out of control, and the cracks in their relationship began to show. One night, after losing more money than he could afford, Peter stumbled into Sofia's apartment, reeking of whiskey and defeat.

"You're better than this, Peter," Sofia said, her voice trembling with frustration. "At least, I thought you were."

Peter sat heavily on the couch, his head in his hands. "I'll fix it," he muttered.

Sofia shook her head, her eyes filled with a mixture of anger and sadness. "I've heard that before."

When she packed her things and left a week later, Peter didn't stop her.

Youngstown and the Fall

By the time Peter moved to Youngstown in 1978, he was running on fumes. The steel industry was crumbling, and the city's economy was being propped up by shadows—organized crime and backroom deals that operated just out of sight. For someone like Peter, desperate and directionless, Youngstown offered both danger and opportunity.

"You've got a knack for numbers," Lou Castellano, a local mob-connected businessman, said one night at a poker game. "Ever thought about using that for something a little more... lucrative?"

Peter raised an eyebrow, his interest piqued. "Like what?"

"Insurance," Lou said with a sly grin. "You sell peace of mind. People pay premiums, but what they don't know doesn't hurt them. You skim a little off the top, and everybody's happy."

It started small—fake policies here and there, a bit of money laundered through his accounts. But as the years went on, the operation grew. Peter opened a legitimate-looking insurance office, complete with glossy brochures and a receptionist. Behind the scenes, however, it was all a front for laundering mob money and pocketing premiums from unsuspecting customers.

Peter knew it was wrong, but the money was intoxicating. He bought a modest house, drove a flashy car, and cultivated an image of success. To the outside world, he was a respectable businessman, but inside, guilt gnawed at him.

It was during this time that he met Maria Kowalski, a jazz singer at a downtown nightclub. Maria was unlike anyone Peter had known— independent, fiercely intelligent, and unafraid to call him out on his nonsense.

"You've got secrets," she said one night as they sat in her dimly lit apartment, her voice low and teasing.

"Don't we all?" Peter replied, his smile not quite reaching his eyes.

Maria stayed with Peter longer than most, perhaps sensing the good man buried beneath the layers of regret and deceit. But even she couldn't ignore the danger surrounding him.

When the FBI began investigating Peter's operation in 1985, Maria left, warning him that he was playing a losing hand.

Arrest and Prison

The knock came late one night in October 1986, sharp and unrelenting. Peter opened the door to find two FBI agents standing on his porch, their expressions grim.

"Peter Di Lonzo, you're under arrest for insurance fraud and money laundering," one of them said, as they read him his rights.

The trial was swift. The evidence against him was overwhelming—bank records, fake policies, witness testimonies. Peter was sentenced to 10 years at FCI Elkton, a low-security federal prison in Ohio.

Prison was an extremely humbling and frightening experience. Gone were the flashy cars and tailored suits. Peter found himself in a world where his past accomplishments meant nothing. He spent his days working in the prison library and his nights replaying the choices that had led him there.

One day, while shelving books, an older inmate named Charlie struck up a conversation.

"You read much?" Charlie asked, eyeing the tattered copy of *The Old Man and the Sea* in Peter's hands.

"Not really," Peter admitted.

"You should. Helps pass the time," Charlie said, sliding a copy of *Crime and Punishment* onto the shelf. "Might teach you something about redemption."

The word stuck with Peter. Redemption. Could he ever find it? Could he make amends for the lives he'd hurt and the trust he'd betrayed?

Peter Di Lonzo's rise and fall was complete. The boy who had once carried Wheeling's hopes on his shoulders now sat in a prison cell, his life reduced to a cautionary tale. But deep in the shadows of his despair, the faintest glimmer of hope began to take root. Redemption, though distant, was not out of reach.

Redemption Begins to Stir

Prison was a strange kind of limbo, where days blurred into one another, marked only by the clang of steel doors and the occasional sound of guards barking orders. For Peter, the first year was the hardest. The humiliation of his fall was a constant weight, and the faces of those he'd wronged haunted him in quiet moments.

In the evenings, he'd sit on the edge of his bunk, staring at the cinder block walls. Letters from his family—what few there were—remained unopened in a small pile beneath his mattress. His younger brother Michael and sister Angela had long since given up on him. Their disappointment, Peter imagined, was heavier than any anger they might have felt.

The Prison Library

The library became Peter's refuge. At first, it was just a way to pass the time, but over the years, it became something more. The books he read weren't just stories; they were mirrors, reflections of his own struggles and failings. Hemingway, Steinbeck, and Dostoevsky became his companions, their words stirring something inside him that had long been buried.

"Let me guess," Charlie said one day, nodding toward the copy of *Les Misérables* in Peter's hands. "You see yourself in Valjean?"

Peter smirked, closing the book. "A little. Except I stole more than bread."

Charlie chuckled, his weathered face creasing with amusement. "Redemption's still redemption, my friend. Doesn't matter what you stole."

The word came up again and again: redemption. It followed Peter like a shadow, whispering to him in the quiet hours of the night. He began to wonder if it was possible, if there was a way to make good on the mess he'd made of his life.

Letters from Home

One evening, Peter finally opened one of the letters from Angela. Her handwriting was neat and deliberate, each word cutting into him like a blade.

Peter,

Mom always said you were the golden boy, the one who could make it out of Wheeling and do something great. But look where you are. I don't even know what to say to you anymore. We used to look up to you, you know? Michael and I. Now, we can't even explain you to our kids. They ask where Uncle Peter is, and we don't have an answer that won't make them ashamed to know you.

I hope you think about what you've done. I hope you find a way to make it right. But I don't know if you can.

Angela

Peter read the letter three times before folding it and tucking it back under his mattress. Her words hurt, but they weren't wrong. For weeks, he carried the letter in his pocket, pulling it out to reread it whenever the guilt threatened to overwhelm him.

Turning Point

By his fifth year in prison, Peter had settled into a rhythm. He worked in the library, joined a fitness group in the yard, and kept to himself. But one day, during a group session led by a visiting chaplain, he heard something that stuck with him.

"Redemption isn't about erasing what you've done," the chaplain said, his voice calm but firm. "It's about using the rest of your life to make up for it. To do good, even when no one's watching."

Peter stayed after the session, waiting until the other inmates had filed out.

"You think that's really possible?" he asked, his voice low.

The chaplain studied him for a moment. "Depends on you. But if you're asking, I'd say you're already halfway there."

The Release

When Peter walked out of FCI Elkton in the summer of 1996, he was 45 years old and carrying little more than a duffel bag and a lingering sense of shame. The world had changed while he was inside. The steel mills of his childhood were now skeletons of their former selves, and Wheeling felt like a ghost town in comparison to the bustling place he'd once known.

He didn't go back to Wheeling. There was nothing for him there. Instead, he took a bus to Las Vegas, a place where anonymity was easy to find.

The city was a whirlwind of lights and noise, its energy intoxicating and overwhelming. Peter found work as a valet at a mid-tier casino, parking cars for tourists who had no idea he'd once driven a Cadillac as a self-made businessman. The irony wasn't lost on him.

At night, he went to Gamblers Anonymous meetings, sitting quietly in the back as others shared their stories. Slowly, he began to share his own, each admission of guilt and regret chipping away at the armor he'd built around himself.

Redemption Before the Lottery

The Las Vegas skyline sparkled in the desert twilight; a city built for those who craved reinvention. Peter Di Lonzo stepped off the bus in the summer of 1997 with nothing but a duffel bag and a second-hand suit. His time in prison had left him humbled and alone, but Vegas offered the one thing he needed most: anonymity.

A Modest Life

Peter found work as a valet at the Fremont Hotel, a far cry from his days as a flashy insurance broker in Youngstown. The pay wasn't great, but it kept him afloat. His shifts were long, spent under neon lights and the gaze of tourists whose faces blurred together after midnight.

The nights brought temptation. The slot machines' bright lights beckoned, and the dealers at blackjack tables whispered promises of second chances. But Peter had learned the hard way that gambling offered nothing but ruin. Instead, he went to meetings—Gamblers Anonymous, Alcoholics Anonymous, wherever he could find a chair and a cup of coffee.

One evening at a Gamblers Anonymous meeting, an older man with wiry gray hair and a New York accent sat beside him.

"You're new here," the man said, leaning back in his chair.

Peter glanced at him. "Been coming for a couple of months."

The man smirked. "Couple of months ain't much, kid. But it's a start. Name's Tony Russo."

Peter offered a hesitant handshake. "Peter."

"Peter, huh? Let me guess—cards, dice, or the ponies?"

"Mostly cards," Peter admitted.

Tony chuckled, shaking his head. "The demons never go away. You just learn to muzzle 'em."

Tony became a fixture in Peter's life, a grizzled voice of experience who kept him grounded.

The Diner and Maria Alvarez

In the fall of 1998, Peter discovered the Desert Rose Diner, a small eatery tucked between pawn shops on a side street off the Strip. The place felt like a relic from another time, with red vinyl booths and a jukebox that hadn't worked in years.

"Coffee, hon?" Maria Alvarez asked, appearing at his table with a notepad and a weary smile.

Peter nodded. "And whatever the special is."

Maria was quick-witted and sharp-tongued, the kind of woman who could silence a rowdy table with one raised eyebrow. Over time, Peter became a regular, always sitting in the same corner booth. He learned that Maria was a single mother, raising a 12-year-old daughter, Elena, while working two jobs.

One evening, as Maria refilled his coffee, Peter asked, "How do you do it? Two jobs, raising a kid?"

Maria shrugged, her tired eyes betraying her resolve. "You don't think about it. You just do it. Elena wants to be a doctor, and I'll do whatever it takes to make that happen."

Peter admired her determination, though her words stirred a pang of guilt. He'd squandered his own opportunities, dragging others down with him.

A Quiet Act of Kindness

By 1999, Peter had saved a small amount from his valet job and avoided old temptations. One night, as he sat in his corner booth at the Desert Rose, he pulled an envelope from his jacket and slid it across the table to Maria.

"What's this?" Maria asked, her brow furrowing.

"For Elena," Peter said simply. "Call it a little help toward that doctor dream."

Maria opened the envelope to find $1,000 in cash. Her hands trembled as she looked at him.

"I can't take this," she said.

"You can," Peter replied. "And you will. It's not charity—it's a gift for someone who deserves it."

Maria stared at him for a long moment before tucking the envelope into her apron. "You're a strange man, Peter Di Lonzo."

He smiled faintly. "Maybe. But I know a good investment when I see one."

Friendship with Tony

Peter and Tony Russo grew closer over the years. Tony, a former gambler who had lost everything, saw in Peter a kindred spirit—someone who had been to the bottom and was trying to climb out.

One evening, after a meeting, they sat on a bench outside the community center, the desert air cooling the sweat on their faces.

"You ever think about your family?" Tony asked, lighting a cigarette.

Peter hesitated. "All the time. But they've given up on me."

Tony exhaled a plume of smoke. "Maybe. Maybe not. People got a way of surprising you. Especially if you give 'em a reason."

Peter shrugged, unsure if Tony's words were wisdom or wishful thinking.

The Weight of Regret

By 2001, Peter had carved out a life of quiet solitude. He worked his shifts, attended meetings, and saved what little money he could. But the weight of his past lingered, a constant reminder of the harm he'd caused.

One sleepless night, he wrote letters to his brother Michael and sister Angela.

Dear Michael,

I know I've let you down. I know you probably hate me. But I'm trying to be better. I want you to know that I think about you and Angela every day, and I hope someday you can forgive me.

Peter folded the letters and sealed them, but they never made it to the mailbox. They sat in drawer, their words too raw to send.

The Lottery

On a cold December night in 2002, Peter stopped by a gas station on his way home from work. As he paid for a cup of coffee, the clerk asked if he wanted a Powerball ticket.

"Why not?" Peter said, handing over a crumpled bill.

He didn't think about it again until the numbers were called a week later.

Sitting in his dimly lit apartment, Peter stared at the ticket in disbelief. He checked the numbers once, twice, three times. There was no mistake. He had won.

$500 million.

Peter sank into his chair, the enormity of the moment pressing down on him. The money could change everything—but it wasn't his to squander. He thought of the word that had followed him for years: *redemption*.

This was his chance.

Redemption Fulfilled

Peter Di Lonzo sat in his modest Las Vegas apartment, holding the winning Powerball ticket in trembling hands. December 2002 had been an unremarkable month—until this moment. The ticket, casually purchased at a gas station, was worth $500 million. For a man whose life had been defined by mistakes and regrets, the money felt like both a blessing and a burden.

He poured himself a cup of coffee and stared out the window at the neon-lit skyline. The question lingered in his mind: *What now?*

Peter claimed the prize through a blind trust, ensuring his identity remained secret. His lawyer, an old-school operator named Alan Sharp, handled the logistics.

"You're sitting on a mountain of money, Peter," Alan said during their first meeting in his sleek downtown office. "Most people would be buying yachts and islands by now."

Peter leaned back in his chair; his expression unreadable. "That's not what I'm here for, Alan. I need this money to do some good, not draw attention."

Alan raised an eyebrow. "And by 'good,' you mean?"

"Redemption," Peter said simply.

Alan nodded slowly. "Well, it's your money. Let's make it work."

Peter's first project was close to home. He and Tony Russo had often talked about the need for a safe space for at-risk youth in Las Vegas. Tony, now retired, spent his days mentoring kids and volunteering, but the lack of resources frustrated him.

One evening, Peter sat across from Tony in a dimly lit diner.

"Tony, what if we opened a center?" Peter asked.

Tony frowned, stirring his coffee. "A center? For what?"

"For everything. After-school programs, job training, mentorship. A place where kids can go instead of the streets."

Tony leaned back, his eyes narrowing. "You serious? That kind of thing costs money."

Peter shrugged. "I've got it covered."

Tony stared at him for a long moment. "You hiding something from me, Di Lonzo?"

Peter smirked. "Maybe. But trust me on this."

Six months later, the Russo Community Center opened its doors. The building was state-of-the-art, complete with classrooms, a computer lab, and a workshop for trade skills. Local leaders and community members speculated endlessly about the anonymous donor behind the project, but Peter remained in the shadows.

Peter knew he owed a profound debt to his insurance customers in Youngstown, having swindled them out of their hard-earned money and used their accounts to launder mob funds. Determined to make amends, his first major act through his charity was to anonymously repay as many of his former customers as he could locate. The process was arduous and time-consuming, but with persistence and the help of an expert, he eventually identified all of them. He devised a method to discreetly provide $50,000 to each of the more than 200 customers he had wronged. When the last payment was made, Peter exhaled deeply, finally feeling a measure of relief and redemption for his past actions.

Peter continued his quiet friendship with Maria Alvarez, the waitress who had once served him countless cups of coffee at the Desert Rose Diner. Maria had used Peter's earlier gift to help her daughter Elena attend college, and by 2005, Elena was a year away from medical school.

Maria invited Peter to dinner one evening, her small apartment alive with the smells of arroz con pollo and the sound of laughter. Elena's excitement was infectious as she shared stories about her classes.

"Mr. Di Lonzo, do you know what kind of doctor you'd want to be?" Elena asked, her eyes bright.

Peter chuckled. "One who doesn't faint at the sight of blood. So, not much like you."

Maria laughed, shaking her head. "Peter's too stubborn to faint at anything."

Later, as Maria walked him to the door, she placed a hand on his arm. "I don't know what made you step into the Desert Rose that night, but you changed our lives. Thank you."

Peter smiled; his voice quiet. "You're the one doing the hard part, Maria. I just gave you a little boost."

Peter's philanthropy expanded in the following years. Through his accountant, Marcy Nguyen, he created a network of anonymous giving. His focus wasn't just on big-ticket items but on the small, often overlooked needs of struggling communities.

In Youngstown, he funded the renovation of an old library, adding a new children's wing and a digital media lab. The townspeople speculated endlessly about the mysterious benefactor.

In Wheeling, his hometown, Peter quietly donated to the local food bank and paid off the debt of a struggling Catholic church. When the church's new roof was completed, Father Michael Sullivan thanked the anonymous donor in his Sunday sermon, his voice trembling with gratitude.

In 2010, Peter purchased a modest villa outside Venice, Italy. The countryside offered a kind of peace he hadn't known since childhood. The villa had terracotta roofs, sprawling olive groves, and a small vineyard, all surrounded by rolling hills that seemed to stretch into eternity.

He quickly became part of the local community. Giulia Conti, a widowed schoolteacher, would stop by to share espresso and stories about her students. Franco Bellini, a retired historian, introduced Peter to the region's history, while Marcello Romano, the jovial vineyard owner next door, brought over bottles of wine and hearty laughter.

"Why Venice?" Giulia asked him one afternoon as they sat on the patio overlooking the hills.

Peter sipped his coffee, his eyes distant. "It feels like a place where I can breathe. Where the past isn't chasing me."

Giulia studied him for a moment before nodding. "We all need a place like that."

By 2015, Peter could no longer ignore the estrangement from his siblings, Michael and Angela. The guilt weighed heavily on him, but he knew the letters had to be written.

In his small study, Peter penned the letters by hand.

Michael,

I've spent decades trying to figure out how to say this, and I still don't know if I'm doing it right. I've made mistakes—big ones—and I don't expect forgiveness. But I want you to know that I've tried to make things right, in my own way. I hope we can talk someday.

He sent the letters with no expectation of a response. Months later,

Michael called.

"Peter," Michael said, his voice cautious.

Peter swallowed hard. "Yeah, it's me."

"I got your letter. Angela did too. We…we're not sure what to say."

"Start with hello," Peter replied softly.

In March 2020, as the world grappled with the COVID-19 pandemic, Peter redirected his charity efforts to relief projects. He sent funds to hospitals, purchased PPE for healthcare workers, and covered rent for families on the brink of eviction.

In April, Peter contracted the virus. Despite his age and history of health issues, he resisted hospitalization until his condition worsened.

Tony visited him once, standing outside the glass wall of the isolation unit.

"You stubborn son of a bitch," Tony said, his voice muffled but clear. "You've done too much good to leave now."

Peter smiled faintly and raised a hand in acknowledgment.

Peter passed away quietly on April 15, 2020. His will and autobiography were released weeks later, revealing the full scope of his generosity.

Michael and Angela sat together as the lawyer read the details.

"He gave all of this away," Angela whispered, tears streaming down her face. "And he never asked for anything."

Michael nodded, his expression a mix of sadness and pride. "Maybe we didn't know him, but the world did."

Months later, an envelope arrived at the Russo Center, addressed to Tony Russo. Inside was a handwritten note from Peter, dated a week before his death:

Tony,

Thanks for keeping me grounded all these years. The center wouldn't exist without you. It's yours now. Do something great with it.

Also enclosed was a deed, transferring ownership of Peter's villa in Italy to Tony. The note concluded with: Take a vacation for once. God knows you've earned it.

Peter's name became synonymous with quiet generosity. Scholarships, community centers, and restored libraries bore his influence, though his identity remained unknown to most.

In the quiet hills of Italy, Marcello Romano placed a plaque near Peter's villa:

"To the American with a heart big enough to fill the world."

Peter's anonymous generosity touched countless lives in profound ways, often in places that needed it most. In small, struggling towns like Wheeling, West Virginia, he paid off overdue utility bills for dozens of families during harsh winters, ensuring they could heat their homes. In Youngstown, Ohio, where he once walked a darker path, Peter funded scholarships for children of laid-off steelworkers, opening doors to futures their parents had once dreamed of. His donations revitalized local libraries, rebuilt community centers, and restored dignity to neighborhoods long forgotten by prosperity. Every act was deliberately uncredited, done in the shadows to allow the recipients to feel gratitude without obligation.

On a deeply personal level, Peter found ways to extend his kindness to his estranged family. Without ever revealing the source, he sent significant financial aid to his sister Angela and brother Michael during moments of need, helping Angela through mounting medical expenses and assisting Michael's son with college tuition. For years, they had no idea who the mysterious benefactor was, but the gifts allowed them to weather storms that might have otherwise overwhelmed them. Peter's quiet way of reconnecting with his family through these acts was as much for their benefit as it was for his own healing.

Perhaps his most heartfelt efforts were directed toward former inmates like himself. Drawing from his own experience, Peter funded reentry programs for incarcerated individuals, creating opportunities for education, job training, and housing. At the Russo Community Center in Las Vegas, he launched a mentorship program that paired ex-offenders with business leaders and skilled tradespeople, giving them the tools to rebuild their lives. For those who had nowhere else to turn, Peter became a lifeline, though they never knew his name. His ability to transform his wealth into hope for others was a quiet revolution of redemption, one that rippled through individuals and communities for years to come.

Peter's story ends not in fame or recognition, but in the quiet satisfaction that redemption, though hard-earned, is always possible.

WINTER SHOES

It was 1936 and the Depression raged on across America. In the coldest December days in Beaver Falls, Pennsylvania, the town seemed frozen in time. Snow clung to the steep hillsides and rooftops of shuttered factories, blanketing the quiet streets where laughter was rare, and hope hung thin in the air. Felix Gianinno tugged his wool coat tighter against the bitter wind as he trudged down Seventh Avenue. At ten years old, he had grown used to the bare shelves at home and the endless sacrifices his parents made just to keep a loaf of bread on the table. But his heart remained warm—kept alive by small joys: the scent of his mother's baking, a game of marbles with his best friend, or the flicker of light from the wood stove in their tiny apartment above his father's barbershop.

"Hey, Felix!" A familiar voice cut through the wind. Felix turned to see Sammy Callahan sprinting down the street, his skinny legs slipping in the snow. Sammy's shoes—if they could still be called shoes—flapped noisily as he ran, the worn leather barely holding together with patches and string. Felix's chest tightened as he noticed the boy's socks, frayed and thin, poking out from the open toes.

"Sammy, you're gonna freeze to death running like that," Felix called, his voice tinged with concern.

Sammy grinned, brushing a strand of hair from his face as he stopped next to Felix. "Can't freeze if you're moving, right? Besides, Ma made soup for dinner last night. I feel like I'm flying."

Felix forced a smile, though his eyes lingered on Sammy's feet. "Flying with wings that've got holes in 'em," he muttered under his breath. Louder, he said, "C'mon, let's get to the welfare tent before the bread's all gone. My ma says the lines've been extra-long this week."

They walked together, their breath forming clouds in the frosty air. Sammy's laughter was quick and easy, but Felix noticed the winces when his friend's feet slipped into icy puddles. Sammy's shoes had been falling apart for weeks, but now they seemed beyond saving.

When they reached the tent at 10th Street, the line of families snaked out into the road. Mothers clutched their children close, and fathers shifted awkwardly, avoiding eye contact as they waited for their turn. Felix and Sammy squeezed into the back of the line, chatting quietly to pass the time. But Felix couldn't shake the image of Sammy's bare toes, blue and raw against the snow.

That night, Felix sat by the wood stove in their apartment, the warmth barely reaching his small corner of the room. His father had already gone to bed, exhausted from a long day of giving haircuts on credit to men who could barely afford to pay. His mother hummed softly in the kitchen, rolling out dough for the next day's bread. Felix stared down at his own shoes—old but sturdy, a little too big for him but warm and whole. His mind wandered back to Sammy, shivering in the cold.

"Sammy's got it worse than me," Felix whispered to himself, his breath curling in the chill of the room. "I don't need new boots—I've got my shoes. He doesn't have anything."

His decision came quickly. Felix rummaged under his bed for an old rag, pulling it out along with a tin of polish his father had given him. He worked quietly, wiping and buffing the leather until the shoes shone faintly in the dim light of the stove. He tied the laces neatly and wrapped them in a scrap of newspaper he found in the kitchen, knotting the package with a piece of twine. His heart felt lighter as he held the bundle in his hands, imagining Sammy's face when he opened it.

On Christmas Eve, the snow fell in thick, silent flakes as Felix crept through the streets toward Sammy's house. The town seemed deserted, the windows glowing faintly with candlelight as families huddled together against the cold. Felix's feet were wrapped in layers of rags—his makeshift solution until he could figure out what to tell his father. They slid uncomfortably on the icy ground, but he pressed on, clutching the bundle tightly to his chest.

When he reached Sammy's porch, Felix knelt and set the package carefully by the door. He raised his hand to knock, hesitated for a moment, then rapped sharply before darting around the corner to hide. His heart pounded as he waited, his breath coming in short, visible puffs.

The door creaked open, and Sammy's mother stepped out, her thin frame wrapped in a patched shawl. She bent down to pick up the package, her face etched with surprise. "Sammy!" she called, stepping back inside. "Come see this!"

Felix peeked around the corner, a smile tugging at his lips as he watched Sammy tear into the paper. "Mama, look! Shoes! Real shoes!" Sammy held them up, his eyes wide with wonder. "Who could've done this?"

Sammy's mother clutched her hand to her chest, her eyes brimming with tears. "An angel, that's who," she said softly. "A real Christmas angel."

Felix turned away, his smile spreading as he hurried back down the street. The snow bit at his wrapped feet, soaking through the rags, but he hardly noticed. His mind was filled with Sammy's joy, the sound of his friend's laughter echoing in his ears.

As he rounded the corner to his apartment, Felix slowed. The light from the barbershop window spilled onto the snowy street, and in the doorway stood his father, arms crossed and eyebrows raised. Felix stopped in his tracks, his heart sinking as his father's eyes traveled down to his feet.

"Felix," his father said, his voice steady but laced with concern. "Where are your shoes?"

Felix froze in place, his breath curling in the frosty air like smoke. His father stepped forward, his boots crunching in the snow, arms still folded tight. The yellow glow from the barbershop behind him cast long shadows on the icy street.

"I asked you a question, Felix," his father said, quieter this time but no less firm. "Where are your shoes?"

Felix shifted nervously, his rags-wrapped feet curling against the cold. He tried to think of an excuse, something that wouldn't give away his secret, but when he looked up into his father's weathered face, lined with exhaustion and worry, the truth tumbled out before he could stop it.

"I gave them to Sammy," Felix said, his voice trembling. "His shoes were worse than mine, Papa. He needed them more."

For a long moment, his father said nothing. Felix's heart thudded painfully as he braced for a scolding. Instead, his father crouched down, his hands rough but gentle as he gripped Felix's small shoulders.

"You gave away your only shoes?" his father asked, his voice low, the faintest trace of disbelief and something else—something like pride— underneath.

Felix nodded, his eyes brimming with tears. "I couldn't stand to see his feet like that, Papa. It's Christmas."

His father's face softened, the hardness melting away like frost in the morning sun. He sighed deeply, then pulled Felix into a hug. "You've got a good heart, my boy. Too good for this world, maybe." He stood and ushered Felix inside, closing the door firmly against the bitter cold.

Inside the apartment, the scent of fresh bread and oregano filled the air. Felix's mother looked up from the kitchen table, a rolling pin in hand. "What's this?" she asked, her eyes darting from Felix to her husband. "Why's he got no shoes?"

Felix's father explained quietly, and his mother's stern expression softened into something tender and sad. She walked over, kneeling to check Felix's makeshift rags. "Your heart's in the right place, Felix," she murmured, tying the rags more securely. "But what will you wear? You can't go out barefoot in this weather."

Felix shrugged, trying to look brave. "I'll figure it out, Mama. I don't need much."

His father rubbed a hand over his face and muttered something in Italian before looking at Felix with a small, wry smile. "You take after your grandmother, you know. She'd have given away the roof over her head if someone needed it more."

Felix beamed at the compliment but stayed silent. He didn't want to admit how cold his feet were, or how the snow had soaked through the cloth, leaving his toes numb.

That night, word of Felix's act spread quietly across town. It began with Mrs. Callahan, who told her neighbor while they collected water from the pump. By the time the evening soup line formed outside the welfare tent on Seventh Avenue, nearly everyone had heard.

"Can you believe it?" Mrs. Novak said, tucking a jar of beans into her coat. "That Gianinno boy gave his only pair of shoes to Sammy Callahan."

"His only pair?" Mr. O'Connor, the cobbler, shook his head as he ladled soup into a tin cup. "That boy's got more kindness in his heart than most men I know."

Mrs. O'Connor nodded, her eyes sparkling with determination. "We can't let him go without, especially not at Christmas. What do you have to spare, Novak?"

By the next morning, the people of Beaver Falls had formed a quiet plan. Neighbors stopped by the cobbler's shop to contribute a coin or two from their meager savings. Mrs. O'Connor donated a pair of wool socks she'd been saving for her own husband, and Mr. Novak added a dollar he had stashed away in case of emergencies. The local grocer, hearing the story from a customer, handed over an old wool scarf, and a fireman from the Presbyterian church offered a pair of leather gloves worn but warm.

That evening, the cobbler sat in his tiny shop, carefully working a piece of leather into shape by the light of a single oil lamp. He hummed softly as his fingers stitched with practiced precision, crafting something sturdy and beautiful. The boots that emerged were not fancy, but they were solid—a pair that could withstand the harshest winters Beaver Falls could throw at them. He polished them until they gleamed, then wrapped them in brown paper tied with string

"We'll give it to him tomorrow," Mrs. O'Connor said as she handed the bundle to Mr. Novak.

"The boy deserves something special."

By Christmas morning, the quiet plan had turned into a full rally. Felix, unaware of the commotion brewing in the town, sat by the wood stove with a cup of weak tea, his feet still wrapped in rags. Outside, the snow fell in soft, lazy flakes, muffling the usual noises of the street. His mother was humming softly in the kitchen, and his father was tinkering with an old razor in the barbershop below.

A knock came at the door, sharp and urgent. Felix looked up, puzzled. "Who could that be?" his mother asked, wiping her hands on her apron.

Felix opened the door to find a small crowd gathered outside, bundled in coats and scarves, their breath fogging the air. In front of them stood Mr. Novak, holding the neatly wrapped package, and Mrs. O'Connor with a bright smile on her face.

"Merry Christmas, Felix!" she said, her voice warm and cheerful. "We've got something for you."

Felix stared, wide-eyed, as Mr. Novak handed him the bundle. "Go on, lad," the cobbler said. "Open it."

Tearing through the paper, Felix gasped. Inside was the most beautiful pair of boots he had ever seen, the leather polished to a rich shine and the soles thick and sturdy. Tucked into the boots were the wool socks, gloves, and scarf, all carefully arranged.

"These are for me?" Felix stammered, his voice breaking.

Mrs. O'Connor crouched down, placing a hand on his cheek. "You reminded us all what Christmas is about, Felix. You gave everything to help your friend. Now it's our turn to help you."

Tears filled Felix's eyes as he held the boots close, his heart swelling with gratitude. "Thank you," he whispered. "Thank you so much."

Behind him, his parents stood in the doorway, his father's arm around his mother's shoulders. His father gave a small, proud nod. "You've made us all proud, Felix," he said softly.

As the crowd began to disperse, Felix tried on the boots, marveling at how perfectly they fit. His mother wrapped the scarf around his neck, and his father helped him slip on the gloves. For the first time in days, Felix's feet were warm, and his heart felt full.

"Come on, Felix," Sammy called from the street, waving a hand. "Let's go try out your new boots!"

Felix grinned, running to join his friend. The sound of laughter filled the snowy air as the two boys raced down the street, their footprints side by side in the freshly fallen snow.

On Christmas morning, the light of dawn stretched across Beaver Falls, casting golden hues over the thick blanket of snow that covered the streets. Smoke curled lazily from chimneys, and the sound of church bells echoed faintly in the crisp air. Felix Gianinno stood on the stoop of his family's apartment, his new boots gleaming in the pale sunlight. The scarf around his neck was warm, the wool gloves snug on his small hands. But what truly warmed him was the kindness that had enveloped him, the love of a town that had reminded him of the magic of Christmas.

He took a tentative step forward, the boots feeling sturdy and solid beneath him, like they could carry him through any storm. Sammy Callahan bounded up the steps to meet him, his own feet clad in the polished shoes Felix had given him. Sammy grinned; his cheeks red from the cold.

"You ready, Felix? Betcha those boots can outrun anything in town!"

Felix laughed, a bright, unrestrained sound that filled the street. "You think so? Let's find out!"

The two boys tore down the snow-packed road, their laughter trailing behind them like ribbons.

They raced past the welfare tent on Seventh Avenue, where women handing out canned goods paused to smile and wave. They skidded to a stop near the church, where a group of children was building a snowman, and Felix couldn't help but join in, scooping up handfuls of snow with his new gloves. For a moment, the struggles of the Depression seemed to melt away, leaving only joy and the pure simplicity of childhood.

By midmorning, Felix and Sammy were back on Seventh Avenue, watching as families gathered near the fire station for the town's Christmas celebration. There was a tree adorned with handmade ornaments and strings of popcorn, and the faint strains of carolers' voices floated on the air. The entire town seemed to have come alive, united in a rare moment of happiness and togetherness.

Mrs. O'Connor spotted Felix in the crowd and bustled over; her cheeks flushed from the cold.

"Felix, my boy!" she called, her voice carrying above the din. "How do those boots feel?"

"They're perfect," Felix said, standing a little taller. "Thank you, Mrs. O'Connor. I'll never forget this."

She leaned down, her kind eyes twinkling. "You've got a good heart, Felix. It's boys like you that remind us what we're all here for. Now go on, enjoy yourself. It's Christmas!"

Felix smiled and turned back to Sammy, who was eyeing a group of older boys building a sled ramp near the church steps. "Think we can take 'em?" Sammy asked, his grin widening.

"With these boots?" Felix replied, grinning. "We don't stand a chance— they'll never catch us."

The boys spent the afternoon racing down the hill, their laughter carrying over the town like the toll of the church bells. But as the sun began to dip lower in the sky, Felix found himself growing quieter, his thoughts drifting. He looked down at his boots, their polished leather scuffed now from hours of play, and he thought of the sacrifice his parents made every day just to keep their family afloat. He thought of the townspeople, who had given what little they had to make his Christmas special, and of Sammy's face when he'd opened the shoes Felix had left on his porch.

By the time the stars began to prick through the night sky, Felix and Sammy had made their way back to Felix's apartment, where the lights from the barbershop window still burned brightly. Felix's mother opened the door with a smile, her apron dusted with flour from an afternoon of baking. The smell of fresh bread wafted out into the cold, and Felix's stomach growled.

"Come in, boys," she said, ushering them inside. "Dinner's almost ready."

Sammy glanced nervously at Felix. "I don't wanna intrude…"

Felix's father appeared in the doorway, a kind smile on his face. "You're not intruding, Sammy. You're family. Now come sit at the table before the soup gets cold."

The table was modest but warm and inviting. A pot of hearty vegetable soup steamed in the center, flanked by loaves of fresh bread and a small bowl of olives. Felix looked around at his family, at Sammy, and at the simple meal before them, and he felt a swell of gratitude so strong it nearly overwhelmed him.

After dinner, the family gathered by the wood stove, its flickering light casting long shadows on the walls. Felix's mother began to hum a soft Christmas carol, and soon Sammy joined in, his voice strong and clear. Felix's father pulled out an old accordion, its bellows worn but still able to produce music that filled the room with a gentle, nostalgic melody.

Felix leaned back; his boots propped up near the stove to dry. He felt the weight of the day settle into his bones—not the kind of weight that burdens, but the kind that reminds you of how much you must carry forward. His mind wandered to the faces of the people who had helped him, who had reminded him that even in the darkest of times, the light of kindness could shine through.

As the fire crackled and the music swelled, Felix closed his eyes, his heart full. He didn't know what the coming days would bring—more struggle, more sacrifices—but he knew one thing for certain. He would carry this moment with him, this lesson of love and generosity, and he would spend the rest of his life giving it back.

Above the quiet town of Beaver Falls, the stars shone brightly, as if to remind everyone that even in the hardest winters, warmth could be found in the hearts of those who cared. And on that Christmas night, as the Gianinno family sang softly around the fire, the small apartment above the barbershop felt like the brightest place in the world.

THE LAST TRAIN HOME

On a damp and overcast December morning in 1944, Union Station in Seattle buzzed with activity. The grand, cavernous hall echoed with the clatter of footsteps, the murmur of worried voices, and the occasional sharp whistle of a departing train. Outside, a light drizzle soaked the city, casting a gray haze over the skyline dotted with defense plants and naval ships in Puget Sound. Posters urging sacrifice and patriotism lined the walls, their bold slogans a constant reminder of the war's grip on every corner of life.

Private Rafael Delgado stepped into the station, shaking the rain from his army-issued coat. At 22, Rafael was lean and broad-shouldered, with warm brown eyes that betrayed his exhaustion. A tattered duffel bag hung from one shoulder, and in his other hand, he clutched a small, carefully wrapped box. Inside was a hand-carved figurine he had made for his younger sister—a horse rearing on its hind legs, its mane, flowing as though caught in an invisible wind.

His boots scuffed softly against the polished tile floor as he moved toward the departure board. His heart pounded with anticipation. He had been dreaming of this moment for weeks—making it home to his family in Eastern Washington for Christmas. He could already picture the glow of the small wood stove in their modest home, the smell of his mother's tamales steaming on the table, and the sound of his younger siblings laughing as they tore through handmade gifts.

Reaching into his pocket, he pulled out a telegram from his mother, the words almost worn away from the number of times he had read them: *"We can't wait to see you. The little ones are counting the days."* A small smile tugged at his lips, but it quickly faded as he read the departure board. The train to Eastern Washington was marked with a single, ominous word: "Delayed."

A sinking feeling settled in Rafael's stomach. He approached the ticket counter, where a harried station worker was fielding complaints from a crowd of disgruntled passengers. The man barely glanced up as Rafael reached the front of the line.

"The train to Wenatchee—how long?" Rafael asked, his voice tinged with urgency.

"Indefinite," the worker replied flatly. "Snow's blocking the pass in the Cascades. Could be hours, could be tomorrow." He waved Rafael aside, already turning to the next passenger.

Rafael stepped back, disappointment pressing down on him like a weight. He found an empty bench near the center of the station and sank onto it, setting his duffel at his feet. Around him, the station swirled with movement—families huddled together, servicemen in uniforms like his own pacing restlessly, and lone travelers sitting silently with tired eyes. The air was thick with the smell of damp wool coats, coffee, and the faint metallic tang of the railway tracks.

As Rafael sat there, trying to tamp down his frustration, he became aware of a small figure edging closer to him. A boy, no older than ten, plopped down on the bench beside him. The boy's dark hair stuck up in uneven tufts, and he clutched a toy airplane made of scrap metal.

"Are you a real soldier?" the boy asked, his wide brown eyes staring up at Rafael with awe.

Rafael couldn't help but smile. "Yeah, I'm a real soldier." He pointed to the patches on his sleeve. "See these? They're from my unit."

The boy leaned in closer, his face lighting up. "Wow! Have you ever been in a tank? What about an airplane? Did you see any battles?"

Before Rafael could answer, a soft laugh interrupted them. He looked up to see a woman standing nearby, her arms crossed and an amused smile on her face. She was dressed in a plain but neat coat, and her hands, raw and chapped from work, clutched the handle of a small suitcase.

"Looks like you've got yourself a fan," she said, her voice warm and teasing.

"Looks like it," Rafael replied, chuckling.

The woman walked over and held out a hand. "Evelyn Carter. I'm a nurse."

"Rafael Delgado," he said, shaking her hand.

Evelyn pulled a piece of candy from her pocket and handed it to the boy, who accepted it eagerly. "And who's this?" she asked, crouching slightly to meet the boy's eyes.

"Luis Ramirez," the boy said proudly. "I'm going to see my dad in Bremerton. He works at the shipyard."

Evelyn smiled. "Nice to meet you, Luis. That's a fine airplane you've got there."

Luis beamed, holding up the toy. "My dad made it. He said I could keep it to remind me of him."

As the three of them chatted, the bench began to feel less like a place of frustration and more like a refuge. Luis's enthusiasm was contagious, and Evelyn's calm presence seemed to anchor them both. Rafael found himself relaxing, the edges of his disappointment softening as their voices filled the space between train announcements.

A short distance away, an elderly couple shuffled toward them. The man, dressed in a worn wool coat, carried a small basket covered with a checkered cloth, while his wife leaned on his arm for support. They paused near the bench, exchanging glances.

"Excuse us," the man said hesitantly. "Would you mind if we sat here? My wife could use a rest."

"Of course," Evelyn said, moving her suitcase to make room.

The couple settled onto the bench, the woman sighing with relief as she adjusted her threadbare scarf. The man offered a small smile. "We're the Hensleys. Headed to Spokane to see our grandkids for Christmas. Brought them some cookies." He patted the basket.

Luis's eyes lit up at the mention of cookies, and Mrs. Hensley chuckled. "Would you like one, young man?"

Luis nodded eagerly, and she handed him a cookie, then offered the basket to Rafael and Evelyn.

As the hours passed, the unlikely group began to feel like a small family. They shared snacks and stories, their laughter cutting through the heavy mood of the station. Rafael found himself opening up about his family, describing his siblings' antics and his mother's Christmas traditions. Evelyn spoke of her work in the military hospital, the long shifts and the bonds she had formed with her fellow nurses.

By the time the next train announcement came, the gloom of the delay had faded, replaced by a quiet sense of camaraderie. For the first time since arriving at the station, Rafael felt a spark of hope. They were strangers brought together by circumstance, but in that moment, they were something more.

The hours stretched on, and the distant chime of the station clock echoed like a taunt in Rafael's ears. Outside, the rain had given way to a wet snow that clung to the tracks and coated the city streets in a gray-white slush. Inside Union Station, the air was heavy with frustration. Harried announcements crackled over the loudspeaker, most of them apologizing for delayed trains, as travelers shuffled about with weary resignation.

Rafael leaned forward on the bench, resting his elbows on his knees, staring at the polished floor beneath his scuffed boots. Around him, the group that had gathered seemed to settle into a rhythm. Evelyn sat beside him, rubbing her sore hands and stealing glances at Luis, who was sprawled on the floor in front of them, zooming his scrap-metal airplane through an imaginary sky.

"Rough crowd, huh?" Evelyn murmured, nudging Rafael with a slight smile.

He chuckled dryly, shaking his head. "I'd take a battlefield over this mess. At least there, you know what you're up against."

Evelyn laughed, the sound warm and genuine. "Spoken like someone who hasn't worked a hospital ward during a bombing run."

Rafael raised his hands in surrender. "Point taken."

Across from them, Mr. Hensley adjusted his wife's scarf as she rested her head on his shoulder, her eyes closed. The old man caught Rafael's eye and gave him a knowing smile. "Patience, son," he said softly. "The trains'll run when they run. They always do."

Rafael nodded politely but couldn't hide the flicker of doubt in his expression. He couldn't shake the gnawing anxiety in his chest, the thought of missing Christmas with his family. He glanced at the clock—another hour had passed, and still no word on their train.

Luis jumped to his feet suddenly, clutching his toy airplane. "I'm hungry," he announced, his voice breaking the somber silence.

Evelyn reached into her coat pocket and produced another candy, but Luis frowned. "Real food," he clarified, looking pointedly at Rafael.

Rafael smirked. "Guess that's my cue."

He stood and stretched, the stiff muscles in his back protesting. "I'll see what I can find."

"I'll come with you," Evelyn offered, grabbing her coat. "No sense wandering around alone in this crowd."

They made their way through the bustling station, weaving between clusters of travelers. The smells of coffee and wet wool mingled with the faint aroma of something warm wafting from a small food stand near the far wall. The line stretched long, but Rafael and Evelyn joined it, grateful for something to do.

"Where're you headed?" Evelyn asked after a moment, breaking the silence.

"Home," Rafael said simply. "Eastern Washington. Small town near Wenatchee. My family's there." His voice softened. "It's been over a year since I've seen them. My sister was just a baby when I left. She probably doesn't even remember me."

Evelyn's expression softened. "They'll be glad to have you home. Families don't forget, no matter how long it's been."

"What about you?" Rafael asked. "Where's home for you?"

"Spokane," she said, her voice tinged with nostalgia. "Haven't been back in years, not since I started nursing school. My parents run a small boarding house there. I used to help out before the war, cooking breakfast for the lodgers. My mama says the place isn't the same without me."

Rafael smiled. "I bet she's right."

Evelyn shrugged, but her eyes glistened with emotion. "I'm just hoping I make it in time for Christmas. It'd be nice to see everyone again. Even if it's only for a day."

The line moved forward, and soon they had two bowls of steaming soup and a loaf of bread between them. They carried the food back to the group, where Luis's face lit up at the sight of the bread. "Finally!" he exclaimed, tearing off a piece before Rafael had even set it down.

"Easy, kid," Rafael teased, sitting back down. "There's enough for everyone."

The group ate in companionable silence, the warmth of the soup taking the edge off the chill that had seeped into their bones. Even Mrs. Hensley seemed to revive a bit, smiling faintly as her husband fed her small bites of bread.

As they finished, Luis looked up at Rafael with wide eyes. "Do you think the train will come soon?" he asked, his voice tinged with worry. "My dad said he'd be waiting for me at the station. What if he thinks I'm not coming?"

Rafael hesitated, unsure how to answer. He glanced at Evelyn, who leaned forward, her voice gentle. "Trains have a way of finding their way, Luis," she said. "And if they don't, people have a way of making things happen. Your dad will understand."

Luis seemed to consider this, nodding slowly before returning to his toy airplane. Evelyn leaned back, letting out a quiet sigh.

Hours passed, and the group fell into a quiet rhythm. Luis entertained himself with his airplane, darting around the benches and making whooshing sounds that occasionally drew chuckles from the adults. Evelyn busied herself with a small notebook, jotting down what looked like letters or lists. The Hensleys dozed off, their heads tilted together like two halves of the same coin.

Rafael found himself staring at the clock again, the minutes ticking by with agonizing slowness. He clenched his fists, frustration bubbling up. "What if it doesn't come?" he muttered, more to himself than anyone else.

Evelyn looked up, her gaze steady. "Then we figure something out. But sitting here worrying won't get you home any faster."

Rafael opened his mouth to respond, but before he could, the station loudspeaker crackled to life. "Attention passengers: Train 457 to Wenatchee is now boarding at Gate 3. Repeat, Train 457 to Wenatchee is now boarding at Gate 3."

A hush fell over the group, and then Rafael shot to his feet, grabbing his duffel. "That's me," he said, his heart pounding.

The Hensleys stirred, and Mrs. Hensley reached out to grasp his hand. "Safe travels, son," she said softly. "Give your family our best."

Luis looked up, his face a mix of excitement and sadness. "Are you coming back?"

Rafael crouched down to his level, resting a hand on his shoulder. "I'll be back," he promised. "And when I am, I want to hear all about what you and your dad are building."

Luis nodded, his grip tightening on the toy airplane. "Okay. Deal." "I want you to have this," Luis added. Rafael was surprised. "I can't take your toy airplane that your dad made for you." Luis pressed the airplane into Rafael's hand. "Yes you can. Dad can make me another. This way you'll remember me." A lump caught in Rafael's throat as he carefully placed the airplane in this coat pocket. "Okay, Luis. It's a deal! I will always remember you."

Evelyn stood, pulling Rafael into a quick, firm hug. "Merry Christmas, Rafael," she said, her voice steady but warm. "Go home. Your family's waiting."

He nodded, his throat tight. "Merry Christmas, Evelyn. And thank you."

As he made his way to the gate, the sound of their voices followed him. He turned once to wave, his heart full, before stepping onto the train. The whistle blew, and the train lurched forward, carrying him into the snowy night.

The train swayed and groaned as it climbed through the snow-draped Cascades, its whistle cutting through the icy silence of the mountains. Rafael leaned his forehead against the frosty window, watching the darkened landscape roll past in ghostly shapes. The rhythmic clatter of the wheels on the tracks should have been soothing, but instead, his thoughts raced.

The delay had stolen hours, and the train was running behind schedule. Rafael's heart clenched with every mile, fearing the worst. Would he arrive to find the house dark, his family already gathered and asleep? He pictured his siblings sitting at the table, their hopeful faces falling when they realized he wasn't coming.

A man seated across the aisle—a grizzled logger, judging by the sawdust still clinging to his coat—lit a cigarette and gave Rafael a sympathetic look. "You headed home for Christmas, soldier?"

Rafael nodded, dragging himself out of his thoughts. "Yeah. Hoping I can make it in time."

The man took a long drag, exhaling slowly. "Well, these old trains have a way of surprising you. Got stuck on one last winter, blizzard up in the mountains. Figured I'd be stranded until New Year's, but somehow they got us through."

Rafael forced a tight smile, appreciating the effort but finding little comfort in it. "Thanks," he muttered, returning his gaze to the window.

The train lurched to a stop in the small town of Skykomish, a whistle signaling the pause. Passengers grumbled as conductors moved through the car, announcing a temporary delay to clear snow from the tracks ahead. Rafael's fists tightened on his knees. Another delay.

A young mother seated nearby jostled her crying infant, murmuring soft reassurances as she tried to calm him. Rafael turned away, desperate to keep his frustration in check, and reached into his duffel bag. His fingers brushed against the carefully wrapped figurine. The touch steadied him, reminding him of why he needed to get home.

Minutes stretched into nearly an hour before the train jerked forward again, the slow climb resuming through the snowy peaks. The air inside the train felt thick, every passenger caught in their own quiet tension. Rafael closed his eyes, leaning his head back against the worn seat.

He must have dozed off because the next thing he knew, a conductor was gently shaking his shoulder. "Wenatchee's the next stop, son. Better get your things ready."

Rafael blinked, disoriented for a moment before the words sank in. His heart leapt. He grabbed his duffel, slinging it over his shoulder, and headed for the door as the train began its slow descent toward the town. Outside the window, the first pale light of dawn crept over the snow-covered fields, painting the world in soft shades of gold and pink.

The train hissed to a stop, steam rising in great clouds around the platform. Rafael stepped off, his boots crunching against the ice-crusted ground. The station was small, its wooden beams frosted with ice, but the sight of it sent a flood of relief through him. He had made it.

Scanning the platform, Rafael felt his stomach tighten. Where was his family? His pulse quickened as his eyes darted from one face to another, none of them familiar. Panic began to rise, the fear he had tried to suppress during the journey threatening to overwhelm him.

"Rafael!"

The voice cut through the crowd, high-pitched and joyful. He turned sharply, his heart soaring as he saw a small figure darting through the sea of passengers. His youngest sister, Maria, barreled into him, her tiny arms wrapping around his legs.

"Mijo!"

His mother's voice came next, thick with emotion. She emerged from the crowd, her shawl pulled tightly around her shoulders, tears streaming down her face. Rafael scooped Maria into his arms just as his mother reached him, pulling him into a fierce embrace.

"You made it," she whispered, her voice trembling. "You made it."

Rafael buried his face in her shoulder, breathing in the familiar scent of flour and lavender soap. "I'm here, Mamá," he said, his own voice cracking. "I'm here."

His father appeared next, his weathered face breaking into a rare smile as he clapped a hand on Rafael's shoulder. "We were starting to think you wouldn't make it, son."

Rafael shook his head, his throat too tight to speak. He set Maria down as his other siblings crowded around, their laughter and chatter filling the cold morning air. He handed the figurine to Maria, watching her eyes light up as she unwrapped it.

By the time they reached the family's small home, the sun was fully up, casting a warm glow over the snow-covered fields. Inside, the scent of tamales and cinnamon filled the air, and the warmth from the wood stove seeped into Rafael's chilled bones. He sat at the table, surrounded by his family, the sound of their voices blending into a melody he had missed more than he realized.

As the day wore on, Rafael couldn't stop thinking about the strangers who had helped him. Evelyn, Luis, the Hensleys—they had been more than companions on a delayed journey. They had reminded him of the strength found in kindness, of the bonds that could form between strangers in the unlikeliest of circumstances.

That evening, after dinner, he stepped outside, the cold air biting at his cheeks. The stars above were bright, their light glinting off the snow like a field of diamonds. Rafael reached into his pocket and pulled out the small toy airplane Luis had given him, turning it over in his hands.

He whispered a quiet thank-you, not just to the people who had helped him, but to the universe for carrying him home.

The whistle of a distant train echoed across the still night, a sound of departure and return, of journeys ending and beginning anew. And as Rafael stood there, surrounded by the warmth of home and the memory of those who had shared his path, he felt a deep and abiding peace. He was home.

Epilogue

Twenty years had passed since that long, snowy night at Union Station. It was December 25, 1964, and the Delgado family home in Eastern Washington was alive with the sounds of Christmas. Laughter rang out from the living room, where Rafael's children raced around the tree, their excited voices blending with the soft crackle of the fire. The air was filled with the scent of tamales, cinnamon cookies, and pine, a comforting reminder of the traditions Rafael's mother had started so long ago.

Rafael, now in his early forties, sat in a worn armchair near the hearth, a steaming mug of coffee in his hands. His dark hair was tinged with silver at the temples, and his face bore the lines of a life well-lived. Yet, his eyes held the same warmth and kindness they always had. He watched his youngest daughter carefully hang an ornament on the tree, her small hands adjusting the placement until it was just right. It was a simple wooden horse, carved in the same style as the figurine he had given his sister so many years ago.

As the children laughed and played, Rafael's thoughts drifted to another

Christmas—one marked not by the warmth of home but by the uncertainty of a delayed train and the kindness of strangers. His gaze fell on the mantle above the fireplace, where two objects stood out among the family photos and holiday decorations: a toy airplane made of scrap metal and a framed note, its ink faded but still legible.

"The world's a tough place, but people like you make it better. Never forget that kindness is the greatest gift you can give."

Rafael stood and walked over to the mantle, picking up the airplane. Its metal wings were slightly bent, but its significance had never dulled. He ran a thumb along its edge, his mind filling with memories of Luis Ramirez, the wide-eyed boy who had given it to him as a token of friendship.

"Dad?"

Rafael turned to see his eldest son, Marco, standing nearby. At 18, Marco had the same broad shoulders and determined gaze Rafael had once carried into the world as a young soldier. Marco gestured toward the airplane. "I've always wondered about that. You never told us where it came from."

Rafael smiled, setting the airplane back on the mantle. "It's a long story," he said, motioning for Marco to sit by the fire. "But I think it's time you heard it."

As the family gathered around, Rafael began to recount the events of that Christmas Eve in 1944. He spoke of Union Station, of Evelyn Carter, Luis Ramirez, and the Hensleys, of the delays, the frustration, and the unexpected bond they had formed. He told them about the toy airplane, Evelyn's encouragement, and the sacrifices those strangers had made to ensure he made it home.

His voice softened as he spoke of the note Evelyn had slipped into his pocket, a message that had stayed with him ever since. "She taught me something that night," he said, his gaze sweeping over his children. "Kindness isn't about grand gestures or flashy words. It's about showing up for people, even when you're tired, even when you're struggling yourself. It's about making the world a little lighter, one small act at a time."

When he finished, the room was quiet, save for the crackling of the fire. His youngest daughter, Sofia, crawled into his lap, her eyes wide. "Did you ever see them again?" she asked.

Rafael shook his head, a bittersweet smile on his face. "No. But I think about them every Christmas. And I hope, wherever they are, they've found the same kind of happiness they gave me."

Years later, during a trip through Spokane, Rafael would stumble upon a plaque outside a hospital: *"Evelyn Carter Memorial Wing."* The sight brought a lump to his throat. He stood there for a long moment, remembering the nurse who had given him hope on that snowy night.

He also found Luis's name in an old newspaper article, listed among the decorated pilots of the Korean War. A sense of pride swelled in him, knowing the boy's dreams of flight had come true.

Back in 1964, as the evening wore on, Rafael stepped outside, the cold air biting at his cheeks. The night was still, the stars scattered across the sky like shards of light. He stood on the porch, hands tucked into his pockets and listened to the faint sound of a distant train whistle.

His wife joined him, slipping an arm around his waist. "What are you thinking about?" she asked, her voice soft.

Rafael smiled, his breath clouding in the cold air. "About how far we've come. And how much of it started with the kindness of strangers."

She rested her head on his shoulder. "It's a good lesson to pass on."

"It is," he said, glancing back toward the warm glow of the house. Inside, their children were still laughing, the joy of Christmas filling the air. "And I hope they'll carry it forward."

The train whistle echoed again, a reminder of the journey that had brought him here. And as Rafael stood there, surrounded by the life he had built, he felt a deep and abiding peace. Kindness had carried him home then, and it continued to guide him now.

THE SHOEMAKER'S SONG

The year was 1910. The flickering light of the oil lamp cast long shadows across the walls of the small workshop at the back of the Ferrante family's tenement. The room smelled of leather and wax, mingling with the faint scent of coal smoke drifting in from the street outside. Giuseppe "Pino" Ferrante leaned over his workbench, his strong hands guiding a needle through the soft red leather of a child's shoe. His movements were steady and deliberate, the rhythmic tap of his hammer punctuating the otherwise quiet night.

Pino hummed an old Italian lullaby, his deep voice rising and falling in tune with the song his father had once sung while crafting shoes in their cobbler shop back in the hills of southern Italy. His brow was furrowed with concentration, but his lips carried a faint smile as he worked. The tiny red shoes he was crafting were for his youngest, Maria—her Christmas gift, though she was too young to understand the significance.

"Pino, è tardi. Devi dormire. Domani hai una lunga giornata." Maria's soft voice broke through the quiet as she appeared in the doorway, her shawl wrapped tightly around her shoulders. ("Pino, it's late. You need to sleep. Tomorrow is a long day.")

Pino didn't look up. He carefully knotted the thread, inspecting the stitch before responding. "Non posso dormire, Maria. Non finché questi non sono perfetti." ("I can't sleep, Maria. Not until these are perfect.")

Maria sighed and stepped into the workshop, her footsteps light against the worn wooden floor. She placed a gentle hand on his shoulder, her touch warm despite the chill that crept through the poorly insulated walls. "I bambini sarebbero felici con qualsiasi cosa. Non devi fare tanto." ("The children would be happy with anything. You don't have to do so much.")

Pino finally looked up, his dark eyes meeting hers. "È Natale, <aria. Una piccola magia non fa mai male." He smiled, the corners of his eyes crinkling. ("It's Christmas, Maria. A little magic never hurts.")

Maria shook her head but couldn't help returning his smile. She admired his determination, even if it worried her. Life in Utica, New York had been harder than they ever imagined when they left Italy five years ago. The promise of opportunity had turned into endless hours of labor for meager pay, and Pino's workshop was more a labor of love than a thriving business. Yet, he never wavered in his efforts to provide for their children.

"Ricordi quando tuo padre faceva scarpe per tutti i bambini del villaggio?" Maria said, her voice soft with nostalgia. "Non aveva niente, ma ogni bambino si sentiva speciale a Natale." ("Do you remember when your father made shoes for all the children in the village? He had nothing, but every child felt special at Christmas.")

Pino nodded, his smile growing wistful. "Lo ricordo. E voglio che i nostri bambini sentano lo stesso." ("I remember. And I want our children to feel the same.")

Maria leaned down, pressing a kiss to his cheek. "Ma non dimenticare di dormire, Pino. Hai bisogno di forza per affrontare domani." ("But don't forget to sleep, Pino. You need your strength for tomorrow.")

She left him to his work, her figure disappearing into the dimly lit hallway. Pino returned his attention to the shoe in his hand, running his fingers over the soft leather. He could already picture Maria's face when she saw them, her chubby little hands reaching out to touch the shiny red surface. The thought warmed him, giving him the strength to keep going.

The next morning, the Ferrante family gathered in their small kitchen for breakfast. The room was filled with the hum of activity: the clinking of cups, the scrape of knives on bread, and the chatter of children. The table was set with their usual fare—simple bread and coffee, a meal that stretched thin in times like these.

Antonio, the oldest at ten, looked at the bread and frowned. "Perché non possiamo avere carne come la famiglia Santoro?" he asked, his voice tinged with longing. ("Why can't we have meat like the Santoro family?")

Maria, who was pouring coffee into Pino's chipped cup, paused. She set the pot down and turned to her son, her expression gentle but firm. "Antonio, le cose sono difficili adesso. Dobbiamo essere grati per quello che abbiamo." ("Antonio, things are hard right now. We must be grateful for what we have.")

Pino reached over and ruffled Antonio's dark curls, a smile softening his weathered face. "Un giorno avremo tutto, Antonio. Ma per ora, lavoriamo sodo e non perdiamo speranza." ("One day, we'll have it all, Antonio. But for now, we work hard and hold onto hope.")

Antonio sighed but nodded, picking up his bread and taking a bite. Sofia, his younger sister, leaned over to whisper in his ear, trying to make him laugh. Angela, seated in Maria's lap, clapped her tiny hands together, giggling at the sight of her father's animated gestures.

Pino leaned back in his chair, watching his family with quiet pride. Life in America was hard, but it was moments like these—simple and full of love— that reminded him why he worked so tirelessly. He caught Maria's eye across the table, and she gave him a small, knowing smile.

"Farò tutto per loro," Pino thought to himself, his resolve hardening like the leather beneath his hands. ("I will do anything for them.")

As the family finished breakfast, Pino stood and kissed each of his children on the head before heading to his workshop. The day's work awaited, and the holiday shoes weren't going to make themselves. But as he closed the door behind him, he carried the sound of his children's laughter with him, a melody that would keep him going through the longest of days.

The cold of winter had settled deep into Utica, wrapping the city in a stubborn, icy grip. Snow swirled outside the tenement window as Pino sat hunched over his workbench, the lamp casting a weak, flickering glow. The red shoes for Maria were done now, placed carefully in a box lined with tissue paper. But his work was far from over. On the bench before him lay a mound of heavy, worn leather—an order for factory boots that had to be completed by Christmas Eve.

Pino stared at the boots, his hands aching just looking at them. He could feel the weight of time pressing down on him. The hours were slipping away, and with every tick of the clock, the strain in his chest grew heavier. His promise to finish the holiday shoes for Antonio and Sofia still loomed large, and the thought of breaking it gnawed at him. The boots were important, though. The pay would buy coal for the stove and food to last them through the New Year.

From the corner of the room, Maria's voice broke the tense silence. "Pino, sei sicuro di poter fare tutto?" she asked, worry softening her tone. ("Pino, are you sure you can do everything?")

Pino didn't look up. "Non ho scelta, Maria. I bambini si aspettano le scarpe, e dobbiamo pagare l'affitto." His voice was steady but tired. ("I don't have a choice, Maria. The children expect the shoes, and we need to pay the rent.")

Maria crossed her arms and leaned against the doorframe, her brow furrowed. "Stai lavorando troppo. Non voglio che ti ammazzi per questo." ("You're working too hard. I don't want you to kill yourself over this.")

Pino turned to her, his expression a mix of exhaustion and determination. "Non posso fallire. Non ora." His voice broke slightly, betraying the strain he was under. ("I can't fail. Not now.")

Maria stepped forward and placed her hands on his shoulders. "Non stai fallendo, Pino. Hai già dato tutto per questa famiglia." She paused, her voice softening. "Ma i bambini hanno bisogno di te vivo, non solo delle scarpe." ("You're not failing, Pino. You've already given everything for this family. But the children need you alive, not just the shoes.")

For a moment, Pino allowed himself to lean into her touch, his eyes closing as he let out a long, weary sigh. But the weight of his responsibilities quickly pushed him back into action. He pulled away gently and returned to his workbench, picking up a hammer.

"Dormirò quando sarà finito," he said quietly, more to himself than to Maria. ("I'll sleep when it's finished.")

The next evening, Pino sat in the workshop, his head bowed low over the boots. His hands were raw, his fingers cramped from hours of stitching and hammering. Outside, the wind howled, rattling the thin windows. The clock on the wall ticked relentlessly, reminding him that time was slipping through his grasp.

A knock at the door startled him. Pino straightened, rubbing his tired eyes as Maria entered, her face pale. Behind her, Antonio peeked around the corner, his expression hesitant.

"Mamma mi ha detto che hai bisogno di aiuto," Antonio said, stepping into the room. ("Mama said you need help.")

Pino frowned, his instinct to shield his son from the burden of his work kicking in. "No, Antonio. Questo è lavoro da uomo." ("No, Antonio. This is a man's work.")

Antonio squared his small shoulders, a determined look crossing his face. "Voglio aiutare. Non voglio vedere mamma preoccupata." ("I want to help. I don't want to see Mama worried.")

Pino stared at his son, torn between pride and guilt. After a moment, he nodded and handed Antonio a small, worn brush. "Va bene, ma puoi pulire questo." ("Alright, but you can clean this.")

Antonio took the brush eagerly and began scrubbing one of the finished boots. Pino watched him for a moment, a lump rising in his throat. He turned away quickly, focusing on his work.

As the hours wore on, Antonio fell asleep on a pile of leather scraps, the brush still clutched in his hand. Maria came to collect him, her eyes meeting Pino's as she lifted their son. No words were exchanged, but the worry in her gaze spoke volumes.

Pino continued to work, his movements slower now, his body begging for rest. At one point, his vision blurred, and he had to steady himself against the workbench. His breath came in shallow gasps as he forced himself to keep going. The faces of his children danced in his mind—Angela's innocent giggle, Sofia's bright eyes, Antonio's determined scowl. They were his reason for everything.

But as the night stretched on, doubt began to creep in. The boots were nearly finished, but the shoes for Antonio and Sofia remained untouched. Pino buried his face in his hands, the enormity of his failure crashing over him. "Che tipo di padre sono?" he whispered to the empty room. ("What kind of father am I?")

The next morning, as Pino sat slumped over his workbench, a knock came at the door. He lifted his head, expecting Maria, but instead, it was Mr. Santoro, their upstairs neighbor. The elderly man stepped inside, carrying a bundle of leather scraps.

"Pino, ho sentito che hai bisogno di aiuto," Mr. Santoro said, his voice warm. ("Pino, I heard you need help.")

Before Pino could protest, Mrs. Nowak from down the hall appeared, holding a basket of thread and needles. "For the children," she said simply.

One by one, the neighbors filed in, each carrying something—a pair of scissors, a jar of polish, a box of nails. The tiny workshop filled with the hum of voices and the rhythmic sound of work. Pino stood frozen for a moment, overwhelmed by the outpouring of support.

Maria stepped up beside him, her hand slipping into his. "Non sei mai solo, Pino," she whispered. ("You are never alone, Pino.")

As he watched his neighbors work tirelessly to help him, a spark of hope ignited in his chest. Maybe, just maybe, he could finish what he had started. And maybe, despite the struggles, there was still magic to be found in their small corner of the world.

The night before Christmas dawned colder than any the Ferrantes could remember. Snow fell heavily on Utica, blanketing the streets in silence as though the world itself held its breath for what was to come. Inside the small workshop, the flickering light of the oil lamp illuminated tired faces and busy hands. Neighbors bustled in and out, their movements a symphony of determination. Mr. Santoro hammered soles to boots, Mrs. Nowak carefully stitched seams, and young Antonio, barely awake, polished finished pairs until they gleamed.

Pino stood in the center of it all, his eyes scanning the room as though memorizing every face. His heart swelled with gratitude so fierce it almost hurt. He had never asked for help, yet here they were—his neighbors, his friends, his community—working as if the shoes were for their own children.

"Maria," Pino whispered, his voice thick with emotion. She looked up from where she was cutting strips of leather, her cheeks flushed from the cold air seeping into the room.

"Sì, Pino?" she asked softly.

"Non ho mai saputo che avessimo così tanto," he said, his voice breaking. ("I never knew we had so much.")

Maria's lips curved into a small smile, her eyes glistening. "Non è quello che hai, Pino. È quello che condividi." ("It's not what you have, Pino. It's what you share.")

As the clock struck midnight, the last pair of boots was finished. The neighbors began to trickle out, each offering quiet words of encouragement before stepping back into the snow-covered streets. Pino slumped into his chair; his body too weary to move. Maria brought him a steaming cup of coffee, her touch warm against his cold fingers.

"Vai a letto, Pino. Hai fatto abbastanza," she murmured. ("Go to bed, Pino. You've done enough.")

But as Pino sipped his coffee, his gaze fell on the small pile of unfinished shoes meant for Antonio and Sofia. His stomach twisted with guilt. How could he let them down on Christmas? How could he face their hopeful eyes?

"No," he said aloud, setting the cup aside. "Non posso fermarmi ora." ("I can't stop now.")

Maria opened her mouth to protest but stopped when she saw the fire in his eyes. She nodded silently, kissed his forehead, and left him to his work.

The hours ticked by. The snow outside thickened, muffling the sounds of the city. Pino worked with a singular focus, his hands moving as though guided by something greater than himself. His father's voice echoed in his memory, urging him on.

"Ogni cucitura, ogni passaggio, racconta una storia," his father had once said. ("Every stitch, every step, tells a story.")

As dawn approached, the shoes were done. Pino stared at them, his vision blurring with exhaustion and pride. The pair for Antonio was sturdy and practical, with a polished brown finish that gleamed like chestnuts. Sofia's shoes were delicate and bright, with small ribbons that fluttered like whispers of joy. They weren't perfect, but they were made with love—and that made them enough.

Pino placed the shoes under the small tree in the corner of their apartment, beside the tiny red shoes he'd made for Maria. The sight of them filled him with a peace he hadn't felt in years.

Christmas morning came with the first rays of sunlight cutting through the heavy snow clouds. The children woke early, their laughter ringing out as they raced to the tree. Maria squealed with delight as she clutched her red shoes, her tiny hands tracing the soft leather. Antonio held up his boots, his eyes wide with wonder.

"Papà, li hai fatti tu?" he asked, his voice filled with awe. ("Dad, did you make these?")

Pino nodded, his throat too tight to speak. Antonio threw his arms around his father, holding him tightly. "Grazie, Papà. Sono perfetti." ("Thank you, Dad. They're perfect.")

Sofia twirled in her new shoes, her laughter like music. "Guardami, Papà! Sono una principessa!" she cried. ("Look at me, Dad! I'm a princess!")

Maria watched from the kitchen, her heart full as she prepared their modest breakfast. She caught Pino's eye and smiled, mouthing the words, "Sono orgogliosa di te." ("I'm proud of you.")

Later that evening, the Ferrantes' small apartment was filled with the warmth of family and the glow of their shared joy. Pino picked up his old guitar, the one he had carried all the way from Italy, and began to play a soft, familiar tune. The children gathered around him, their voices joining his in song.

Outside, the snow fell quietly, blanketing Utica in a peaceful hush. Neighbors passing by stopped to listen, their hearts warmed by the melody drifting through the cold night air. It was a song of resilience, of hope, of love—a song that carried the spirit of their small Italian village into the heart of their new American home.

As the last notes faded, Pino looked around at his family, at the laughter and light that filled their little apartment. For the first time in years, he felt something he hadn't dared to hope for: contentment. Despite the struggles, despite the hardships, they had everything they truly needed.

He set the guitar aside and pulled Maria close, his voice low but steady. "Non importa quanto sia difficile la vita, Maria. Finché abbiamo questo, abbiamo tutto." ("No matter how hard life is, Maria. As long as we have this, we have everything.")

Maria rested her head on his shoulder, her voice soft. "Sì, Pino. E la tua canzone ci ricorderà sempre." ("Yes. And your song will always remind us.")

And as the snow continued to fall, the Ferrantes' laughter and song carried into the night, a testament to the enduring strength of love, family, and the simple magic of a shoemaker's song.

THE WINTER QUILT

The snow fell softly over Harmony, New Hampshire, blanketing the narrow streets in a crisp, quiet stillness. It was 1918 and World War I raged on. The faint chime of the church bells echoed through the air, mingling with the distant whistle of the evening train. In the corner of the frosted windowpanes, golden light spilled from the town hall, promising warmth and camaraderie within. Eliza Mae Sullivan pulled her scarf tighter around her neck, her breath forming wisps in the frigid air as she carried her basket of fabric scraps through the snow. The basket bumped against her side with every step, and she gripped it tighter as the chill seeped through her woolen gloves.

Inside the town hall, the scene was a stark contrast to the frosty stillness outside. The hum of sewing machines blended with the soft murmur of conversation. A fire crackled in the stone hearth, casting a warm glow over the women gathered at the long tables. The air smelled of wool, lavender sachets tucked into sewing baskets, and the faint metallic tang of scissors and pins.

"Eliza Mae!" Mrs. Henderson's voice rang out cheerfully, cutting through the hum of the room. The elderly organizer waved her over, her silver hair glinting in the firelight. "There you are, my dear! I thought the snow might've kept you in tonight."

Eliza managed a small smile as she approached, setting her basket on the table. "The snow's no bother," she said softly, her voice nearly drowned out by the chatter around her. "I had some fabric left from my sister's old dresses. Thought it might do."

Mrs. Henderson beamed, her hands deftly sorting through the scraps. "Lovely, lovely. These will make fine patches, Eliza Mae. Sit, sit. There's plenty of work yet to be done."

Eliza found a seat at the far end of the table, away from the center of attention. The other women were chatting animatedly, their voices overlapping in a comforting symphony of community. "Did you hear about the Johnson boy?" one woman asked. "Sent home on a hospital ship last week. Poor thing lost his leg."

"Better to lose a leg than his life," another replied, her hands busy stitching a patch of blue calico.

Eliza kept her head down, her fingers steady as she began to sew. The fabric felt warm and familiar in her hands, but her thoughts were far from the town hall. Her mind wandered to Andrew Harper, his easy smile and the way his hand lingered a second too long when he handed her a letter. He'd been the boy next door, all freckles and laughter, until war had turned him into something else—something she couldn't quite reach. His letters had been her anchor, filled with his hopes for the future, his dreams of returning to Harmony. But then the letters had stopped, swallowed by the abyss of war. She assumed the worst because hope, she had learned, was a dangerous thing to cling to.

"Ladies!" Mrs. Henderson's voice rose above the din, her tone commanding but kind. "I have a small request. Each of you should include a note with your quilt—just a line or two to let the boys know we're thinking of them. A kind word can warm a heart even more than the finest wool."

There were murmurs of agreement, though a few women exchanged hesitant glances. Eliza's heart quickened, her hands faltering on her stitch. She had never been good with words, especially words meant for strangers. She focused on her sewing, hoping the task would pass unnoticed.

"Eliza Mae," Mrs. Henderson called, her sharp eyes catching her in the act of retreat. "You'll write one too, won't you? I know you have just the right touch."

The room seemed to quiet as Eliza's cheeks flushed. She nodded quickly, not trusting herself to speak. She picked up a scrap of paper and a pen, her fingers trembling slightly. The noise around her faded as she stared at the blank page, willing the words to come.

Finally, she wrote:

To the brave soldier who receives this quilt, know that every stitch is sewn with care and hope. May it bring you warmth and remind you of home.

She hesitated, her pen hovering over the page. On impulse, she signed it: *Yours, Eliza Mae Sullivan, Harmony, New Hampshire.*

She folded the note carefully, tucking it into the quilt's corner before returning to her work. The room around her buzzed on, but for Eliza, the act of writing felt like something monumental—like the start of a thread being pulled through the fabric of her life, ready to unravel the grief she had carried for so long.

The icy wind whipped through the town of Harmony as the snowstorm raged on, its fury rattling the windows of Eliza Mae's farmhouse. The next morning, she awoke early, her fingers still aching from the hours she had spent stitching the night before. The quilt now lay neatly folded on her small kitchen table, its vibrant patchwork a stark contrast to the gray dawn light filtering through the frost-covered panes.

As Eliza poured herself a cup of coffee, the knock at the door startled her. She set her cup down, wiped her hands on her apron, and opened the door to find Clara Henderson, Mrs. Henderson's granddaughter, bundled in a thick woolen scarf.

"Eliza Mae," Clara greeted breathlessly, her cheeks pink from the cold. "Gran sent me to fetch the quilts. She said if we don't get them to the station by noon, they'll miss the shipment."

Eliza nodded and motioned for Clara to step inside. "It's on the table," she said, her voice soft but steady. "Let me wrap it for you."

Clara lingered by the hearth as Eliza carefully tied the quilt with twine, her fingers working deftly. "Gran says your stitches are some of the finest she's seen," Clara offered, her tone light. "She says the soldier who gets your quilt will be the luckiest one of all."

Eliza's hands paused for the briefest moment before she resumed tying the knot. "It's just a quilt," she murmured. But even as the words left her mouth, she felt the weight of the note tucked into its folds—a weight she couldn't quite name.

Clara beamed, oblivious to Eliza's hesitation. "I'll make sure it gets there safely," she said, taking the bundle from Eliza's hands. "The train leaves at two sharp."

Eliza watched as Clara disappeared into the snowy morning, the quilt cradled in her arms like something precious. As the door closed behind her, the farmhouse fell silent again, the only sound the faint crackle of the fire. Eliza stood there for a moment, her heart heavy with questions she couldn't answer. Would the quilt even reach its destination? Would the soldier who received it feel the care she had poured into every stitch? And would they— could they—know it was more than just fabric? That it carried a part of her, a piece of herself she hadn't been able to give in words?

Across the ocean, in a field hospital near Amiens, France, the scene was a world away from the quiet farmhouse in Harmony. The makeshift ward was cold and damp, the air thick with the metallic scent of antiseptic and the low moans of the wounded. Rows of cots stretched out in every direction, each one occupied by a soldier bearing the scars of war—some visible, others not.

Andrew Harper lay on one of those cots, his leg elevated in a sling, the pain a constant throb that no amount of morphine could dull. He stared at the ceiling; his mind numb from weeks of the same endless routine. Nurses shuffled between beds, their faces drawn with exhaustion, their voices quiet as they whispered words of reassurance to the men who clung to life around them.

The sound of a trolley rolling across the floor caught Andrew's attention. He turned his head slightly, watching as a nurse unloaded a pile of quilts onto a nearby table. Her voice carried over the hum of the ward.

"These just arrived from the States," she announced, her tone brisk. "Fresh from New England."

Andrew's eyes flickered with interest. Quilts meant warmth, and warmth meant a brief reprieve from the biting cold that seeped through the hospital's thin walls. As the nurse began distributing the quilts, Andrew closed his eyes, expecting little.

But when his turn came, and the quilt was draped over him, something caught his attention. The fabric was soft, its patchwork of colors and patterns unlike anything he'd seen in months. He ran his fingers over the stitches, each one meticulous, each one speaking of care and patience.

And then he found the note.

Frowning slightly, Andrew unfolded the small piece of paper tucked into the corner of the quilt. The handwriting was neat but unpracticed, the words simple yet profound:

To the brave soldier who receives this quilt, know that every stitch is sewn with care and hope. May it bring you warmth and remind you of home.

He read the words twice, his chest tightening as he reached the signature. *Yours, Eliza Mae Sullivan, Harmony, New Hampshire.*

His breath caught. Eliza Mae. The name was a thread that pulled at his memory, unraveling months of silence and darkness. He could see her now— the way her laughter lit up the room, the warmth of her hand in his, the promises they had made before the war stole him away.

Andrew clutched the quilt tightly, his eyes stinging. The pain in his leg receded, if only for a moment, as something long buried stirred within him. It wasn't just a quilt. It was a lifeline, a tether to a world he thought he had lost forever.

He turned to the nurse, his voice hoarse. "Miss, is there any way to write back?"

The nurse blinked, surprised by the urgency in his tone. "We can try," she said carefully. "But it's hard to get letters through these days."

Andrew nodded, determination hardening his features. "Then I'll try," he said. "I'll try."

Back in Harmony, Eliza Mae sat by the fire, her hands idle for the first time in weeks. The storm outside had subsided, leaving a stillness that felt almost oppressive. She stared into the flames, her mind restless. She thought of the quilt, now thousands of miles away, and the soldier who might be holding it at this very moment.

A knock at the door broke her reverie. Eliza rose, her heart inexplicably quickening as she opened the door to find the postman standing there, a letter in his hand.

"For you, Miss Sullivan," he said, tipping his hat before retreating into the snow.

Eliza stared at the envelope, her fingers trembling as she broke the seal. The handwriting was unfamiliar, the ink smudged in places, but the words were clear:

Eliza Mae,

Your quilt found me in a place where hope was a scarce thing. Your words reminded me of home, of a world beyond this war. And of you. I am alive, thanks in part to your care. And if I can, I will find my way back to Harmony. Back to you.

Yours, Andrew Harper.

Eliza's knees buckled, and she sank into the nearest chair, her breath coming in uneven gasps. She clutched the letter to her chest, tears streaming down her face. For the first time in years, she allowed herself to hope. Andrew was alive. And maybe, just maybe, he would come home.

The air in Harmony buzzed with anticipation as spring began to melt the snow that had blanketed the small New England town. The church bells rang in celebration of the armistice signed months earlier, but for many families, the war still cast its shadow. Eliza Mae Sullivan sat on the porch of her farmhouse; her hands wrapped around a steaming cup of tea. She stared at the horizon, her mind a whirl of emotions since the letter from Andrew had arrived weeks ago.

He was alive. That fact alone was enough to upend the quiet, predictable rhythm of her days. The words he'd written—simple but full of warmth—had ignited a flicker of hope in her heart. But with each passing day, that flicker dimmed. The rational part of her warned not to expect too much. After all, letters often got lost. Promises made in the fog of war could fade like the morning mist.

Still, she found herself scanning the dirt road leading to the farmhouse every morning, half expecting to see Andrew walking toward her.

Weeks turned into months, and the spring flowers began to bloom. One warm April afternoon, as Eliza tended to her small vegetable garden, the distant sound of a carriage drew her attention. She straightened, brushing dirt from her hands, her heart pounding in her chest.

The carriage came into view, the wheels creaking as it slowed to a stop at the gate. The driver, an older man with a wide-brimmed hat, tipped it in greeting before stepping down to help his passenger.

Eliza froze.

Andrew Harper stood there, leaning heavily on a cane, his face thinner than she remembered but unmistakably his. His uniform was gone, replaced with simple civilian clothes, but the way he carried himself—the quiet strength in his posture—hadn't changed.

For a moment, neither of them moved. Eliza's breath hitched as their eyes met, and suddenly the weight of all the years apart pressed down on her. The letters. The war. The quilt. Everything she'd bottled up surged to the surface.

"Andrew…" she whispered, her voice barely audible.

He smiled, that familiar, boyish grin she thought she'd never see again. "Eliza Mae," he said, his voice steady despite the tremor in his hands. "I told you I'd find my way back."

She ran to him, her feet barely touching the ground, and when she reached him, she hesitated for only a second before throwing her arms around him. The cane clattered to the ground as Andrew held her tightly, as if letting go might break the fragile moment.

"I thought…" she began, but her voice broke.

"I know," he murmured. "I thought the same."

They stood there for a long time, the world around them fading as they held onto each other. Finally, Andrew pulled back, his hands still on her shoulders. He reached into the satchel slung across his chest and pulled out the quilt.

"This saved me," he said, his voice thick with emotion. "Not just the warmth, though God knows I needed that. But your letter, Eliza. It reminded me of everything I was fighting for. Everything I'd almost forgotten."

She touched the fabric, her fingers tracing the stitches she'd sewn so many months ago. Her eyes welled with tears, but this time, they were tears of joy. "I never thought you'd read it," she admitted. "I never thought it would find you."

Andrew chuckled softly, shaking his head. "It did. And I can't explain it, but it felt like fate. Like I was meant to come home. Meant to find you."

That evening, they sat on the porch together, wrapped in the quilt as the sun dipped below the horizon. Andrew told her about the war—the friends he'd lost, the battles he'd fought, the day he was wounded and thought he might never see home again.

"It wasn't just the pain," he said quietly. "It was the loneliness. The feeling that I was just another nameless soldier in a war too big to understand."

Eliza listened, her hand resting over his. "But you weren't nameless, Andrew," she said softly. "Not to me."

He looked at her, his expression unreadable for a moment, and then he nodded. "No. Not to you."

As the stars began to dot the sky, the weight of their shared history seemed to lift, leaving only the present—a quiet moment full of possibility. Andrew turned to her; his voice steady but laced with vulnerability.

"Eliza Mae, I know I've been gone a long time. And I don't know if I can ever make up for that. But if there's still a place for me here…with you…"

She didn't let him finish. "There's always been a place for you," she said, her voice firm but tender. "Always."

The next day, the townsfolk of Harmony buzzed with news of Andrew Harper's return. Mrs. Henderson couldn't stop smiling as she told anyone who'd listen about the quilt that brought him home. Clara ran to the farmhouse with a loaf of fresh bread, beaming as she embraced both Eliza and Andrew.

The quilt became a symbol in Harmony—a reminder of the power of kindness, hope, and the connections that endure even in the darkest times. And for Eliza and Andrew, it was more than a quilt. It was the thread that had woven their lives back together.

As the seasons turned and the war became a distant memory, the farmhouse filled with laughter and love once more. And on quiet nights, when the world seemed still, Eliza and Andrew would sit by the fire, the quilt draped over their laps and remember how it had all begun—with a simple note stitched into a patchwork of hope.

SECRETS OF THE CUYAHOGA

The Last Echoes of the Cuyahoga

The lecture hall at Cleveland State University was silent, save for the rustling of notebooks and the occasional cough from the audience. Fall quarter 2024 had just begun. Dr. Nikan Waaseya stood at the podium, his dark eyes scanning the room. Behind him, a projection of the Cuyahoga River twisted across a yellowed map, its curves resembling a sinewy snake cutting through the city's urban sprawl.

"This river," Nikan began, his deep voice steady, "was once more than a boundary or a resource. It was a lifeline for the Late Woodland peoples, the ancestors who walked this land long before settlers claimed it. To them, the Cuyahoga was alive—an entity with secrets and stories we may never fully grasp."

A hand shot up from the audience. It belonged to a young graduate student, glasses perched crookedly on his nose. "Dr. Waaseya, you've mentioned the mysterious disappearance of the Late Woodland people from this region in the late 1600s. Are there definitive theories about what happened?"

Nikan clasped his hands behind his back, his posture thoughtful. "Theories abound," he said. "Some suggest disease, brought by early European traders, decimated the population. Others believe intertribal conflict drove them away. But there's another possibility—one rooted not in history books but in the oral traditions of my people."

He paused, letting the weight of his words settle. "These stories speak of a decision—a choice to leave this physical realm, to merge with the land and sky, to become part of the spirit world rather than face annihilation. It's a story that science struggles to measure but one I cannot ignore."

The room was quiet. A few students scribbled notes, but most stared, unsure whether to question or accept his words. Nikan knew his audience well—young minds eager to dissect the past but hesitant to embrace anything that blurred the lines between science and myth.

The Call to the Museum

Later that evening, as the Cleveland skyline flickered in the distance, Nikan's phone rang. The voice on the other end belonged to Dr. Margaret Lansing, a curator from the Cleveland Museum of Natural History.

"Nikan," she said, urgency in her tone, "you need to see this."

"What's 'this'?" he asked, leaning back in his chair. He could hear the faint hum of activity in the background—museum staff, perhaps, or the distant murmur of an exhibit.

"Artifacts," she replied. "Excavated from a site along the Cuyahoga River. Potsherds, tools... and something else. Something I think you'll want to examine in person."

Curiosity piqued; Nikan agreed to meet her the next morning.

The Effigy

The museum's artifact lab was a world of organized chaos. Shelves lined with tagged items, microscopes glowing under fluorescent lights, and the faint aroma of dust and earth filled the air. Margaret greeted Nikan with a firm handshake and led him to a table where several items lay spread out on a white cloth.

"These were unearthed last month," she explained. "The usual pottery fragments and tools, nothing surprising—except for this."

She gestured to a carved effigy about the size of a human hand. It was a Thunderbird, its wings outstretched, etched with intricate patterns. Nikan stepped closer, his breath catching as his eyes traced the grooves in the stone. There was something about it—something almost alive.

He reached out, his fingers hovering above the surface. "May I?"
Margaret nodded.

As soon as his skin touched the effigy, a strange sensation coursed through him. It wasn't a shock, exactly, but a tingling warmth that traveled up his arm. For a moment, the room seemed to fade, replaced by the sound of rushing water and the faint echo of voices—whispered words in a language he couldn't consciously understand but instinctively recognized.

He pulled his hand away, his heart pounding. Margaret raised an eyebrow. "Are you all right?"

"Yes," Nikan replied quickly, though he wasn't sure if it was true. He picked up the effigy again, this time steadier. "This… this is Late Woodland, no doubt about it. The Thunderbird was a powerful symbol, often associated with transformation and protection. Where exactly was this found?"

"Near the old canal path, just off the river," Margaret said. "A small mound we almost missed during initial surveys."

Nikan nodded, his mind racing. "This could be significant—a ceremonial piece, perhaps. It's rare to find something this intact."

But he didn't mention the faint voices, the feeling of connection that had struck him so deeply. That, he knew, would sound absurd to anyone else.

Skepticism Among Peers

The next day, Nikan presented his findings to a small group of colleagues, including Dr. Helen Kline from Case Western Reserve University and Dr. Alan Crawford from Cleveland State. Both were respected archaeologists, though their perspectives were firmly rooted in empirical evidence.

"This effigy," Nikan began, holding up a photograph of the Thunderbird, "suggests a ceremonial context, possibly tied to the spiritual practices of the Late Woodland people. Its discovery raises questions about their final days along the Cuyahoga."

Helen frowned. "Questions we can't answer without further evidence. Artifacts are objects, Nikan, not conduits to the past."

"Are they?" Nikan challenged, his voice calm but firm. "Every object carries a story. Some are just harder to read."

Alan leaned back in his chair. "Look, we all know the Late Woodland people were likely displaced by European expansion or succumbed to disease. It's tragic, but it's not a mystery."

"Unless we're missing something," Nikan countered. "This effigy isn't just a trinket—it's a symbol of transformation. What if their disappearance was a choice? A spiritual migration rather than a physical one?"

Helen sighed. "Nikan, you're romanticizing. We must stay grounded in data."

The meeting ended in frustration, with Nikan feeling the familiar sting of dismissal. But as he walked out of the conference room, he couldn't shake the feeling that the effigy held secrets waiting to be uncovered—secrets that might finally reveal the truth about his ancestors.

The stage was set. The whispers of the past had found their way to him, and Nikan knew he couldn't ignore them. As he prepared to return to the excavation site, the line between science and spirit blurred further, drawing him deeper into the mystery of the Cuyahoga.

Faint Voices from the Earth

The Cuyahoga River wound through the heart of Cleveland like a forgotten artery, its waters darkened by years of industrial labor yet still holding the echoes of an older time. As Dr. Nikan Waaseya approached the excavation site, he felt the tug of history, not just as an academic pursuit but as something deeply personal. He wasn't just uncovering artifacts; he was uncovering pieces of himself.

The site was modest—just a small clearing by the riverbank surrounded by skeletal trees, their branches bare against the gray winter sky. Two graduate students from the Cleveland Museum of Natural History were methodically sifting through dirt, their gloves caked in mud. They nodded in acknowledgment as Nikan arrived, but their attention quickly returned to the ground.

Margaret Lansing was already there, crouched near a shallow pit where the Thunderbird effigy had been found. "You're just in time," she said, standing and brushing dirt off her knees. "We've started unearthing more items, and I think you'll want to see this."

Nikan knelt beside her; his breath visible in the cold air. She handed him a piece of pottery, its edges jagged but its surface smooth, with faint etchings that appeared to be waves. He traced the pattern with his thumb, a sense of recognition stirring within him.

"It's Late Woodland," he murmured. "These waves—they're not just decorative. They symbolize water, movement, perhaps even migration."

Margaret tilted her head. "Migration? You mean they were leaving this area?"

Nikan hesitated. "Not in the way you might think. There's a story my grandfather used to tell me, about a time when our people faced forces they couldn't overcome—disease, displacement, conflict. He said they didn't vanish; they chose to merge with the land, to let their spirits become one with the earth and sky."

Margaret's expression softened. "That's a beautiful story, Nikan, but..."

"But it doesn't fit the data," he finished for her, a hint of frustration in his voice. He stood, looking out at the river. "I'm not asking you to believe it. I'm asking you to consider the possibility that there are truths we can't measure with carbon dating or stratigraphy."

The Unearthed Secrets

As the afternoon wore on, the team uncovered more artifacts—a bone awl, fragments of a stone pipe, and what appeared to be a ceremonial blade. Each item seemed to whisper of a life once lived, a story interrupted but not entirely erased.

Then came the most startling find of the day. One of the graduate students called out, his voice tinged with excitement. "Dr. Waaseya! Over here!"

Nikan hurried over, his heart racing. The student pointed to what looked like a series of stones arranged in a deliberate pattern. As Nikan carefully brushed away the soil, he realized it was a small circular mound, its center marked by a single larger stone etched with the same spiral design he had seen in his dreams.

Margaret joined him, her brow furrowed. "What do you think it is?"

"A marker," Nikan said, his voice low. "A symbol of cycles—birth, death, and rebirth. This wasn't just a settlement. It was a sacred site."

The air seemed to grow heavier, as if the land itself was holding its breath. Nikan placed his hand on the spiral stone, and for a moment, everything around him faded—the students' voices, the sound of the river, even the bite of the cold air.

The Vision

He was no longer at the excavation site. Instead, he stood in a clearing surrounded by people—his ancestors. They wore deerskin tunics and beads, their faces painted with ash and ochre. In the center of the gathering stood a shaman, a man with piercing eyes and feathers braided into his hair. Nikan knew his name without being told: Red Sky.

The shaman raised his arms, and the crowd fell silent. He spoke in a language Nikan didn't fully understand, yet the meaning was clear.

"Our time here is ending," Red Sky said. "But we are not ending. We will leave our bodies, our homes, and our tools, but we will not leave this land. We will become the wind in the trees, the fish in the river, the fire in the sky. We will become the Cuyahoga itself."

Nikan's chest tightened with emotion as the vision shifted. He saw his ancestors dismantling their homes, burying their sacred items, and walking toward the horizon, their figures fading like mist. The last to leave was Red Sky, who turned to Nikan and said, *"Tell them. Tell the story. They must know we did not vanish."*

Doubt and Skepticism

When Nikan came back to himself, he found Margaret staring at him with concern. "Are you okay?" she asked. "You looked... distant."

"I'm fine," Nikan lied, though his hands trembled slightly. He couldn't bring himself to explain what he had just experienced, knowing how it would sound.

Later, at a meeting with Helen and Alan, he tried to convey the significance of the spiral stone and the other artifacts. "This site isn't just about daily life. It's a place of transition, a crossroads between the physical and spiritual."

Helen sighed, her patience clearly wearing thin. "Nikan, you're reading too much into this. The Late Woodland people were practical, not mystical."

"And how do you know that?" Nikan shot back. "Because we haven't found the tools to measure their beliefs? Artifacts aren't just objects—they're fragments of a worldview. A worldview we can't fully understand if we dismiss their stories as mere folklore."

Alan folded his arms. "So you're saying they willingly disappeared? That they just... became one with the land?"

"I'm saying there's more to their story than what we can see under a microscope," Nikan said, his voice firm. "And if we ignore that, we're doing them—and ourselves—a disservice."

The Pull of the Past

That night, Nikan returned to the excavation site alone. He knelt by the spiral stone, the moonlight casting long shadows across the ground. He traced the grooves of the spiral with his fingers, his heart heavy with both awe and sorrow.

"Red Sky," he whispered, his breath visible in the cold air. "I'm trying to tell your story, but they won't listen. How can I make them understand?"

The wind picked up, rustling the trees and carrying with it a faint, melodic chant. Nikan closed his eyes, letting the sound wash over him. For the first time, he felt truly connected—not just to his ancestors, but to the land itself.

He didn't know if his colleagues would ever believe him. But he did know one thing: he wouldn't stop trying. The secrets of the Cuyahoga were too important to be forgotten.

The mystery deepens as Nikan's personal and professional struggles intertwine, setting the stage for the climactic final act.

The Line Between Science and Spirit

The winter wind cut through the bare trees along the Cuyahoga River as Dr. Nikan Waaseya stood alone by the spiral stone. The excavation site was eerily silent, the usual hum of activity from graduate students and colleagues replaced by the quiet murmur of the river. Nikan's breath fogged the cold air, but he barely noticed. He was waiting—for what, he wasn't entirely sure.

The spiral stone had drawn him back, a magnet pulling at something deep within. It wasn't just an artifact anymore; it was a doorway, a tangible link to a past that refused to remain buried. His dreams of Red Sky and the vision of his ancestors had been hauntingly vivid, and though they defied scientific explanation, they had left him with an undeniable truth: the Late Woodland people had not simply vanished. They had chosen a different path.

Confrontation at the Museum

The next morning, Nikan presented his findings to a formal panel at the Cleveland Museum of Natural History. Helen and Alan sat on either side of the room, flanked by other skeptical archaeologists. Margaret Lansing stood near the back; her expression unreadable.

Nikan held up a photograph of the spiral stone, its intricate design projected onto the screen behind him. "This symbol is not merely decorative," he began. "It represents cycles—of life, death, and renewal. It's a map, a story, and a declaration all in one."

Helen folded her arms. "And yet, we have no written records to confirm that interpretation."

"That's because you're looking for confirmation in the wrong places," Nikan replied, his voice calm but firm. "The Late Woodland people communicated through symbols, oral tradition, and the land itself. This site is their final message—a place where they marked their transition, not just out of this region, but out of this physical realm."

Alan sighed audibly. "Nikan, you're romanticizing again. It's far more likely they were displaced by European expansion or succumbed to disease."

"Likely," Nikan conceded, "but not certain. And isn't it our responsibility as archaeologists to consider every possibility? Even the ones that challenge our methods?"

The room fell silent, the weight of his words hanging in the air. Margaret finally spoke, her tone measured. "Nikan, you're asking us to take a leap of faith. But faith isn't part of our discipline."

Nikan met her gaze. "Maybe it should be."

The Ritual

That night, Nikan returned to the excavation site with a small bundle in hand. Inside were offerings: tobacco, cornmeal, and a feather he had found during one of his hikes along the river. He wasn't sure why he felt compelled to bring them, but it seemed right—as though Red Sky himself had whispered instructions in his ear.

The moon hung low, casting silvery light over the spiral stone. Nikan knelt beside it, arranging the offerings in a circle. He closed his eyes and began to hum softly, a melody his grandfather used to sing—a song of gratitude and connection to the earth.

The wind stirred, rustling the trees. It grew stronger, howling through the clearing until it became almost deafening. Nikan opened his eyes, and the world around him shifted.

He was no longer at the excavation site. He stood in a vast field under a sky streaked with crimson and gold. His ancestors surrounded him, their faces solemn but serene. Red Sky stepped forward, his eyes glowing with a wisdom that seemed to span centuries.

"You have done well, Nikan," Red Sky said, his voice like the rumble of distant thunder. "You have heard us when others could not."

Nikan's throat tightened. "What do I do now? How do I make them see?"

Red Sky placed a hand on Nikan's shoulder. "You cannot force them to see. But you can tell our story. Speak of us not as relics of the past, but as voices still alive in the land, the water, the air. That is your purpose."

As quickly as it had begun, the vision ended. Nikan was back at the excavation site, the wind now a gentle breeze. He looked down at the spiral stone, its grooves glistening faintly as though touched by dew—or tears.

A New Understanding

The following week, Nikan published a paper combining the scientific data from the site with the spiritual narratives he had experienced. He knew it would be polarizing. He knew Helen and Alan would dismiss it as speculative at best, unscientific at worst.

But he also knew it was the truth.

Margaret approached him after reading the paper. "It's... unconventional," she said, her tone hesitant. "But it's compelling."

"Compelling enough to change minds?" Nikan asked.

Margaret gave a small smile. "Maybe not. But compelling enough to make people think. And sometimes, that's all it takes."

The Closing Scene

On his final visit to the excavation site, Nikan brought his grandfather's old drum. He sat by the spiral stone, its grooves now protected by a plexiglass cover, and began to play. The steady rhythm echoed across the river, blending with the sounds of nature—the rustling leaves, the gentle flow of water.

As he played, a hawk soared overhead, its wings catching the last rays of sunlight. Nikan smiled, a sense of peace washing over him. The secrets of the Cuyahoga were not his to solve, but to share. And as long as he kept telling the story, his ancestors would never truly be forgotten.

In the distance, the city lights of Cleveland twinkled like stars, a reminder that the past and present were always connected, if one only knew where to look.

Epilogue: Secrets of the Cuyahoga

The excavation site is quiet now, long since packed up and returned to the rhythms of nature. Snow fell softly on the spiral stone, the flakes melting as they landed on its ancient grooves. Dr. Nikan Waaseya stood on the riverbank, bundled against the winter chill, staring at the place where his ancestors had left their final mark. The site had been covered to protect it from erosion, but to Nikan, its energy was still palpable, humming faintly beneath the earth.

His paper on the Cuyahoga artifacts had sparked a quiet ripple in the academic world—small, but undeniable. Some colleagues dismissed his conclusions outright, labeling them speculative and unscientific. Others, however, found themselves drawn to his blend of archaeology and storytelling, appreciating the depth it brought to a field often focused solely on material evidence.

It wasn't validation, exactly, but it was enough.

The Return to the Classroom

Back at Cleveland State, Nikan stood before a lecture hall filled with anthropology students, many of them fresh-faced and eager. On the projector behind him, an image of the spiral stone glowed against a dark background.

"Archaeology," he said, pacing slowly, "is the study of what people leave behind. But let me ask you this: What if what they left behind wasn't just objects? What if they left behind questions—messages meant to be uncovered not just with tools, but with imagination?"

A student raised her hand. "Dr. Waaseya, do you believe the Late Woodland people really disappeared the way you described in your paper?"

Nikan paused, his gaze drifting to the window, where the trees swayed gently in the wind. "What I believe," he said carefully, "is that their story didn't end. It changed. And it's our responsibility to listen—not just to the evidence, but to the land, the symbols, the stories. They all carry a truth, even if it's not one we can measure."

The class was silent, some scribbling notes, others simply watching him with wide eyes. Nikan knew some of them would leave the room unconvinced, but he also knew that others would carry his words with them, just as he carried the whispers of his ancestors.

A Quiet Revelation

That evening, Nikan returned to his grandfather's house on the outskirts of Cleveland, a modest structure nestled among tall pines. The house smelled of cedar and tobacco, a comforting reminder of the man who had shaped so much of his identity. On the mantle, his grandfather's drum sat untouched, its skin worn but sturdy.

Nikan picked it up, running his fingers over its surface. He hadn't played it since that night at the spiral stone. But now, in the quiet of his family home, he felt the urge rise again.

As the first beat resonated through the room, he closed his eyes. The rhythm was steady, a heartbeat that connected him to something larger than himself. He thought of Red Sky, of the vision, of the ancestors walking into the horizon. He thought of the Cuyahoga, winding its way through time, carrying their story.

And for the first time, he didn't feel the need to explain it.

Bridging Two Worlds

Months later, Nikan stood at the Cleveland Museum of Natural History, where a new exhibit had been unveiled: *Echoes of the Cuyahoga*. Artifacts from the excavation were displayed in glass cases, alongside digital renderings of the site and an interactive map of the Late Woodland migration patterns.

At the center of the exhibit was the Thunderbird effigy, its wings spread wide, glowing softly under the museum lights. Beside it, a plaque read:

"The Late Woodland peoples left more than artifacts. They left a legacy—a story of resilience, transformation, and connection to the land. We invite you to explore their world, not just through objects, but through the stories they carried with them."

As visitors moved through the exhibit, Nikan watched from a distance. A young boy pointed at the Thunderbird, tugging on his father's sleeve. "What does it mean, Dad?"

His father shrugged. "It's a symbol, I guess. Maybe of power, or hope."

The boy pressed his hands against the glass, staring at the effigy as if it might come alive. Nikan smiled, knowing the artifact had already done its work.

The Final Reflection

Years later, long after the exhibit had closed and the site along the Cuyahoga had been overgrown with new life, Nikan returned one last time. The spiral stone remained, now weathered by time and the elements. He knelt beside it, placing a hand on its surface.

"Your story is safe," he whispered. "I told it the best I could."

The wind stirred around him, carrying with it the faintest echo of Red Sky's voice: *"You have done well, Nikan."*

Rising to his feet, Nikan looked out at the river, its waters flowing endlessly toward the horizon. It wasn't closure he felt, but something better—a sense of continuation, of belonging. The secrets of the Cuyahoga were no longer his burden alone. They were part of the world now, woven into the fabric of history and memory.

And as he walked away, the river whispered its gratitude, carrying his ancestors' story forward, one ripple at a time.

STORIES FROM DREAMS

The Dreams Begin

It was January 21, 2024, and Don sat at his writing desk in his Auburn Lakes home, two days past his seventy-third birthday. Snow blanketed the ground outside, muffling the outside sounds. His desk lamp cast a golden glow over the cluttered surface—notes for a poetry book here, a stack of photographs waiting to be organized there. He stared at the blank page on his Mac desktop, fingers poised but unmoving over the keyboard. His thoughts felt scattered, weighed down by the world outside—a world of political division, greed, and indifference.

Lately, Don wondered if the books he poured his soul into mattered at all. I spend my life writing. My life is writing.

The clock on the credenza ticked softly, marking the minutes as he wrestled with his doubts. Then, without warning, the air in the room grew heavier, and a faint chill crept along the back of his neck. He glanced at the window, expecting to see it cracked open, but it was shut tight against the winter wind.

That night, sleep came uneasily. When it finally did, the dreams began.

The First Dream

Don found himself standing in a dense forest. The trees were impossibly tall, their branches weaving together to form a canopy that blocked out the sky. A faint glow filtered through the leaves, casting shadows that moved like living things. The air was alive with hushed sounds—not words, exactly, but the hum of countless voices just out of reach.

From the shadows emerged an old man. His face was lined like tree bark, his eyes sharp and penetrating. He wore a cloak of woven fibers that shimmered faintly as though lit from within. When he spoke, his voice was both deep and soft, resonating like a distant drumbeat.

"You seek meaning," the man said, his gaze locking onto Don's. "You wonder if your words can change the world."

Don tried to respond, but no sound came from his mouth. He felt rooted to the spot, like a tree unable to bend or move.

The man smiled faintly. "The stories you seek will find you. But you must keep them secret until they are complete. Only then will their purpose be fulfilled."

Before Don could ask what he meant, the man raised a hand and gestured toward the forest.

Figures began to emerge from the shadows—men, women, children, each carrying an object: a quilt, a sled, a soldier's letter, a pair of shoes. Their faces were blurred, yet Don felt he knew each of them. They stood silently, watching him.

"Write their stories," the old man said. "And remember: You are not writing alone."

The old man seemed familiar to Don in a strange sort of way, maybe an archetypal muse or alchemist. Perhaps someone he knew in his seventy-three years.

The forest faded, and Don woke with a start, his breath catching in his chest. His room was silent, the only sound the faint ticking of the clock. Yet the dream lingered, vivid and unsettling.

The Stories Take Shape

The next night, the dreams returned. This time, Don found himself in a dimly lit workshop, the smell of leather and wood shavings filling the air. A boy sat at a bench, meticulously carving a toy airplane from scrap wood. The boy's hands moved with precision, but his face was streaked with tears.

"It's for my brother," the boy said, not looking up. "He always wanted to fly, but now he can't."

Before Don could ask what had happened, the scene shifted. He was standing in a hospital ward filled with wounded World War I soldiers. A ghostly figure of a soldier knelt beside one of the beds, his hand resting on the shoulder of a dying comrade. The ghost's voice was soft but firm: "You are not alone. I'm here."

Each dream was different yet connected. Don saw glimpses of an immigrant mother holding her child tightly as she arrived in Cleveland, her face a mix of hope and fear. He saw a Native American elder sitting by a fire, lamenting the loss of his people's land but speaking of the resilience of the human spirit. He saw a young boy during the Great Depression, offering his only pair of shoes to a friend in need.

Every dream felt real, as though he were living these moments alongside the characters. And every morning, Don woke up with an urgent need to write. He began drafting stories at a pace that startled him, the words flowing effortlessly as though they were being dictated. He felt like a vessel, channeling something far greater than himself.

The Mystery Deepens

As the dreams continued, strange things began to happen during Don's waking hours. He would catch glimpses of movement out of the corner of his eye, only to turn and find nothing there. His writing room would grow unexplainably cold, and he often felt the sensation of someone standing behind him, though the room was empty. Don's thoughts returned to the old man in the forest. Could this presence be the old man's ghost?

One afternoon, as he reviewed his notes, he noticed something strange. The characters in his stories seemed to overlap in subtle ways—a name mentioned in one dream would appear in another, or an object from one story would show up in the background of another. It was as though the stories were part of a larger tapestry, threads weaving together to form a picture he couldn't yet see.

Don's wife Mary noticed the change in him. "You've been quiet lately," she said one evening. "Are you working on something new?"

Don hesitated. The old man's warning echoed in his mind: *You must keep them secret until they are complete.* "Just some ideas," he replied. "Nothing ready to share yet."

Don's phone conversations with his friends Dan and Steve in Denver, Richard in Martins Ferry, and Don in Las Vegas were similarly stingy with details. While Mary and his friends pressed him to explain his inspiration for this short story collection, he knew he had to honor his commitment to the old man in the forest to keep the source of his ideas a secret.

But the truth was, Don wasn't sure what to share even if he wanted to. Were the dreams simply his imagination, or was something—or someone—guiding him?

One night, after finishing a particularly emotional story about a soldier and his lost love, Don sat back in his chair, exhausted but content. As he reached to turn off his desk lamp, the room suddenly filled with the faint sound of voices—not whispers this time, but a melody, haunting and beautiful. Tilly, the family calico cat with symmetrical gold swirls on both sides of her black and gray body, thymically swished her tail to the music. She heard it and responded with tail movements as she did so often when Mary and Don sat in the living room in the evening, listened to music, and shared the highlights of their days. Tilly heard the music in the room.

Don froze, his hand hovering over the lamp switch. The melody grew louder, filling the room, and for a moment, he thought he saw figures standing in the shadows—familiar figures, holding their objects and watching him. At that point, Tilly leaped from the green recliner and raced out of the room.

Then, as quickly as it had come, the sound vanished. Don was left sitting in silence, his heart pounding.

What was happening to him? And what would happen if he stopped writing?

The Struggle Between Belief and Doubt

The snow fell heavier the next morning, blanketing the streets outside Don and Mary's home in Auburn Lakes. Inside, the air was warm and smelled faintly of coffee. Don sat at his desk, staring at the pile of handwritten notes and drafts accumulating beside him. He didn't know how to explain what was happening—not to himself, and certainly not to anyone else. The stories were flowing too perfectly, the characters too alive, their voices too real.

He leaned back in his chair, running a hand through his long thin white hair. The old man from his first dream still haunted him. *The stories will find you. But you must keep them secret until they are complete.* It had seemed like a simple instruction at first, but now it felt like a heavy weight pressing down on him.

The Fracture Between Dreams and Reality

The dreams grew more vivid, more insistent. That night, Don dreamed he was sitting in a courtroom, though it looked nothing like a modern one. The walls were rough-hewn logs, the benches filled with shadowy figures whose faces flickered like candle flames. A judge with a stern face, wearing a tattered robe, banged a gavel carved from bone.

"This is the case of truth," the judge intoned. "The accused is the storyteller."

Don looked down and realized he was the one standing at the defendant's table. His hands were bound, but he didn't feel afraid—only confused. A figure stepped forward to testify. It was the young boy from the Great Depression story he had written.

"You have to tell them," the boy said, his voice trembling. "People need to know there's still good in the world."

Another figure emerged, the Native American elder. He held a burning branch, its flames licking the air as he spoke. "But beware. Some stories demand a price."

Don woke with a start, drenched in sweat. The room was dark except for the faint glow of his laptop on the bed, still open to the draft he had been working on before bed. He glanced at it and froze. The last paragraph he had typed was gone. In its place were words he didn't remember writing:

"You cannot stop now. The stories are your burden and your gift."

The Whispered Warnings

The next day, Don decided to confide in Mary, though he didn't tell her everything. "I've been having strange dreams," he said over breakfast. "They're… vivid. And they're giving me ideas for stories."

Mary looked up from her coffee, her brow furrowing. "Strange how?"

"It's like the characters are alive. They speak to me, and when I wake up, the stories are already written in my head. But…" He hesitated, unsure how to explain the whispers, the shadows, the eerie feeling that someone—or something—was watching him.

"But what?" she prompted.

"I feel like I'm not alone when I write. Like the stories are coming from somewhere else."

She gave him a skeptical look but said nothing. Instead, she reached across the table and squeezed his hand. "Maybe you're just more creative than you give yourself credit for."

Don nodded, but her words didn't comfort him. If anything, they deepened his unease. He wanted to believe it was just his imagination, but the evidence was mounting against him.

Unexplained Connections

That afternoon, Don decided to research one of the characters from his dreams: the young immigrant mother from early 1900s Cleveland. He had written her story in a single sitting the day before, her name, Rosa Schmidt, and her struggles as clear to him as if she had been sitting beside him.

He turned on his computer and began digging through old census records online. After an hour of searching, he froze. There it was: a listing for Rosa Schmidt, a German immigrant who had arrived in Cleveland in 1908. She had lived on the city's west side and worked in a garment factory, just as he had written.

The hairs on the back of his neck stood up. He hadn't made up Rosa's story; he had *remembered* it.

A Haunting Message

That evening, as Don sat at his desk, the shadows in the room seemed to grow deeper. He tried to focus on his writing, but the whispers began again— soft at first, then louder, more insistent. He covered his ears, but the voices seemed to come from inside his head.

"We are you. You are us. Tell our stories."

He turned off his computer and stepped away, pacing the room. The voices subsided, leaving only silence, but when he glanced back at his desk, he saw something that made his heart skip a beat. His computer screen had turned itself back on, and on it was a single line of text:

"Not all stories are safe to tell."

Don stared at the screen, his pulse racing. Was it a warning? A threat? An artificial intelligence intrusion from the Web into his computer? He didn't know. But one thing was clear: whatever force was guiding him; it wasn't going to let him stop.

The Stories Tighten Their Grip

The next few days were a blur. Don wrote feverishly, barely stopping to eat or sleep. The stories seemed to pour out of him faster than he could type, each one more powerful and more unsettling than the last. He wrote about a boy in the 1950s who built a sled to bring his fractured neighborhood together. He wrote about a soldier from World War I who comforted a dying comrade in a French hospital. He wrote about a Native American archaeologist who helped answer the perplexing question of what happened to the Late Woodland peoples in northeast Ohio

The dreams continued, more vivid than ever. One night, Don dreamed he was standing at the edge of a vast canyon. On the other side stood the old man, flanked by the characters from his stories.

"You are the bridge," the old man said. "Without you, the stories are lost."

Don tried to ask what that meant, but the canyon began to crumble beneath his feet, and he woke up gasping for air.

Don began to notice changes in himself. His hands shook when he wasn't writing, and he felt a constant pull toward his desk, as though it were a magnet and he was made of iron. The faint voices followed him everywhere now—not just in his writing room, but in the kitchen, the living room, even outside during walks with Mary through Auburn Lakes.

One night, he couldn't take it anymore. He stood in his writing room and shouted, "What do you want from me?"

The room fell silent, and for a moment, he thought the whispers were gone. Then, from the shadows, a voice spoke—a voice that was both familiar and alien.

"Finish the book."

And then the lamp on his desk flickered and went out, plunging the room into darkness.

Don sat at his desk in the dim light of his writing lamp, the snow outside his window thickening into a silent white curtain. His fingers hovered over the keyboard, trembling as if they no longer obeyed his will. He had one story left to write. It was the story that had come to him in fragments over the past few days, the story he had been avoiding.

This one felt different—darker, heavier, as though it carried the weight of something too profound to fully comprehend. It wasn't just a story; it felt like a confession, a revelation he wasn't sure he was ready to make.

The Last Dream

The previous night, Don had dreamed of the old storyteller again. This time, the man wasn't alone. He was surrounded by the characters from Don's stories—each one vivid, alive, and watching him with a mix of expectation and sorrow. The storyteller stepped forward; his face lined with an ageless wisdom.

"You have done well," the man said, his voice echoing as though it came from a vast, empty canyon. "But the final story is the hardest. It is the thread that ties them all together."

"What is it?" Don had asked, his voice breaking. "Why does it feel like it's meant for me?"

The storyteller smiled faintly. "Because it is you."

Don had jolted awake, his heart pounding. He didn't understand what the storyteller meant, but the weight of the words lingered, pressing down on him like an unseen hand.

The Final Story Emerges

Now, as Don stared at the blank screen, the story began to pour out of him, unbidden and unstoppable. It was about a man—an aging writer—who spent his days crafting stories to bring light into a dark world. The man was haunted by dreams, visions of people from different times and places, each whispering their tales into his ear.

As he wrote, Don realized the man in the story was himself. The dreams, the whispers, the shadows—they were all reflections of his own struggles, his fears, and his hopes. But there was something else, too. A connection. The characters in his dreams weren't just figments of his imagination. They were pieces of him, fragments of his soul scattered across time.

The story took him back to a moment he had long buried—a night during his childhood when he had stood in the darkness of his family's backyard, staring up at the stars. He had felt small, insignificant, yet deeply connected to something vast and incomprehensible. That night, he had whispered a question into the void: What is my purpose?

Now, decades later, he felt the answer.

A Revelation

As Don finished typing the last words, a chill swept through the room, though the heater was running. The lamp on his desk flickered, and for a moment, he thought he saw a shadow move in the corner of his eye. He turned, his breath catching in his throat.

Standing in the doorway was the storyteller, his tall figure translucent, his eyes filled with both sadness and gratitude. Behind him stood the characters from Don's stories—Rosa Schmidt, the Native American elder, the boy with the sled, the soldier from World War I. They were all there, silent but present, their forms shimmering like reflections on water.

"You've done what we could not," the storyteller said. "You've given us a voice."

Don swallowed hard; his mouth dry. "Who are you?"

The storyteller tilted his head, as if the answer were too simple and too complex at the same time. "We are the stories. And now, so are you."

"Donnie, we know each other from Tucson, Prescott, the LA Forum West,

Rocky Point in Mexico, Indian country in the Midwest, the Rock and Roll Hall of Fame, and from the many dreams where we visited. Now you know me as the old man in the forest. I am Derk, I am your muse. Derk was Don's best friend who changed lanes on the universe's vast superhighway on February 27, 2014 in Prescott, Arizona.

The room seemed to hum with energy, a vibration that filled the air and coursed through Don's body. He felt a profound sense of connection, as though he were part of something infinite. Tears streamed down his face, but he didn't know if they were tears of joy, sorrow, or something else entirely. The loss of his friend Derk felt much larger, but also different because together they had produced twenty remarkable stories bringing hope to the world.

The Book is Released

The next morning, Don sent the completed manuscript to his publisher. The book, titled "Kindling Hope: Stories Awakening the Heart," was released quietly a few months later, without fanfare. But word of mouth spread quickly, and soon, letters began pouring in from readers across the country.

"I cried reading the story of the Tremont kids and the sled," one letter said. "It reminded me of my own childhood, of the hope I had forgotten."

"The story of Rosa Schmidt felt like it was written just for me," another reader wrote. "My grandmother was an immigrant, and your words brought her memory back to life."

Don read each letter carefully, his heart swelling with a mixture of pride and humility. The book was doing exactly what he had hoped: reminding people of the goodness that still existed in the world, even in the smallest acts of kindness.

The Final Dream

On the night of the book's release, Don had one last dream. He was back in the canyon, standing at the edge of the cliff. The storyteller stood on the other side; his hand outstretched.

"It's time," the man said.

"For what?" Don asked, his voice trembling.

"To let go."

Don hesitated, looking down at the canyon below. It was filled with light, not darkness, and he felt an overwhelming sense of peace. He reached out, and as their hands touched, the canyon disappeared, replaced by a vast, endless sky.

An Ambiguous Ending

Don woke with a start, his heart pounding. The dream lingered in his mind, vivid and undeniable. He looked around the bedroom, half expecting to see the storyteller or the characters from his stories. But the room was empty, except for Mary by his side and the faint rustle of the wind outside.

He got up, walked to his writing room, sat at his desk and turned on his computer. The final line of his book stared back at him: "Goodness exists in all of us. It is our task to bring it forth, one story, one act, one life at a time."

Don leaned back in his chair, a faint smile on his lips. He didn't know if the dreams were real or just his imagination. But in the end, it didn't matter. What mattered was the stories, and the light they brought into the world.

As the snow continued to fall outside, Don closed his eyes, feeling a sense of peace he hadn't felt in years. The voices were gone, but their message remained, etched into his soul.

And somewhere, in the quiet corners of the world, the characters in "Kindling Hope" smiled.

ABOUT THE AUTHOR

Don Iannone is a highly respected author and expert in economic development and public policy. "Kindling Hope: Stories Awakening the Heart" is Don's first fiction book. Its twenty stories awaken the heart by reminding us of the goodness in ourselves and others. Don's earlier 2024 book, "The Civil War Yesterday and Today in Poetry," uses poetry to paint a vivid picture of Pre-Civil War America, Civil War America, and Post-Civil War America. It raises the prospect of a new civil war in America, caused by the insurmountable gulf in American's beliefs, values, and expectations for America in the future.

His "America's Dream at a Crossroads: The 2024 Presidential Election and Beyond," became a bestseller due to its appeal in view of the 2024 presidential election. Since the book's release on July 8, 2024, Don was interviewed about the book and the upcoming election by over 50 media sources nationwide.

Don worked in economic development and public policy for over forty years. Since 2020, he has taught graduate business students at the European Union-based Transcontinental University. Don has authored five nonfiction books and numerous articles and monographs on economic development and public policy. He is also the author of eleven poetry collections and ten photographic essays. He holds a doctorate in philosophy and several other degrees. He serves on the board of Seeds of Literacy, a nonprofit dedicated to improving adult literacy in Greater Cleveland. He is active in the International Economic Development Council (IEDC), Cleveland Civil War Roundtable, Literary Cleveland, the Authors Guild, the Academy of American Poets, and the Poetry Society of America. Don and his wife, Mary, a retired Cleveland Clinic executive, live in the Greater Cleveland area.